# Music
# to Die For

**Center Point
Large Print**

**This Large Print Book carries the
Seal of Approval of N.A.V.H.**

# Music
# to Die For

## Radine Trees
## Nehring

CENTER POINT PUBLISHING
THORNDIKE, MAINE

This Center Point Large Print edition
is published in the year 2007 by arrangement with
St Kitts Press.

The text of this Large Print edition is unabridged. In other
aspects, this book may vary from the original edition. Printed in
Thailand. Set in 16-point Times New Roman type.

ISBN-10: 1-58547-928-4
ISBN-13: 978-1-58547-928-3

Library of Congress Cataloging-in-Publication Data

Nehring, Radine Trees, 1935-
    Music to die for / Radine Trees Nehring.--Center Point large print ed.
        p. cm.
    ISBN-13: 978-1-58547-928-3 (lib. bdg. : alk. paper)
    1. McCrite, Carrie (Fictitious character)--Fiction. 2. Country musicians--Fiction.
3. Tourism--Fiction. 4. Kidnapping--Fiction. 5. Large type books. 6. Ozark
Mountains--Fiction. I. Title.

PS3614.E44M875 2007
813'.6--dc22

2006030220

# Acknowledgments

This book is my tribute to the wonderful people who have worked hard over many years to make the Ozark Folk Center in Stone County, Arkansas, such a special place. The Folk Center is a living display of the unique talents and skills Ozarks dwellers have relied on since they first came into the area from the Appalachians during the 1840's.

My husband, John, and I have enjoyed special programs, classes, nature hikes, and holiday celebrations in and around Folk Center State Park for many years, and did so long before I considered setting a novel there. What fun it has been to make a story come alive in a place I love, and to write about fellow humans whose ingenuity, strengths, and abilities I learn from and admire.

Now to specifics—beginning with the artists, teachers, and staff at the Folk Center itself.

First, special thanks to Elliott Hancock, Assistant Manager, who has encouraged and helped me in so many ways and took the time to fill in memory gaps by e-mailing pictures of hiding places around the auditorium.

To Mary Gillihan, Harmony musician; Park Interpreter and Elderhostel Coordinator, Ozark Folk Center State Park.

To Bill Young, Ozark Folk Center General Manager, who is out there working, wherever there's a need.

To Dr. Bill McNeil, folklorist and expert on Ozarks

music and musicians. (He knows the history.)

To Kay Blair Thomas, Crafts Coordinator, musician, mystery lover.

To Orthrene Fletcher, seamstress and manager of the Dressmaker's Shop in the Folk Center craft grounds. (Don't worry about blood stains on the floor of your shop, Orthrene.)

To Wanda Baird, Gift Shop Manager.

And thanks, as well, to many more Folk Center friends and teachers, some from the past. All are treasured in memory. I can't name them all, but here are a few:

Deb (I knew her as Mullins) Carbone, musician and former Public Information Officer for the Folk Center

Tina Marie Wilcox, herbalist

James Toney and Scott Riedy, blacksmiths

Jack Thomas, knife maker

Lori Woodard, woodcarver

Jean Jennings, Folk Center musician, dulcimer teacher

Jimmy Driftwood, musician, poet, historian, who, so many years ago, helped get things rolling toward preservation of the Ozarks ways.

And biggest and best of all, to Ozark Folk Center State Park itself. Sorry, old friend, if I've moved around a few insignificant things in your grounds and buildings . . . you're still recognizable, and, I believe, just as lovable.

Other experts also helped guide my way, including:

Arleen Knoderer, Spavinaw Literacy Council Executive Director, and Barbara Mortensen. These strong women shared information about dyslexia.

Susan McPherson, Branch Manager, Arvest Bank, Gravette, who helped me explain why Chase couldn't get ransom money on Saturday.

Chief Trent Morrison and Sergeants Lonnie Ash and Kurt Banta, Gravette Police Department. They taught me details of Arkansas law enforcement.

Danny Trammell, Head Jailer, Stone County Sheriff's Department, who confirmed jurisdictions for the various law enforcement agencies covering the Mountain View area, the National Forest, and Ozark Folk Center State Park.

Robert Honderich, Director of Nursing, Gravette Medical Center Hospital, and Dr. Billy V. Hall, Gravette Medical Associates, Ltd., who answered my questions about knife wounds.

Ann Behnke, Home Economist, Benton County Extension Service, who gave recipe advice.

You will find knowledge from these people within the pages of *Music to Die For*. Any mistakes in details are mine, not theirs.

**Thank you, one and all,**
*Radine Trees Nehring*

For more information about the Ozark Folk Center, go to www.ozarkfolkcenter.com or phone 1-870-269-3851. For a free packet of information about Arkansas, including a book with information about all state parks and a highway map, phone 1-800-NATURAL.

# Dedication

To my St Kitts editors
Laurel B. Schunk and Diana Tillison.
I am more grateful than even
an author's words could ever say
for their talent, skill, support, and friendship.

# Introduction

The doll was smiling. Dolls always smiled, didn't they? Her Mandy always smiled. Momma said Mandy was a happy doll.

She looked at the teddy bear. Teddy bears weren't like dolls. Mostly they didn't smile. Only Pooh bears smiled.

She turned back to the doll, who looked a lot like Mandy, but it wasn't Mandy. Mandy was back at Grandma's house, waiting for her. This doll was sitting on a bed she'd never seen before.

She wondered if Momma was waiting for her. They were s'posed to go play music. Was it time to do that? Was it time for Momma to come get her?

Was it time for supper?

She wouldn't cry, 'cause Daddy said it was wrong to cry when you were with strangers, even if crying was what you wanted to do, and you had to snuffle and swallow and that made your singing bubbly.

Daddy said she must smile at the strangers, even when they smelled stinky and reached out hands to grab her or patted her head like she was Grandma's doggie, Bounce. Bounce liked patting. She didn't. She'd tried to imagine she was Bounce, which would be fun, but it wasn't any good. She still didn't like patting.

But she did want to do what Daddy said, so she learned to make a scrunchy-face smile, even when

11

people hugged too tight or their hands went places she didn't like.

Her feet took her to the bed. It was a big bed and had a quilt with red squares. The red was pretty . . . like Christmas.

She climbed up and sat, remembering to keep her shoes over the edge so they wouldn't touch the red quilt. She looked at the doll, blinked her eyes, swallowed, and picked up the teddy bear. She didn't want to hold a smiley doll.

Maybe, if she was very quiet, it would be okay to take Teddy for a walk. Outside. There were woods outside, she could see them through the window.

She'd pushed at the window. It didn't open, so she and Teddy could play like being ghosts. They'd walk through the door and go hide in the woods. Daddy hadn't said hiding from strangers was wrong, everyone knew hiding was a game.

She slid off the bed and her shoes made a small click as they hit the floor. Oops. Shhh.

She and the teddy bear moved across the room. Shhh, shhh. Each foot up, over, down; and up, over, down. Running would have been better, but the strangers might hear her, so she must be as quiet as Teddy, quiet as a ghost.

Now she and Teddy were at the door. She reached up, held on to the knob as tightly as she could, and twisted.

Oh. It was one of those that took two hands.

She sat Teddy on the floor by her feet and put both hands on the knob, wrapping her fingers around the cold metal and swinging her body to help her fingers make the knob move.

The knob turned. She tugged, but the door didn't open. After several more tugs she picked up the teddy bear and backed away from the door so the two of them could think about why it didn't open. Was it like outside doors on a house? Did it need a key?

She was thinking about keys when the floor on the other side of the door creaked. Something went "chunk." A whimpering noise rolled up inside her, and she lifted a hand to cover her mouth as she watched the knob turn.

Her eyes were wet now, but she was a good girl. When the stranger came into the room, she remembered what Daddy had said. She put her hand down—and she smiled.

# Chapter I

The droning stopped, and popping noises erupted.

Whoops!

Carrie jerked out of a comfortable doze and saw that the speaker was nodding his head to acknowledge applause. She began clapping and hoped the dim light in the auditorium had concealed her own nodding head.

What on earth had the man been talking about?

She turned pages in her convention program. Ah, there he was: "Chamber of Commerce, Tuckatoo, Arkansas, Rice-growing Capital of the United States: *Honeymooning Among the Rice.*"

For good garden seed! What next?

She looked. "Chamber of Commerce, Bean, Arkansas: *The Yearly Bean Bottoms Festival, Featuring our Famous Catfish Calling Contest.*"

Oh, my!

For three days she'd listened and taken notes. She'd collected stacks of brochures to take back to the tourist information center in Bonny, Arkansas. But now . . .

The program coordinator called the final afternoon break, the auditorium lights brightened, and Carrie picked up her briefcase. Smiling at nearby colleagues, she hurried up the aisle toward the back of the room.

Once out in the hall she turned left, joining a cluster

of women headed for the pink door with a bonnet painted on it.

She allowed several women to get in line ahead of her, then backed away from the chattering crowd. Five steps beyond the pink door she backed around a corner, pushed against a plain grey door, and slipped through the opening into sunshine. The door clicked shut and locked.

Carrie had learned long ago that it paid to explore buildings where meetings were being held.

She took a deep breath and stood still, letting bird calls and the scent of damp brown leaves replace the sounds and smells of the auditorium. Ahhhhh.

She could hear a titmouse and . . .

Music?

Was she imagining . . . ? No, it *was* music! Faint, ghostly, from some stringed instrument . . . but where?

Then, as if the player had been strangled, it was gone. Maybe the music had been a trick of the breeze, or her imagination. She shook her shoulders to dispel the eerie memory and started downhill toward the cluster of cabins.

As manager of an Arkansas highway tourist information center, Carrie McCrite couldn't skip the yearly Department of Parks and Tourism Convention. But the towns being covered this afternoon were in the southeastern corner of the state, and right here, all around her, was a forest begging to be explored.

At least the department was holding this year's meeting at the Ozark Folk Center State Park near

Mountain View, rather than among crowds and concrete in Little Rock.

Carrie had moved from Tulsa, Oklahoma, to the Arkansas Ozarks five years earlier, partly to get away from crowds and concrete. Her other reason for leaving the city was murder.

The violent death of her husband had pushed her out of a quiet existence as Mrs. Amos McCrite, dependent wife and part-time librarian, into a choking fog of worried widowhood, with too little confidence, too little peace, too little money, and far too much mystery.

Then one spring day, while looking through old photographs, she'd realized that the bride, the young mother, the dutiful wife she saw there were all history now. Surely there must be a new Carrie waiting somewhere inside the veneer of her former life. All she needed to do was find and free that Carrie.

So she packed up everything, including her courage, and fled to the Ozarks. She found a job with Parks and Tourism, built a home on land she and Amos had bought for their retirement, and set about discovering the new Carrie.

Though both Amos and her friend JoAnne had been killed near where she now lived, the comfort of the natural world all around her had almost wiped out the horror of their deaths, just as helping discover who killed them had given her confidence and a new-born awareness of her own strength.

She was content in her small house above Walden

Valley. Living in the woods had turned out to be just right for her, in spite of dire predictions from city friends and family when she'd told them her plans.

And, she thought, as she unlocked the door of her room, tossed her briefcase on the bed, and started to peel off too-tight slacks and blazer jacket, friendship with her neighbors in and around Walden Valley was also just right.

Carrie's lips twitched in a smile. Oh, yes, the very best, the most right thing, was friendship with her nearest neighbor, retired Kansas City police detective, Henry King. JoAnne's brutal murder had brought Henry into her life. Now, possibilities lay before them.

Henry and two other Walden Valley neighbors, Jason and Eleanor Stack, would be joining her tomorrow for the spring opening of the Folk Center's weekend craft classes. Henry and Jason were learning wood carving; she and Eleanor, studying herbs. In the evenings they'd enjoy music shows in the auditorium, and of course there was always the wonderful Ozarks cooking at the Folk Center restaurant.

Thinking about the restaurant reminded her she was hungry, and she glanced at her travel goodie box between the room's two beds. Apples, bananas, fruity fiber bars. Nope, better not. Better save hunger for tonight's banquet. She pulled on elastic waist jeans, breathed deeply, and sat down, reaching for her walking shoes. As soon as the shoes were tied, she picked up the convention schedule.

Dinner tonight included several kinds of smoked

meat, with spring greens, corn bread, black-eyed peas, and the Folk Center's own Apple or Peach Chunky to pile on the corn bread.

As she read she wished she'd paid more attention to the evening program before now. Henry should be here. Country musicians Chase Mason and Tracy Teal were the entertainers, and they were favorites of his. She could have invited Henry to come a day early. The Folk Center Lodge was full until after the convention, but . . .

She looked at her room's unused bed.

Well, it wouldn't have mattered to anyone whether her roommate was Henry or, as originally planned, her friend Beth, who managed the other tourist information center in northwest Arkansas. She and Henry were mature adults. He was divorced and very proper. She was a sensible widow—certainly no ingénue. Besides, it was absolutely amazing what was accepted without comment once your hair was grey.

And Beth was out of the picture. Almost as soon as she'd pulled her car up in front of the lodge office, the department director had come out to ask if she'd fill in as host for the convention's two keynote speakers. Their original host was still at home, dealing with a last-minute emergency. That meant Beth had driven off to the Mountain View Bed and Breakfast Inn where convention speakers were staying, and Carrie was left alone in their very comfortable room with a view of the forest, two rocking chairs, and two beds.

At least she had lots of space for organizing all the

brochures and booklets she was collecting. The top of the second bed was covered with them.

Carrie looked back at the evening's program. It said that, as a special treat, Chase and Tracy's four-year-old daughter Dulcey would perform on her miniature dulcimer, and Chase's mother, old-time fiddle player Aunt Brigid Mason, would be accompanying her family.

The program explained that the Masons were Stone County natives, and Chase and Tracy had started their music careers right here at the Ozark Folk Center. After a year of performing together, they married, and their combined talents took them on a sky-rocket ride to the top of country music charts. They owned a theater in Branson, Missouri, now, but were often away on highly publicized tours.

All this Carrie already knew from Henry, who read everything he could find about the Masons and shared most of the information with her.

Henry had recently reported, with more than casual concern, that there might be dark clouds moving over the Chase and Tracy landscape. Some entertainment writers hinted at temperamental outbursts behind stage and said Chase and Tracy were flying too high for their own good, especially now that they were parents.

"Don't worry," she'd told him, intending comfort, "it's probably only tabloid-style gossip. We can't judge people living in a world we don't understand." (And besides, she'd thought, temperamental music stars are not our problem.)

Well, it really was too bad Henry wasn't here. Maybe they'd have CDs for sale; she could buy one for him and get it autographed.

But now it was time to be out in the forest. She picked up her walking stick and eased the door open. There were three people in the distance, going into another guest cabin. They'd probably escaped the convention's afternoon sessions too. They wouldn't matter.

She headed toward a worn path leading into the woods surrounding the cluster of cabins, striding quickly, swinging her walking stick in time to her steps. She didn't look around until she was safely out of sight of the Folk Center buildings.

As soon as she was alone in the comforting tangle of the forest, she slowed her pace, looking to see what spring wildflowers were visible. Sarvis had bloomed at home, as well as rue anemone, bluet, and spring beauty. It was almost the season for redbud and dogwood, and maybe there would be creamy spikes of bloodroot, which she rarely saw in her own woods.

She lost track of time as she strolled along, soaking up the peace that nature's quiet acceptance of life always brought to her. She watched a tortoise making its way through a tiny forest of beginning May apples and smiled at a pair of chickadees flirting among green buds.

At the edge of a deep hollow she stopped, looking down at wisps of ground fog that were beginning to float among the ghostly cedar trees below her. She left

21

the path to sit on a large rock, shutting her eyes, listening to bird chatter. She heard no human sounds from either the town or Folk Center. The rest of the world could be a million miles away.

But it wasn't. Behind the crisp bird notes, the sliding, sad music came again, floating like the ground fog. Yes, something strummed, and now she recognized the melody, since she'd heard it dozens of times on Henry's car radio. It was "Lying to Strangers," a folk song that had become a theme for Chase and Tracy. Someone was playing the tune on what sounded like a mountain dulcimer, creating music both eerie and beautiful. It seemed a part of the breeze that was beginning to shush above her in the treetops. Carrie opened her eyes and looked around. The notes came from no direction. It was impossible to decide their source.

Then, just like before, the music stopped as suddenly as it had begun. She continued to sit, this time enjoying the melody's memory on the slow breeze.

Movement caught her eye, and she looked down in the hollow. The form of a woman was just visible through wisps of fog. The musician?

The ghostly shape began climbing the hill without effort or noise. Carrie stood, ready to hurry back toward the lodge. No. How silly to be afraid. This must be one of the Folk Center workers, someone else enjoying the afternoon.

So Carrie stayed where she was and watched the woman climb. She was wrapped in black from bonnet

people were beginning to come out of the cabins, and they were dressed for dinner. She'd better hurry if she was going to catch up.

## Chapter II

Only a few stragglers were still finding seats when Carrie arrived at the convention dining area, and she was glad she'd worn her blue dress instead of the stand-out red.

She slid between tables and was dropping into a single vacant chair near the back when she heard her name.

Oh, bother! There was Beth at a front table, waving an arm and pointing to the empty seat next to her.

Nothing to do but smile and walk past the seated diners to the front of the room. Maybe the ones who didn't know her would think she was some late-arriving dignitary, though she knew quite well she didn't look like anyone's idea of a dignitary.

Beth was whispering frantically before Carrie's behind hit the chair bottom.

"Carrie, Chase and Tracy haven't shown up yet! We've called his mother's number and no one answered, and that was *ages* ago! They were supposed to be here early to rehearse."

She pointed to four vacant chairs at the head table. "And," she finished, stating the obvious, "they weren't. The director asked if I could find out what happened and says if they aren't here soon we'll have to begin without them. I hate sitting here doing nothing but worrying, but I'm supposed to stay with the men from the auto club."

Carrie looked at the two empty chairs across the table and turned back to Beth, who whispered, "Well, I can't exactly go with them to the men's room, now can I? Come on, think of something! They'll be back any minute."

"Where does the mother live?" Carrie asked. "Is it very far from here?"

"I don't know exactly," Beth said, shaking her bottle-blond curls, "but I remember hearing that the Masons lived out in the country. Do you suppose you could notify someone, Folk Center officials, or . . ."

She paused and glowered toward the man seated at the center of the head table.

"Darn it—excuse me, Carrie—but I'm getting stuck with this. The director came over, said he had the convention dinner to manage, and would I please find someone to check on the Masons since, of course, he didn't want me to go off and leave the auto club men without their host."

"It is an honor to be selected as a host," Carrie said, feeling a twinge of jealousy, even though she knew she'd have hated the assignment.

"Well, maybe, but I feel more like their chaperone if you want to know. Last night they listened to musicians on the square downtown until all hours. They kept singing along like they knew what they were doing, and neither of them can carry a tune in a basket.

26

I could have died of embarrassment. Oh, look, there they come, talking their way across the room as usual. Quick, Carrie, what can we do?"

A tingle of excitement was already beginning to bounce along Carrie's backbone. Here was a challenge, a mystery. She thought back to JoAnne and Amos' deaths and how she . . . well, she and Henry . . . had discovered who killed them. There had been danger and some really awful moments, though to be honest, she'd brought those on by just being stupid. It would never happen again.

The mystery that delayed the Masons would probably turn out to be nothing more than a flat tire, but at least she might have a chance to meet them and tell Henry what they were really like.

Oh, phooey, Henry should be here. She pictured her large, comfortable room and its two beds.

"Carrie, why on earth are you smiling *now?*" Beth asked, looking grumpy. "This is serious, aren't you paying attention?"

"Of course I am." Carrie thought for a moment longer, then whispered, "I'll go see what I can find out, but be sure they leave food for me. I don't want to miss dinner. Are there speeches?"

"The director, and you know he's good for at least twenty minutes. There'll be an invocation and comments by the head of the Folk Center. You have about forty minutes."

Carrie had already spotted baskets of cornbread and plates of butter along the center of the table, as well as bowls of Peach and Apple Chunky. She reached for a piece of cornbread, buttered it, plopped on a generous amount of Peach Chunky, and, realizing it was going to drip, wrapped the sticky mass in her napkin. Pushing the napkin in her purse, she smiled sweetly at a woman who was staring at her, then got up and left the room.

She stopped at the cash register in the public dining room and asked the hostess if anyone there knew Aunt Brigid Mason, Chase, or Tracy.

"Goodness, I don't," said the hostess, who looked about sixteen in her long calico dress and ruffled pinafore, "except I've seen them perform. Haven't they come yet? Some other lady was looking for them a bit ago."

"No, they haven't," Carrie said, "and I wondered if anyone around here knew them well enough, friends or something, who might help us locate them."

"Well," the girl said, "Farel Teal, Tracy's cousin, works over at the auditorium sometimes. He's in charge of organizing the evening performances, and they're rehearsing tonight. Try there."

Carrie thanked the girl and hurried out, hoping she could find her way to the back of the auditorium through the administration-classroom building and the fenced craft village behind it. If everything there was locked, there would be no access to the auditorium from the top of the ridge. She'd have to walk all the way down the hill and back up on the other side—in her dressy blue shoes.

She did the best she could when she bought dress shoes, and these heels were only an inch high, but her toes still felt pinched. More than once she'd wanted to ask a shoe manufacturer why anyone might think normal toes would fit comfortably in what they were offering. And—also more than once—she'd wondered what would happen if she wore lace-up walking shoes to a fancy occasion.

As Carrie hurried across the loop driveway, she wished she'd started her shoe revolution tonight.

But, thank goodness, the door of the administration building was unlocked. Someone must be working late, maybe a cleaning crew getting ready for the spring opening.

A few dim lights were on, but she didn't see anyone as she hurried down the hallway past the open doors of the small auditorium, classrooms, and offices. The click of her heels echoed in the dark building, and, in spite of squished toes, she began to tiptoe. The furtive action brought back an image of the woman who had moved so silently through the forest.

"The gowerow has taken the child."

Surely the strange woman was only a harmless local character, but her message was so weird.

At last Carrie reached the back door of the building. It wasn't locked either. She shoved the heavy door open and peered out. The craft village looked deserted, and the buildings were just one-dimensional humps against glaring security lights on the back of the main auditorium, but there was enough light to see the concrete walkway.

Now, before she left the building . . . She took the napkin out of her purse and was chewing sticky, peach-soaked cornbread as she slipped through the heavy door and let it click shut.

The hexagonal craft huts huddled close to the walk on either side of her, but their blank fronts made them all anonymous. They offered no hint of the rich displays of the potter, iron worker, weaver, and other inheritors of the Ozarks' traditional self-sufficiency that would be showing their skills when the area opened to the public.

The dark patches of the Heritage Herb Garden spread down the hill in raised beds on her left, and Carrie spent a moment wondering what mysteries might be unveiled there during the coming weekend. She looked forward to learning more about the preparation and use of traditional herbs grown here.

She came to a final turn in the walk just as she was finishing the last bite of cornbread and wiping peach syrup off her fingers. She could see the stage door at the back of the auditorium and the dark shape of the outdoor stage next to it.

The glow of a cigarette came and went. Someone was standing in the shadows at the edge of the outdoor stage, smoking. Probably one of the performers. Smoking wasn't allowed inside. At least that meant the back door would be unlocked.

Ignoring the person with the cigarette, she walked up the ramp and pulled on the stage door. It didn't open. She tugged again, rattling the door, then knocked on the metal with her fist.

"Kin I he'p you?" a male voice said from behind her.

She jumped at the sound. She'd been concentrating on the closed door. "Well, yes, I'm looking for Farel Teal."

"Ain't here. Who's askin'?"

"I am," Carrie said stiffly. "And who are you?"

The cigarette was pinched out, and a man walked toward her out of the shadows.

As he came into the light over the stage door, she saw that he was probably about her age, in his sixties, and his face had the weathered look of a man who spends most of his time outdoors.

"Name's Ben. I work here, backstage. T'aint nothin' around here I don't know about, and I kin tell you Farel Teal won't come rushin' through the door 'til the last minute. He's not one fer doin' anythin' extra, and comin' in early is too much extra fer him."

Ben stopped and glared into her face, which was easy, since his stooped form was only a few inches taller than her own five feet two, and he now stood less than three feet in front of her. She could smell the stale tobacco on his breath.

"So I'm askin' agin," he said, "who's lookin' fer Farel Teal?"

"How do you do, Ben?" She extended her hand toward him. "I'm Carrie, and I'm lookin' . . . looking for Farel Teal because his cousin Tracy and her hus-

31

band, mother-in-law, and daughter are needed over in the dining room. They're performing at a banquet there tonight and were supposed to arrive some time ago, but no one has seen them. I thought Mr. Teal might know where they are."

Ben didn't seem to see her extended hand. He snorted, spraying moisture, and Carrie jerked backwards.

The man didn't act like he noticed that either. "Chase 'n' Tracy 'n' Aunt Brigid are around here somewheres. I seen 'em earlier, but like I said, Farel ain't. They was lookin' fer him too. I told 'em what I'm tellin' you, Farel ain't here.

"'N' you're sniffin' the wrong trail 'bout Farel knowin' where his cousin is all the time. Tracy and him may have growed up playin' together like two pigs in a pen, but there's been no playin' and no love lost neither since she married Mason.

"He's a bad 'un," Ben concluded, dropping his voice to a raspy gurgle.

"Oh," Carrie said, wondering which of the two men, Chase Mason or Farel Teal, was supposed to be bad. Her backbone was tingling again, but she didn't have time to ask this odd little man about who was bad and who wasn't.

"Well, Ben, I just know I'm supposed to find the performers for the Department of Parks and Tourism banquet, and," she looked at her watch, "I have twenty minutes to do it. Did you say you'd seen the Masons?"

"Yup, 'bout fifteen minutes ago. Don't know where

they was headed after they left the auditorium though. They seemed mighty anxious to find Farel themselves. He's peculiar popular all of a sudden."

He fell silent but looked thoughtful, and Carrie wondered if he was deciding to tell her something that might help.

She waited, shifting her weight back and forth to relieve her complaining toes.

But, after a pause, the man just repeated, "Sorry, can't he'p you," and turned away, taking a key from his vest pocket. He unlocked the auditorium door and, without looking at her again, slipped inside. The door shut firmly behind him.

Well, then, that was that. Maybe the Masons had gone to the dining room some other way. She hoped so, because she had no idea what to do next.

Carrie retraced her path through the craft area toward the back door of the administration building. She'd started to pull the door open when a shouted *"no"* came through the small crack. What on earth? Was someone saying she couldn't come through this building now?

She was about to open the door farther to see who had shouted at her, but the hidden voice went on, obviously not speaking to her at all.

She stopped where she was, trying to decide what to do next, holding the heavy door open just enough so she could hear what was being said. If it was a private conversation, maybe she should knock or say hello before she went in.

A woman was talking. She wasn't crying, but Carrie could hear tears behind her words. "No! He won't hurt her, Chase." A pause. "He loves her! I know him, and if we raise a fuss it'll only make things worse. He'll get stubborn and up the ante. Don't you see, if we just pay, he'll bring her right back. All he really wants is money. He'd never harm Dulcey."

A man's voice now, shaking, furious. "Oh, sure you know him, Tracy, you *know* him all right. But how do you know he's not on drugs? Does he still drink too much? And Dulcey is supposed to perform with us tonight. How're we gonna explain her being gone? I'm heading for his house right this minute. Y'all can go ahead and start the program without me. It's pretty obvious you don't give a . . ."

*"No."*

The woman screamed the word.

A lower, older woman's voice broke in, spreading like molasses over the echoing "No."

"Well, son, you know these folks are paying you to perform, so that's exactly what you're goin' to do. You'll fulfill your contract. Besides, Tracy's right, Farel'll be good to Dulcey, 'n' she's always enjoyed being with him."

Silence. Carrie shoved her knee against the crack in the door to help hold its weight. If she let the door shut now, they'd notice the click.

The male voice came again, and this time it was almost a whine. "Well, is this what you want us to do? You want us to sit and smile at the audience and say,

34

'Sorry, our daughter's been kidnapped by her mother's crook of a cousin and he wants a huge sum of money, so that's why our little star, Dulcey Mason, isn't with us tonight. We're so sorry.' Trace, you know he hates me. And it was your fault for letting her go out in Momma's yard alone. Anyone could have kidnapped her."

"Chase, Chase." It was the younger woman's voice, still sounding of tears . . . pleading. "It isn't really like kidnapping, and what else can we do? Farel's good with Dulcey; you know she's safe. Let's just pay him and get it over with. It's not that much money, not for us now. All we have to do is pay and he'll bring her back. He's desperate to have money to start over with. I told you, but you wouldn't listen, wouldn't loan him the money, and that's why he did this."

"Oh-h-h no, Trace, you can't fly that rooster in my coop! And, if ol' cousin Farel is so great, why's he want to leave the state in such a hurry anyway? Why the threats? On the phone he said if we didn't pay the ransom he'd take Dulcey far away. That sounds like a threat to me."

"He didn't mean it. For heaven's sake, Chase, go ahead and pay him. We don't want any police or publicity. You know that wouldn't be good for us, so what else is there to do?"

"Of course you're taking the side of your scummy relatives."

There was a gasp, then the older woman's voice.

"Now, now, son, there's no call for that. Of course

35

it's worrisome, but we have a show to do and we're gonna do it. Let's go, we're mighty late already. We'll say Dulcey has a cold and we had to find a sitter. Come on. I don't see what else to do fer now. Besides, I bet Dulcey's having fun with Uncle Farel. She's purty independent, 'n' used to bein' with other folks when you two's out on the road."

Carrie heard movement and the scrape of a chair. She pulled back hurriedly, letting the door click shut, then opened it wide and stepped into the hall, releasing the door so it would slam behind her.

There was light coming from the room on the right. A man looked out. Chase Mason. She recognized him, of course.

"Well, h-hello there," Carrie said, thinking her voice sounded much too loud in the empty building. She swallowed, wondering if her halting words would give her away as an eavesdropper. But then, they were probably used to people being overwhelmed by their fame and would think that's what was causing her discomfort. She cleared her throat, spread her lips in a smile, and continued more steadily, "I'm your escort. The convention banquet is about to start. Shall we go eat?"

# Chapter III

Silence.

For a moment, Chase Mason stared at Carrie as if she were some threatening being that had suddenly materialized out of the air. Then his look of suspicion faded, his head jerked in a nod, and he turned back to the lighted room. Following him, Carrie saw that all three performers were picking up instrument cases, but still, no one said even a small "hello."

Well, somebody should say something!

"I'm Carrie McCrite, and I work for the Arkansas Department of Parks and Tourism. I'm your escort this evening—I guess I said that, didn't I? We're so glad you're going to play for us tonight. It's quite an honor."

She knew she must seem like a babbling fool, but why wouldn't they say anything?

Finally Aunt Brigid Mason spoke, sounding as if she had just awakened and remembered what was expected in moments like this. "Pleased to meet you, Miz McCrite."

"Ah, uh, we're certainly looking forward to hearing you play."

Silence.

Carrie tried again. "Isn't Dulcey going to be here?"

Three voices spoke together: "Sick." "She has a cold." And, the friendliest: "Oh, we're so sorry, the little one has a slight cold, and we thought it best to leave her at home with a babysitter. We're a bit late on account of it."

That was Aunt Brigid Mason, of course, and after Carrie had murmured sympathy, the silence returned.

Carrie was leading the way into the main hall when Tracy said, almost whispering, "Y'all go on, I'm gonna stop in the restroom here. I'll catch up to you."

Chase turned toward Tracy and reached out as if to grab her arm, but she was already headed down the side hall. He glanced at Carrie, shrugged, and said, "Okay."

Carrie started toward the front door again, and as she walked, she heard the snick of a latch as a door clicked shut. Odd. Carrie was familiar with public restrooms in almost any building where she'd spent much time, and she knew, without thinking about it, that the public restrooms here had doors with automatic closers that went shut with a shush and a soft thunk. Wherever Tracy had gone, it wasn't to the restroom, but why the lie?

She shook the question aside and, as she pushed through the front doors of the building, thought once more about the woman in the woods. She decided that, somehow, the Masons should be told about the eerie message. Hearing about a kidnapped child twice in one day was just too much coincidence. Everyone could be talking about the same child. But how would she bring the subject up without admitting she'd overheard some of their conversation?

"We'll be sorry to have missed seeing Dulcey."

No response.

"I'll bet she enjoys playing with you."

A murmured, "Yes," from Chase, but nothing more. Carrie pursed her lips in frustration. What now? The strange warnings came too close to the reality of what she had just overheard to be completely dismissed as the product of a fertile or twisted imagination. That

38

woman might really know something about the kidnapping of Dulcey Mason.

It would have been easy to bring the forest encounter into almost any type of conversation. Since the Masons were native to the area, quizzing them about odd folk lore and a kidnapper called a gowerow would fit right in.

But neither Chase nor his mother offered an opportunity for any conversation at all, let alone questions about a spooky woman who spoke of kidnapping. They remained silent to the point of rudeness.

If only Henry were here right this moment. Then there'd be someone to share this with and another head to think about what to do next.

It had sounded like Tracy and Aunt Brigid thought Dulcey was quite safe—even having a good time, sort of a kidnapping game—but as far as Carrie was concerned, that was carrying fun and games too far. Chase was the only one who had seemed worried, and he was doing a good job of concealing his feelings now.

Oh, well, phooey on them. The Masons probably had so much money that they could pay the ransom without pain, and the public would never know about the abduction of a famous child.

She told herself to forget the whole thing. None of her business. But her spine was still tingling and her mind buzzing with concern as she led the Masons into the dining room.

A breathless Tracy caught up with them just as the convention director was finishing his speech, and after he had acknowledged polite applause, Carrie ushered the three to their seats, whispered their explanation for tardiness in the director's ear, then went to her own chair.

She had taken a bite of her salad before Beth, who was staring at her with what looked like awe, could murmur, "Where were they? Was something wrong?"

After repeating the public explanation for the performers' lateness and acknowledging Beth's thanks with what she hoped was a casual smile, Carrie turned her attention to the food in front of her. She had no difficulty appreciating the meal in spite of the fact that her thoughts were picking through the odd events of the afternoon and evening, and she was trying to sort out what to do next.

Maybe it was none of her business but, after all, she *had* been the one to encounter the woman in the forest and, what's more, that woman had chosen to communicate a message to her. Didn't some responsibility go with that?

Even if she had to admit to the Masons that she'd heard just a teeny bit of their conversation, she really should tell them what the woman had said. By the time her plate was empty she'd worked out a way to do it. After the performance she'd continue pretending to be their hostess and leave with them to escort them to . . . where? They knew this area a lot better than she did.

Well, she'd fake it. She was very good at faking things, as she knew Henry would affirm, without meaning his affirmation as a compliment. Whatever. She was good at acting. She'd just walk out with them and say something like: "By the way, I was in the woods this afternoon and I saw an unusual woman. I wonder if, being native to this area, you might understand what she was talking about . . ."

A waitress took away her dinner plate and put down a fat piece of huckleberry pie with sugary purple juice oozing out each side. Oh, my! She was beginning to feel stuffed, but she took a few bites of pie anyway and went back to thoughts about the missing child.

Finally she looked up to see Beth glaring at her and realized she'd been responding to her friend's attempts at conversation almost like the Masons had responded to hers a few minutes earlier.

She reached over to squeeze Beth's hand. "Sorry, my thoughts have been a million miles away."

"Well, I can sure tell *that*," Beth said, "and I was wondering if Henry had called and said he couldn't come tomorrow."

Carrie laughed. "Goodness, no. I'm making plans for using some of the new ideas we've heard this week. Sorry, guess I can't stop thinking about my tourists. I was also thinking I should try and pick more huckleberries next summer and freeze them to make pies."

These were explanations Beth could understand, and she smiled at Carrie, displaying teeth that were stained purple with berry juice. Then she nodded and returned to her piece of pie, leaving Carrie to feel only slightly guilty about telling such outrageous lies—though Beth would probably remember any minute that Carrie was no cook and never made pies. Oh, well. She would explain everything later, when all this was over and the child was safely home.

Surely that would be soon.

After the dessert plates had been removed, the convention director presented Tracy Teal, Chase Mason, and Aunt Brigid Mason with the flourish their fame deserved, repeating lavish and obviously memorized accolades for each of them.

Once more Carrie was aware that Henry, not she, should be the one listening to this program. Hoping to remember some detail or musical specialty to tell him about, she turned her full attention to the performance.

For the first time she looked closely at the Masons. Tracy was petite, with delicate features, creamy skin, and what Beth would call a Scarlett O'Hara waist. She had long blond hair, worn in a simple ponytail. Her small waist was enhanced by a full country skirt and ruffled blouse.

Chase and his mother were darker. He was tall and a little too thin to be a real pin-up. Aunt Brigid was sturdier than her son, and the gathered skirt and shawl she wore went well with her full figure, though—Carrie looked back at Tracy—the same type costume showed off a petite figure too.

None of the three seemed conscious of their looks, but they were obviously quite conscious of their music. They're really accomplished professional musicians, Carrie thought. At least for the moment, the problem of Dulcey seemed not to be affecting them at all.

The audience stood to applaud and cheer after the last song. Then a few people began calling, "Lying to Strangers, Lying to Strangers," and soon almost everyone in the dining room, including Carrie, was chanting the name of Chase and Tracy's best-known recording.

Finally Chase held up a hand.

"Thank you, thank you all very much. As you know, no music written after 1940 is performed here at the Ozark Folk Center, and," he laughed and looked at Tracy, "since Tracy and I wrote the song, we can't claim it's that old."

He paused to allow the audience to laugh too, then continued. "But seein' as how this is a private party . . ."

Applause interrupted him. The three musicians exchanged glances, then looked down at their instruments until the noise subsided and the dining room fell into an expectant hush.

In a moment the familiar melody began on Tracy's guitar, then Aunt Brigid lifted her fiddle and joined in, playing harmony. Chase strummed the rhythm on his banjo and started to sing, very softly:

"When she was only one day old
She stole her daddy's heart.
And by the time that she was four
They were n'er apart.

43

"But she'd be lying to strangers,
Lying to strangers.
Never any other man,
He's the main one in her heart."

Carrie marveled at the smiling, bland faces that Tracy and Aunt Brigid turned to the audience as they accompanied Chase. These women were incredibly good actresses.

"And after her own momma left,
People saw 'twas true.
She would always stay by him,
He was the only man she knew.

"And she was lying to strangers . . ."

Carrie looked around the room. Everyone was gripped by the emotion that had now begun to fill Chase's words.

"A sixteen year old's beauty
Turned many a young man's head,
But still the same old story came,
'I'm Daddy's, I'll not wed.'"

Aunt Brigid and Tracy were still cool—mere background figures. Chase wasn't. What if Dulcey had been here? Would Chase have sung the song to his four-year-old daughter? That would certainly touch every heart in an audience.

44

"Then, when she was twenty-one
The stranger came to town.
He swore that he would make her his,
She'd wear his wedding gown."

As the next chorus began, Tracy's voice, then Aunt Brigid's, backed up Chase's strong tenor.

"But she kept lying to strangers,
Lying to strangers.
'Daddy's the only man I love,
The main man in my heart.'

"The stranger stayed a single man.
He bought the farm next door.
The years went by, the two would smile.
Folks saw that and nothing more.

"And she kept lying to strangers,
Lying to strangers.
'Daddy's still the only man,
The main one in my heart.'

"When the two were fifty-one
Daddy died in his own bed.
Three months later she became a bride.
'What a shock' folks 'round there said.

"But they'd been lying to strangers,
Lying to strangers.

The man next door was not strange,
He was the main one in her heart.
The main man in her heart."

As the last note faded, the entire audience rose to its feet again, stirred, Carrie knew, not only by beautiful music, but by an emotion most would never know the reason for.

Finally, Chase held up his hand for quiet.

"I should tell you that the term 'lying to strangers' originally had nothing to do with this love song. It comes from a popular saying among us hill folks . . . 'We only lie to strangers.' But," he continued over the laughter, which his voice quickly silenced, "I'm not lying when I say how much Tracy, Momma, and I enjoyed performing for you. Thanks, and good night."

Before anyone in the audience had time to ask for another encore or could rush forward to meet the stars, the three of them had cased their instruments and left the room.

Caught by surprise, Carrie leaped to her feet. Whispering to an astonished Beth that she needed to escort the Masons, she picked up her purse and jacket and hurried out of the banquet hall.

The performers had halted at the opposite side of the darkened public dining room. Carrie saw Tracy say something to Chase and hand him her guitar case before she turned to walk down the hallway leading to the public restrooms. Carrie hesitated, watching Chase and his mother go out the front door of the

46

building, then decided to follow Tracy. The ladies' room would be a good place to talk.

As soon as she reached the hall, Carrie discovered with dismay that Tracy wasn't headed for the ladies' room after all, but for a nearby public telephone. She had her back to Carrie and was punching in a number.

Carrie slowed her steps, hoping to overhear what Tracy was saying, but when Tracy looked toward her, she pulled open the door marked "Women." She could think of no other reason for being behind Tracy.

Carrie had often wondered how soundproof restroom doors were, and now she found that this one was certainly soundproof. She couldn't hear anything outside, even with her ear against the door.

What should she do? She didn't want to lose the opportunity to talk with at least one of the Masons. Gambling that Tracy would come in after finishing her conversation, Carrie went into one of the stalls, shut the door, sat down, and waited.

Eventually it became obvious she had gambled and lost. Too much time had passed. She left the stall and opened the restroom door. The hall was empty. She looked at the pay phone and saw a guitar pick lying on the shelf. Well, it was a small thing, but it did give her a reason to follow, and that was exactly what she was going to do! She stuck the guitar pick in her pocket and headed out the door and across the driveway to the administration building. She assumed the Masons' vehicle was parked in the employee parking lot on the far side of the auditorium.

But, she discovered, the front door of the administration building was now locked.

Since the Masons were on foot, there must be another opening to the craft area. Carrie walked around one side of the building and saw only a weathered board fence glowing silver in the moonlight. She shivered, wishing she had worn her heavier jacket, and circled back around the front of the building, continuing past the entry doors to the other side.

There, a utility gate! Trying the latch, she found the gate was unlocked.

She hesitated. Even someone as unmusical as she was would probably realize that returning a guitar pick wasn't worth following Tracy all over the Ozark Folk Center complex. Many in the Masons' audiences would probably treasure such a souvenir and take it home to show off. She could save it and give it to Henry. Besides, it was dark, it was cold, and this was getting ridiculous.

But . . .

She felt the thing in her pocket. Would a musical novice assume such a pick was specially made for Tracy? She doubted it, but then, she didn't really know. And even if she found Tracy, would the woman talk to her, or would she just take the pick and rush off without so much as a thank you?

Well, Carrie thought, I do know this really *isn't* my business.

Carrie heard a barred owl's call and the return of the call from a distance. Back home she often sat on her deck or stood in the woods and held two-way, or even three-way, conversations with the owls. For some reason she didn't understand, they responded to her mimicry of their "who-hoot hoohoo," and usually came closer to continue the conversation. But she wouldn't break the silence here tonight.

She was just turning away to walk back to the dining room when a soft cry and then a moan came from beyond the gate.

That was enough. Carrie lifted the latch.

## Chapter IV

The moon was now behind a cloud, but she still hadn't expected the area inside the fence to be so awfully dark. What had happened to the security lights? Carrie stood by the gate and tried to figure out just where she was and where everything else in the enclosed area was.

The person who had cried out couldn't be too far away. She waited, listening, afraid to move or make any noise. Then the sound came again. It was definitely a woman, crying, "No, no," very softly. And—maybe it was her imagination since she'd heard her say it earlier—it sounded like Tracy's "No."

But where *was* Tracy? Somewhere ahead. Carrie's impulse was to run forward, but that was impossible in the blinding darkness. All she could do was wait.

At last her eyes began to detect shades and shapes. There was nothing on her left. The ground there seemed to fall away sharply. She could feel the drop with her left foot—the beginning of the terraced herb gardens. The sound hadn't come from that direction anyway.

She knew the administration building was on her right. She could see the outline of a large tree next to it, and, concentrating, she decided the walkway through the craft area must begin under that tree.

She began to slide her feet uphill, keeping her hand against the stone wall of the building. Suddenly her left foot caught on something. She fell, brushing her hand and face against the rough wall and toppling into an area that seemed bare of anything but damp earth.

At least she'd made no noise but a muffled "whump."

There's something to be said for well-padded bottoms, Carrie thought as she sat, assessing damage. Her hand and face tingled and were probably scraped, but, other than a sting in the area where her blue dress met the ground, there seemed to be no other damage, except maybe to the dress. Her behind was probably covered with dirt blobs.

Well. She felt the ground around her and discovered she was sitting in a newly turned square of earth outlined by wooden landscaping timbers. It must be some sort of garden bed, and anything planted in it was probably worse off than she was. Too bad.

She heard another "No . . ." and forgot about the garden and the dirt. She crawled over the timbers on her hands and knees, and, bracing her uninjured hand against the wall, stood and continued uphill until her feet located the edge of the concrete walkway. At the same time, her hand felt the corner of the back door alcove to the administration building. Now she knew where she was, and the building just ahead of her, a dark rectangle against the sky, was the craft area snack shop.

The pale concrete of the walkway was lighter than the ground around it, and she began following its winding trail toward the source of the sounds.

At the front of the snack shop she stopped, moved closer to the wall, and stuck her head around the corner, listening, her eyes sweeping the shades of darkness.

Silence.

Then a glow came from the dressmaker's shop. Somewhere near the floor of the shop a small flame flared, dimmed, went out. The door must be open. She moved toward the door and heard breathing that sounded like gasps, and, once again, a crooned "No-no-no."

"Tracy?" Carrie hoped the person inside could hear her cautious whisper.

For a moment the gasping breaths stopped, then Tracy's voice said, "Momma? Momma Brigid?" There were two or three more gasps before Tracy began to cry—great, rattling sobs that sounded as if they were going to turn her inside out.

Carrie didn't take time to explain that she wasn't Brigid Mason. She went quickly around the door and, guided by sound, knelt next to the woman seated on the floor. "Tracy, where's the light switch? What's wrong?"

Tracy hiccuped. "L-lights don't work. Who *are* you?"

"Carrie McCrite. I walked you to the dinner. Is there trouble?"

"Trouble? Trouble?" Now it sounded like Tracy Teal was laughing.

Before Carrie could say more, the racket stopped. Tracy stood and said in a shaky voice, "Wait, all these shops have candlesticks."

A match flared again, and Carrie gasped before she could stop herself. There was another person in the shop, a large man, lying on the floor. Even in the dim match flame she saw something shiny enough to reflect light. Scissors. It was a pair of scissors, or at least their handles. The rest of the scissors were out of sight because they were in the man's chest. The dark places . . . that would be blood.

The light brightened. Tracy had found the candlestick.

The two women stared at each other over the shuddering flame. For a moment, Tracy returned Carrie's unblinking gaze, then wet streaks dripped down her cheeks as, once more, she began to cry. Carrie got to her feet and reached out to touch the young woman's shoulder before she turned to inspect the man on the floor.

She shut her eyes. Swallowed. Swallowed again.

Steady, she thought, steady. You've faced violent death before. When Amos died, the gunshot wound was uglier than this. Blood spattered everywhere then . . . no, don't think about it. You're strong, as strong as you need to be for this moment.

She could look. She had to. Oh. Oh, yes, certainly things had been worse when Amos died. Blood had simply flowed here, wetting the bright blue shirt and concrete floor.

She bent, felt for a pulse, listened for breathing. The man's skin was warm and soft, but she couldn't detect any heart beat, and his open eyes looked frozen. The broad chest was still, and no new blood came from the wound.

The light had been shaking in Tracy's hand, but now it steadied. She'd put the candlestick on a stool.

Carrie examined the room. She saw lace in glass cases, bolts of cloth stacked on tables, stiff dress forms displaying Ozarks mountain styles. Long dresses. Aprons. Bonnets. Old-fashioned treadle sewing machine. She peered behind the counter and checked inside the single dressing room. No one else was in the shop.

She went to the door, shut it, and turned to study Tracy in the candlelight.

No. Impossible. This woman couldn't have inflicted such a wound. The man was tall, and, even in death, the muscles in the arms and chest under his blue shirt looked powerful. Tracy wasn't any taller than Carrie. She'd have had to raise her arm, aim the blow. She was so tiny, so thin. The wound was in front; the man would have seen her. He could have stopped her easily with one hand.

No, not Tracy.

While Carrie was trying to sort out her thoughts, Tracy began swaying back and forth, crooning, "Dear God . . . make this go away . . . forgive me . . . no, oh, no . . . noooo."

Her words sounded like both a prayer and a cry of the most wretched despair ever heard. She was swaying so far it looked like she was about to topple over, so Carrie reached out and pulled the young woman into her arms. Seeing nothing to sit on but the stool that held the candlestick, she sank to the floor, still holding Tracy, pulling her into her lap like a small child. For a long time they huddled on the floor together while Carrie stroked and patted, murmuring the familiar mother-words, "There-there now, there-there." At last the sobs faded to low moans, and it was time to decide what to do next.

She still hadn't figured that out when Tracy stopped moaning, sniffed, and slid out of Carrie's lap to sit next to her. She took out the cloth hanky that had been part of a perky stage costume only an hour earlier and blew her nose. The emotions and questions on her face were as clear as if she'd spoken aloud.

She's deciding whether or not to trust me, Carrie thought.

But something needed to be done at once. There wasn't time to wait for trust. Carrie began speaking

54

softly, her words coming easily now.

"Do you know who this man is?"

"F-Farel. My cousin, Farel Teal."

She had expected the answer but, because of Dulcey, had hoped her guess was wrong.

"How did you find him? Why is he here?" While Carrie waited for a reply, she remembered Tracy's side trip in the administration building. A phone call? And she'd made another call from the restaurant.

"You called him and asked him to meet you here?"

After a pause and a frown, Tracy said, "Yes."

So she's decided she can trust me, Carrie thought. It's my harmless, grey-haired grandma look.

"I called him from the administration building while you-all were starting to the dining room . . . asked him to meet me here after the performance . . . . bring Dulcey. See, she was, uh, visiting him, and . . . and I needed her back, because Chase, well, he didn't understand. I had to talk to Farel and explain . . . and . . . he said he would meet me. He's . . . he was deputy chief of the Folk Center fire crew, so he has keys to all the shops. This place seemed good, away from where folks would be.

"After we finished the show, I told Chase and Momma Brigid I was going to stop at the dining room phone and call a girl friend here before I forgot—said I'd promised to call. They should go on and we'd meet in the auditorium.

I pretended to use the phone until they left, then I came on here.

55

"But I could barely see. I thought they woulda turned on the post lights by now, but it was dark. I had to feel my way. That's when I saw the light in here."

"Light?"

"Cigarette lighter, but I didn't smell anyone smoking. Farel doesn . . . didn't smoke."

The wet lines on Tracy's cheeks glowed and faded in the candle flame, and now her words began to spurt out as if she were rushing through a just-remembered speech.

"I thought Farel hadn't made it yet, but I started toward the door anyway. I wasn't thinking, you know, and my knees hit the stone wall of the flower planter out there. I must have made a sound because the man with the lighter ran.

"I came around the wall to see what he'd been doing. It was strange. What would he steal here? They don't leave any money. And if he was a workman, why would he run? The light switch didn't work, but I had the package of matches we use in one of our sets at Branson in my pocket. I looked and, um . . . Farel . . .

"I didn't pay any attention to who ran past me. Whoever it was went toward the auditorium real fast. There was no way to tell. It was dark . . . and anyway, there was Farel . . ."

"But you did see that it was a man?"

Tracy stared wide-eyed at Carrie and didn't answer.

She's certainly making sure I know she can't, or more likely won't, identify the person who was in

56

here, Carrie thought, and wondered why, but she only said, "What did you do then?"

"W-went to Farel, you know, to see if he was, um, if I could, uh, help him. And I couldn't." Now Tracy bowed her head and whispered, "Dear God, forgive me."

Carrie turned away from Tracy and crawled over to the body. She looked at it for a long minute and was trying to memorize every detail when she saw a bit of paper clutched in the left hand.

Knowing Henry would not approve of disturbing what might be evidence, and not caring a bit, Carrie pulled the square of paper free and smoothed it out. The words looked as if they had been painted with a brush. "Will you pay enuf to keep the girl alive? Tell no one. See note in blue bird house after tomoro's show starts."

She slid back across the floor toward Tracy, whose head was still bowed. Should she show her the note? If Tracy was frightened and worried now, what would seeing the note do to her? Or did she already know about it? Was this just a continuation of the kidnapping scheme? If so, Tracy probably was a part of it— but how *could* she be? How could she . . .

Carrie prayed for guidance as she thought of the child. She needed a clear plan, needed to act right away. She looked around the shop again. No phone. The administration building was locked, but there was the auditorium. It was probably bustling with people, but it would have phones. She must find a phone where she wouldn't be overheard and call the police.

She looked back at Tracy's bowed head. Well, what else could she do? Henry wasn't here to help, there was no one else to turn to. And she couldn't protect Tracy, not now.

She held the note toward Tracy and said, "Does this look like it was written by Farel?"

At first Tracy didn't move, but then she looked up, stared at the note in Carrie's hand, read it once, twice, and asked, "Where'd you get this?"

"It was in his hand."

Carrie watched Tracy carefully as sadness was replaced by . . . what? Fear? Or was Tracy a good actress as well as a good musician?

She repeated, "Does this look like it was written by Farel?"

"Well, it musta been. It's printed odd, sort of disguised looking, but it musta been him."

After a moment of thought, Tracy lifted her chin. Now she looked stubborn. "But Farel could *spell*." She spit out the defensive words, and, for a moment, reminded Carrie of Ben and his moist snort.

Carrie wondered if Tracy realized what the presence of that note might mean—assuming she wasn't part of the plot that put it there—but she didn't think it was time to mention her own suspicions.

"Where is this blue bird house, and who knows about it?" she asked.

"Just about everyone who works at the Folk Center. It's sort of a joke. Fella who used to make and sell bird

58

houses here said bluebird houses should be blue, so he made a fancy blue one and put it up. Everyone thought it was pretty, but they still bought the plain ones. He stopped making blue houses, but the sample's still up on a pole outside the gift shop. Bushes have grown up around it now, and visitors don't usually see it."

Carrie thought for a moment, biting her lip. Farel Teal wouldn't have had any reason to send a note. He'd already told them he had Dulcey and, from what Chase said, had also explained his demands. So, that meant . . .

Carrie shut her eyes. Had someone killed Farel to take the child? Her heart lurched. Be strong, she reminded herself again and realized she was now up to her ears in this mess and had also accepted, without question, what must surely be her responsibility—helping the Masons.

She crawled back to the body, knowing that Henry, and probably others, would eventually question her. She mustn't miss the tiniest detail. Henry had taught her that the little things could be very important. She needed to remember everything.

The dead man's shirt had a long narrow slit in it that extended at least a quarter inch on each side of the place where the scissors had entered his chest. The candlelight cast tiny ragged shadows where edges of the shirt fabric were lifted up and away from the wound. Even allowing for the blood that had flowed from the wound, why . . . ?

She got to her feet and turned toward Tracy, who

was staring into space, statue-still. "Did you touch anything? Farel? The scissors? Was everything just like this when you got here?"

"Yes, well, um, I touched his wrist and neck like you did. Then I laid my hand on his forehead, like Momma would when we were kids and got sick."

"You touched nothing else at all?"

Tracy dropped her head and spoke softly. "That's all."

"But then, why . . ."

Carrie stopped and looked toward the door. It was opening—a dark form stepping through. Before the shriek in Carrie's throat had time to break out, Chase Mason's voice said, "Good God almighty!"

Instead of rushing to him as Carrie had expected, Tracy bowed her head further and wadded her hands in her lap. She looked like a statue—"Mourning"— posed on a stand.

He'll at least go to her, thought Carrie.

Instead, Chase remained in the doorway, and all he said was, "What happened? Tracy, what happened?" His words were slow, measured, his face and voice without expression.

Several moments passed, and when Tracy stayed as she was, saying nothing, acting as if she hadn't heard her husband, Carrie said, "Farel had evidently just been killed by a person or persons unknown when Tracy came past here on her way to the auditorium. A man she can't identify ran out past her. This note was on the floor."

60

For garden seed, how had she dragged up that "person or persons unknown?" It made her sound like some television cop. Well, maybe that wasn't such a bad impression to give Chase and Tracy right now.

Chase seemed not to have noticed her words. He was reading the note, his face turning to grey steel.

"Dear God, Dulcey."

Then he looked down at Farel. "Evil! Evil rat. He . . ."

A cry from Tracy stopped the words, and both he and Carrie turned toward her. Her eyes were wide and full of panic as she stumbled to her feet. She started toward the door, mumbling something Carrie couldn't understand.

Chase caught her easily and held on as she began to kick and hit, twisting and writhing, trying to free herself. Chase simply held tighter, pinning her arms, though her legs still swung at him. He paid no attention to the blows from her soft shoes.

Finally Carrie heard understandable words as Tracy's voice rose to a shriek, "Go to Farel's, she'll be there . . . I've got to get to her . . . oh, let me go, let me go!"

The noise stopped when Chase loosed his right hand and slapped his wife's face.

"Was that neces . . ." Carrie began, then cut the words off when Tracy collapsed against her husband, dropping like a rag doll.

"Hysterics," was all Chase said as he lifted Tracy into his arms and stood very still, looking down at her face.

Speaking as calmly as she could, Carrie asked, "Do you think Dulcey might still be at Farel's house?"

Chase's sharp eyes turned on her, and she decided that he was going to ask how she was involved in this. But, before he opened his mouth, she saw understanding hit him.

"Farel *didn't* write that note! Someone else has Dulcey!" He looked down at Tracy again. "Good God, what has she done?"

Carrie spoke quickly, taking control, hoping Tracy hadn't heard her husband's condemning words. "We need to act at once. Call the police, or is it the sheriff here?"

"Oh, no, we won't," Chase said. "First we find Dulcey."

She sidestepped that and asked, "Did you go through this area after Tracy left you?"

"Yes. Momma and I did."

"Together?"

His eyes said he caught her implication, but he only nodded. At least he was willing to answer her questions.

"Did you hear or see anything? Anyone in here?"

"No. Just heard owls. The security lights were off, but with the moonlight we could see enough to make our way. We were talking about Dulcey. Wasn't paying attention to anything else. But I didn't see anyone, and I think Momma woulda said if she did."

"Where have you been since then?"

"Back stage. Talking to folks while we waited for

Tracy, asking about Farel. Ben said he hadn't seen him tonight. Uh, that's Ben Yokum, stage hand."

"Yokum? Like Little Abner?" Carrie couldn't help it.

"Yeh, just like that. He came from California not too long ago. Says he's from the Ozarks originally but no one here seems to know him, so he musta not been from this region. Well, anyhow, when Tracy didn't show up, I left Momma talking and came to see, and . . ."

"Have you any idea how long you were in the auditorium?"

"Maybe twenty, twenty-five minutes. Momma mighta noticed the time more exactly."

"But someone was with you and your mother all that time?"

Chase stared at her for a moment, then nodded.

"So then, since I was with Tracy most of that time, you should have no objection to calling the police."

Tracy stirred and murmured, "No," just as Chase said, "It's the sheriff, and we won't call him."

Carrie ignored them and went on. "We have to tell them about Farel right away. You can see they won't suspect you; for one thing, you've both been with other people.

"Surely you don't want the woman who comes to work here tomorrow to be the one to find this. Besides, the sooner the law comes, the better. It's best they get here before anyone else bothers things and destroys some kind of evidence. Or," she looked at

63

each of them, "don't you want them to find Farel's killer?"

Neither of them answered her, and, after a moment, Carrie continued. "I know your first concern is Dulcey's safety, and it's mine too, but that doesn't mean we can ignore a murder.

"Think now. Would there have been someone helping Farel with her, a wife or friend? Where's the rest of his family? Who else might have written the note? The bad spelling may have been faked."

Tracy began to squirm, her voice rising again as she said, ". . . go to Farel's now . . . he was lying about bringing her back . . . musta wanted more money . . . she'll be at his place . . . go there now. Chase, put me down. Let me go!"

Over Tracy's words, Carrie asked, "Where does Farel live? Can we get in his house without breaking in?"

Tracy's head bounced up, her eyes wild, too bright. "Dulcey will be there. We'll find her! He lives alone, but I know where he hides his house key. It'll be easy to get in."

"We won't call the sheriff," Chase repeated as if he hadn't heard them. "You saw the note. And what about the news getting out?" His voice shook. "We're news, oh, my Lord, are we news!"

He looked down at his wife, then at Carrie. "We gotta find Dulcey quick. First thing we do is go to Farel's house." He said this as if it were something he'd just thought of.

Eyes really can blaze with passion, Carrie thought as she watched him. His eyes were reflecting sparks from the candlelight.

"Yes, we'll go there," she said as Tracy finally twisted free of her husband's slackened hold and dropped to the floor, rocking slightly on her feet. Carrie noticed that Chase had moved quickly to wrap controlling fingers in the fabric of his wife's full skirt.

"But I am reporting Farel's murder," she said. "I'll call 911 from a phone in the auditorium. I won't say anything about the kidnapping yet. If we leave now we'll have time to check Farel's house and see if Dulcey might be there alone, or with someone you know. The sheriff won't come until after he's dealt with this.

"But, if strangers are at Farel's, we can't approach the house without help. We'll just stay hidden and keep watch until help comes. We might increase the danger to your daughter if we do anything more—do you understand?"

Neither of them spoke.

She looked at Chase. "Do you have a cell phone?"

He nodded. "In the car."

"Good. We can call for help if we need it."

Now Carrie felt an electric energy moving her. She said, "I'm staying with you. You need a witness to everything you do from now on. And we must talk. I want to tell you about a woman I saw in the woods . . . ."

# Chapter V

Tracy turned toward the door but was stopped by the tug of Chase's fingers on her skirt. A small whimper came from her throat, though she said nothing and froze where she was.

Chase hadn't moved at all. He was staring at Farel, his eyes dark and pensive.

Now they act hypnotized, Carrie thought.

Her son Rob would be ready to take action. At thirty, Rob often seemed older than his mother, and he was more deliberate about making decisions than she was. But, once he'd decided what to do, he'd beat her out the door.

Well, neither Rob—nor Henry—was here. She was on her own.

In comparison with Rob, Tracy seemed so childlike, so unequipped to deal with this tragedy. Perhaps, as a defense against the dreadful circumstances she was facing, her rational mind had shut down.

And Chase? He was arrogant and self-centered. Carrie found it hard to like him, talented and famous or not. She wondered if he went to church, if he ever prayed. As far as she was concerned, not even worry about Dulcey could be an acceptable excuse for the way he was acting.

And there was something else wrong here, something more than Dulcey's abduction. Surely it must be part of her mission to find out what that was . . . and fix it.

It's obvious I've got to stick with them. They need me, she thought, bypassing the knowledge that Chase's own mother was nearby and that both performers, no matter how young, were mature enough to manage successful careers as well as a music theater in Branson.

She reached out and took hold of Tracy's hand, squeezing it hard enough to hurt—which at least got Tracy's attention—and asked, "Where did you find the candlestick? I'll put it back."

Tracy pointed over Carrie's shoulder and she turned, seeing a small shelf on the back wall. Then she whirled back toward Chase, sensing sudden movement from his direction. Quick as lightning he had bent over Farel's body and was reaching toward the scissors. He had a handkerchief in his hand.

Whoa, thought Carrie, he woke up in a hurry! Her sharp command, "Stop," was meant to startle him, and it did. He froze, his handkerchief-wrapped hand only inches from the scissors.

"Don't touch those," Carrie ordered in the firm tone she had used when disciplining Rob. "Tracy didn't touch them, nor did I, and if you didn't . . ." She let the sentence die while her eyes watched him for any further move.

As Chase drew his hand back, Carrie said, "Give it to me," and reached out to take the square of cloth. She was surprised that Chase would think his wife had stabbed Farel, or . . . but no, he'd been in the auditorium with his mother. Who else besides Tracy

67

might he be trying to protect?

She wrapped the handkerchief over her hand and rubbed the metal candlestick as if she were doing a thorough dusting. Surely that would take care of Tracy's fingerprints.

"Wait for me on the sidewalk," she said. "I'll blow this out and follow. As soon as the candle goes out, light a match to show me where you are, and don't move from that spot."

She put the candlestick back on the shelf, blew out the flame, and waited until a match flared outside the door. As she stepped quickly around the dead man, she noticed that shapes and forms were now easy to see in newly unclouded moonlight, though the security lights were still off.

She started through the door, then stopped. She'd touched the inside doorknob. Pushing aside the memory of Henry's instructions about destroying evidence, she polished the knob. Surely the killer hadn't touched it. If that part of Tracy's story was true, the door had been open when he ran out.

She hesitated again, thinking about the light switch. She hadn't touched it, but Tracy had. Well, forget what Henry would say. Tracy had troubles enough, and besides, any fool could see she hadn't killed her cousin.

Carrie rubbed her cloth-covered hand over the light switch, leaving it in the on position. If the killer had left fingerprints there he must have touched lots of other things in the shop too. Henry was still too much a policeman to condone destroying evidence, but if it ever came up, she'd just have to explain about the need to protect Tracy.

Thoughts of Henry reminded her how much she wished he was here right now.

Never mind, he wasn't . . . wouldn't be until tomorrow, so for now it was "Carry On Carrie," just as it had been so many times in years past.

Nodding to herself, Carrie went out the open door and joined the Masons on the sidewalk. They were a pair of statues, waiting for her to lead the way, though they must be very familiar with every part of the Folk Center grounds. She started to walk along the moon-lit path toward the back of the auditorium, talking to them over her shoulder as she went.

"If anyone asks why I'm with you," she said, "just tell them I'm your convention hostess."

"You don't need to come with us." Chase's tone was sullen.

Carrie ignored him. "From now until the police get to Farel's body, you need to be sure someone outside your family can say exactly where both of you were and what you were doing. I'm that outsider. I wasn't with Tracy every minute, but she obviously isn't strong enough to have stabbed her cousin when he was facing her. You were with your mother and other people in the auditorium. The problem is, though, how accurately can officials here decide when Farel was killed? How sophisticated is the sheriff's department or the coroner? Do you have a good medical examiner here? Farel's body was still warm when I first touched it, so he hadn't been dead very long. Do they have the ability to tell the time of death within a few minutes, one way or another? I doubt it, so you could need an alibi for a pretty wide time range."

She stopped at the stage door and turned to see if they understood the importance of what she was saying. Their faces appeared iridescent in the moon-light—two ghostly skulls with dark eye holes. Tracy's lips looked black, and Carrie saw them part several seconds before she heard the moaned, "Ohhh."

As the sound faded, Chase said, "Okay, but then we're *all* gonna go to Farel's house. We'll keep an eye on you too."

Carrie felt a flash of temper and almost opened her mouth to tell Chase she was here because they needed her, not because she was enjoying herself, but she stopped the comment just in time and turned toward the door.

Chase brushed past her and pulled the door open. As light from inside spilled out, Carrie looked back at Tracy. "Wait a minute," she said.

"Tracy dear, spit on this handkerchief. Your eye make-up has dripped into smudges on your cheeks. Let's get rid of that before we go in."

After scrubbing off the marks, Carrie put her arms around Tracy—who looked ready to cry again—and whispered, "There, you'll do, the cheek rub has put in color. You're a good actress, so you can smile. You'll get through this, and we'll find Dulcey soon.

"I've been thinking about the words of one of your recordings, 'He's Got the Whole World in His Hands.' Think 'He's got Dulcey in His hands.' Sing it to yourself now."

She patted Tracy's back, released her, and nodded at Chase. "Okay," she said.

Carrie took Tracy's hand as Chase opened the door, and the three of them stepped into an alcove next to the auditorium stage. There were people everywhere. Bright lights from the front of the stage blinded Carrie temporarily, though she could tell that two adults and two children, probably a family group, were playing and singing in front of the footlights.

Someone shouted, "Next," from the darkness of the auditorium seating area, and the four musicians stepped to the back of the stage. They continued playing while a group of cloggers clunked past Carrie and out into the bright lights.

Neither Chase nor Tracy paid any attention to the activity on stage. Chase grabbed Tracy's free hand and yanked her, with Carrie hanging on behind, toward a side hallway.

Almost like a game of crack-the-whip, Carrie thought, suppressing a desire to giggle as they whizzed down the hall and into an oddly shaped room against the side of the round building.

Several people sat on stools and folding chairs scattered in random disorder around the room. Some were leaning over guitars and other stringed instruments,

71

playing softly to themselves, ignoring everything but their music. One large group sat against the back wall, gathered around Brigid Mason. She was perched on a high stool and seemed to be telling an Ozarks play-party story. As they came into the room she was beginning to growl her lines like a bear.

Almost everyone in the room looked up as Chase, at the front of the human chain, came to a sudden halt, and Tracy, then Carrie—unable to stop their forward motion in time—banged awkwardly into each other and then into Chase's back.

As the three began to untangle themselves, a dry male voice said, "Y'all musta been practicin' yore entrance fur weeks."

Now the room echoed with giggles and hoots of laughter. Chase stared at the floor, and Carrie couldn't tell whether he was angry or embarrassed.

As soon as she could be heard over the laughter, Brigid Mason waved and called out, "Be there in a bit. I'm just finishin' my story." She turned back to the group, and the rising volume of her voice indicated the story was at a crucial point. Once more, she had the full attention of her audience.

A tall young man sitting near the door put down his guitar and rocked back in his chair, staring at Tracy for a long moment. Then he got up and came toward them, his red checked shirt stretching and pulling around broad shoulders and arms as he moved. He punched Chase hard in the biceps. "I see you found 'er, pretty boy. I knew she hadn't run off, seeing as how I wasn't with 'er."

Chase flinched, but now the man ignored him. He had turned to look Carrie up and down. "Well, well, did you go and get Tracy a chaperone? Looks like the poor woman's already been tripped up tryin' to hang on to your . . ."—he paused and turned his eyes toward Tracy—". . . your wife."

He stared at Carrie again. "Got scratches on 'er face and," he bent his head to look insolently at the back of her skirt, "dirt on some-a the rear view. What'd she have to do, Tracy, tackle ya?"

He leaned his head back and laughed.

Tracy's words sounded pinched, almost a squeak. "Shut your mouth, Bobby Lee Logan," she said. "You make noises about nothing."

Bobby Lee seemed not to notice the strain in her voice. "Aw, now, can't take a joke, Tracy m'love?" he said and winked at Carrie.

Chase ignored the man and spoke directly to his mother as groans and laughs from her audience signaled the end of the story. "Come on, Momma, we gotta leave, see how Dulcey's doing."

"Well, you sure are frosty," Bobby Lee said. "Guess fancy man Mason's too big-time now to even say a word to the likes of us. You agree with that, Tracy?"

Carrie looked around the room, which had fallen silent. Several of the faces looking at them appeared hostile.

"Now leave 'em go," said one of the women from her seat near Aunt Brigid. "Their kid's sick. Little Dulcey. Leave 'em go."

73

The room was so quiet it might have been empty. Brigid Mason looked at her son and slid quickly to the floor, forgetting the skirt that had been carefully arranged to fall around her on the stool. The fabric was pulled up and over the top of the stool as her feet hit the floor, revealing a red petticoat and a generous expanse of heavy black pantyhose.

She yanked at the skirt, her mouth held in a firm line, and this time no one laughed. Before she could pick up her fiddle case, Chase had disappeared into the hall, pulling Tracy behind him.

As she waited for Aunt Brigid, Carrie took a good look at the man called Bobby Lee. She hadn't been wrong. Bobby Lee looked like a volcano about to erupt.

## Chapter VI

Chase and Tracy were out of sight by the time the two women reached the stage, but Brigid Mason knew where she was going. She turned behind the stage and headed down a hall bordered by dressing rooms. Though she was hurrying, Chase's mother could still talk without any problem. It was obvious she had sensed her son's anxiety and was also aware that Carrie—though a stranger to the family—was somehow linked to the cause of that anxiety.

"Seems like something's happened," she said without preamble. "Is it to do with Dulcey?"

"Yes, something has happened," Carrie said as she

sidestepped around a boy carrying a tub bass, "but so far as we know, Dulcey's all right. Because of the . . . new development, I need to make a phone call. Is there a phone here I can use?"

"Phone's in the office down this hall. I'll show you. What's happened then?"

"Chase and Tracy may want to be the ones to tell you about it, but we're involved in a bigger problem than Dulcey being missing. That's why I'm here."

Brigid looked at her sharply, but she kept walking, full skirt swirling around her ankles. They came to a group of performers, and as if nothing were amiss, Brigid paused to greet them. While Carrie waited in the background she saw Ben Yokum coming out of what looked like a storage room and said, "Hello," but the man acted as if he didn't recognize her. Well, maybe he doesn't, Carrie thought. He's only seen me once, and the light wasn't good.

When they got to the end of the hall, Brigid stopped, opened a door, reached for a light switch, and pointed. "Phone. Now you tell me what's happened a'fore I go to the car. I won't let on you told when I see the kids."

Carrie looked into the other woman's eyes for a second, wondering what to say. What was this grand-mother feeling? Carrie knew such a kidnapping would worry her to distraction, even if the child she loved was supposed to be with a friendly relative. So, maybe Brigid Mason had a right to know the worst before she went to her children.

"We don't know where Dulcey is yet, though I pray

75

she's all right. Farel Teal, however, is not all right. He's dead. Tracy found him in the dressmaker's shop. Stabbed."

"Lord almighty," said Brigid, putting her hand over her heart. "Poor little gal. No wonder Chase acted so bad. So, you goin' to call Sheriff Wylie? How come we're leavin'?"

"We're going to Farel's house to look for Dulcey. Someone, probably Farel's killer, left a note that makes it look like he, or at least someone connected, has her now. But there's also a chance she's at Farel's."

Carrie saw fear flash into Brigid's round face. The woman struggled with her emotions for a moment, then asked, "When was Farel kilt?"

"Don't know for sure, but he was still warm when I got there. That had to be about 8:30, since your program lasted an hour. Tracy was just ahead of me going through the craft area, and she found him. She says she saw someone in the dressmaker's shop as she walked past. The lights were out, but she thought it was a man. He ran toward the auditorium as soon as he heard her. I came along soon after and found her sitting on the floor of the shop in quite a state. I stayed with her until Chase came, and then I decided to stay with all of you, to see if I could help, of course, but also because I can give Tracy and all of you an alibi until . . ."

Brigid's sharp question stopped her. "How'd you know? Did you think we'd need an alibi 'cause the killin' had somethin' to do with the old feud?"

"Feud?"

"You from around here? What did you say your family name was?"

"Culpeper. I'm Carrie Culpeper McCrite."

"Ohhh, Culpepers. Spelt with two p's and not three?"

"Well, yes."

"Ahhhhh . . . so you're one of *those*." Brigid looked sideways at Carrie, her eyes compressed into slits.

"But I'm not . . ." Carrie stopped. Maybe an imagined family relationship here would help people accept her, confide in her. She wondered, though, if the Mountain View Culpepers were considered good people. Brigid sure had a funny look on her face.

"One can't pick one's relatives," Carrie said, hoping that was the right reply.

Brigid's face smoothed. With a nod, she seemed to dismiss the Culpepers as she asked, "What did the note say?"

Carrie took the paper from her pocket and held it out.

Brigid read it, stared into the distance for a minute, and said simply, "I see," before she handed it back and turned into the hall.

Carrie called after her, "I won't be long, wait for me."

Brigid was nodding agreement as her bright skirt disappeared through the door to the employee parking lot.

Carrie went to the phone on the desk and dialed 911.

A woman answered after one ring. Speaking in a low monotone, Carrie told her there was a dead body in the dressmaker's shop at the Folk Center. She hung up as soon as she had said that, though a sharp, questioning voice was audible in the handset as she lowered it into the cradle. Well, she and Tracy would tell them more as soon as Dulcey was safe.

She was turning away from the desk when she heard a noise from the hall, something that sounded like the scrape of a boot heel on concrete. She hurried to the office door. The hall was empty toward the auditorium entrance, but back the other way she could see several people near the dressing rooms.

She recognized two of them. The man they called Bobby Lee, the one wearing the red checked shirt, was just disappearing around the curve, and Ben Yokum was opening the door to the storage room.

The air was cooling rapidly, and Carrie buttoned her jacket as she left the auditorium. She hoped Farel hadn't lived in some remote mountain cabin—she wasn't dressed for a rough hike. But then, the full ruffled skirts and Mary Jane slippers that Tracy and Brigid wore weren't exactly suitable for an outdoor excursion either. Chase was the only one of them with halfway sensible clothing on, though his fancy boots sure weren't made for hiking.

He was across the parking lot, standing next to a red van. In the glow from the security lights, Carrie could see him putting Brigid's fiddle case in the back, next to the guitar and banjo. The side door was also open, and Brigid called to her, "In here."

As soon as they were settled and the van was moving, Brigid asked, "So, what's goin' on?"

Evidently she really isn't going to tell them we talked, Carrie thought, as Tracy—whose emotions had either evaporated or were under rigid control—gave Brigid basically the same story she'd told Carrie about finding Farel Teal's body.

When the van was halfway down the drive leading to the visitors' parking lot, Chase turned right into a narrow lane. It went around the edge of the Folk Center grounds rather than continuing toward the parking lot and the main road. Carrie had no idea where they were going, but noticed they passed what looked like fair grounds and a park with picnic tables and stone barbecue pits.

As Chase drove through the center of Mountain View and turned south, the three Masons began talking about the best way to approach Farel's house.

Carrie was silent—thinking—asking God to lead them—listening. She wondered if there really was a chance the child was at Farel's now, if, indeed, she had ever been there.

The road began to climb, curving up the side of a mountain. Evidently Farel did live in the country, or . . . were they really going to Farel's?

Carrie began praying harder, hoping to silence concern that was becoming leaping panic. She'd gone and

79

rushed into trouble again. She didn't really know these people at all! Oh, why hadn't she just left things alone, why had she followed Tracy?

Then she remembered the woman in the woods. Of course. All the recent activity had knocked that right out of her head. She had followed Tracy to tell her about the woman.

"What's a gowerow?" she asked when there was a pause in the conversation.

Brigid answered first, though Chase and Tracy had also started to speak. It was obvious that the term wasn't strange to any of them.

"Story-monster," Brigid said, "ugly thing. Large, has tusks. Scare kids with gowerow tales. Why?"

Carrie told them about the woman in the woods.

When she finished, there was complete silence in the car, but even in the darkness Carrie could tell Brigid Mason was looking at her with that slit-eyed hostility again. Finally Brigid said, forming her words as slowly and carefully as if she were addressing a naughty two-year old, "*That* was Mad Margaret. Mad Margaret *Culpeper*."

Carrie was sure her surprise was evident. "But, I don't know her," she said. "I never saw the woman before in my life. You don't think I . . ." She stopped, realizing Brigid Mason just could think she was involved in all this trouble.

But, once again, Brigid's hostile look faded, and she continued, "Margaret Culpeper ain't mad a'tall, she's lots sharper 'n' most folks think. She's said to have second sight. Mebbe you oughta find her house and talk to her. Now, you tell me again—ever-thing she said and did."

Carrie repeated her story.

"You hardly ever see her 'round town," Brigid said, "'n' she lives somewheres in the woods along the ridge back of the Folk Center Park. You could mebbe hike there. I've never been to her place, none I know has, mostly 'cause her sons are unfriendly types and don't care fer visitors. Even the law don't bother 'em. Rye Wylie sez it ain't his jurisdiction, since it's probably town land or grandfathered park land, 'n' I don't think Chief Bolen's ever been there neither. He sez it's county. Not that I'm exactly sayin' the Culpepers'd do anythin' wrong, o'course." She paused, giving Carrie another slit-eyed look. "But I'm sure not sayin' they wouldn't. Yep, if we don't find Dulcey at Farel's, you go talk to Margaret Culpeper! You could do it, bein' a woman, a stranger here, and a Culpeper besides."

"Even if she is a Culpeper," Chase said as he pulled the van off the road, "she'd best take someone with her—someone with a gun."

They were turning into a rocky lane much like the one leading to Carrie's house in Spavinaw County. Chase stopped a few yards from the highway and backed into a small clearing. As he pulled the van around, its headlights reflected on a rusty pasture gate hanging by one wire hinge. "We'll park here," he said. "Momma, you and Miz Carrie stay put 'n' keep the

81

doors locked. Tracy'll come with me, she knows how to find the key."

Brigid and Carrie looked across the seat at each other, and then they slid, Brigid first, followed by Carrie, out the side door. "No way I'm bein' left outa this," Chase's mother said.

Chase made no protest. He was already headed up the bumpy lane leading away from the highway. "This's not the main way to the house," he said, "but someone could be using the other road. Sorry we don't have a flashlight—though maybe it's best we don't." He looked at the sky. "Moon's good for another coupla hours."

Chase set a fast pace, and not long after they began the climb, Tracy dropped back toward Carrie, letting Brigid pass her. Eventually she was at Carrie's side, and Carrie reached out to take hold of her small, cold hand. Any other contact would have been impossible while they were both concentrating on navigating the rough ground.

Tracy clung to Carrie's hand, though that made walking more difficult for both of them. I wonder where this girl's mother lives? Carrie thought as they trudged along.

Well, at least all this activity kept her from feeling cold.

The little group followed the narrow lane, winding their way up the hillside. Carrie tried to avoid the rocks, but was also thinking that, after tonight, she didn't ever want to see her blue shoes again. Finally

Chase stopped, held up a hand, and waited for the women to catch up with him.

They had come to the edge of a clearing where a square wood-frame house was clearly outlined in moonlight. The inside of the house looked dark.

Tracy leaned close to Carrie's ear and whispered, "Farel's lived here alone since Uncle Ted died last year. His ma's been gone for years. I barely remember her, and that's one reason he spent so much time at our house when we were growing up. He was the youngest. His two sisters are married 'n' live away."

Chase's low voice interrupted. "Let's divide up and all come at the house from a different side. Miz Carrie, you stay here at the back. Momma, go to that side. Tracy, come with me and help me find the key, and then take the other side. Each of you sneak up and look in the windows on your side. I don't see curtains or closed shades, so if someone's inside, should be a little light somewhere. If you don't see anything, come around to the front. Now, stay in the woods 'til I give an owl call, 'n' we'll all come in."

Silently, Chase, Tracy, and Brigid faded into the darkness, and Carrie stood alone, staring at the moonlit back of the house with its vacant windows. There were no vehicles in sight but, like the van, they could be hidden in the woods. A wide lane, undoubtedly the main road Chase had referred to, led into the yard at the front of the house.

An owl called. Chase was a good owl mimic, just as good as she herself was.

Carrie left the shelter of the trees and started across the clearing, trying to stay close to the moonshadows of various objects and bushes and almost tripping over a board that was too flat to cast a shadow. One more ding for the blue shoes!

Then she was against the wall of the house, touching the splintery wood with her hands. She moved past the three windows on her side, standing on tip-toe at the edge of each one, peering over the sills. There was no light showing, but, if anyone was inside in the dark, they could surely have seen the shadow of her head in the moonlight. Had Chase thought about that? But no voice or movement challenged her, and there were no sounds anywhere else in the clearing.

She continued on to the corner of the house and looked around, catching a glimpse of Brigid's skirt as it disappeared past the front corner. She followed, and in another minute they were grouped together by the front steps.

Chase held up a key. "Stay here," he said.

Quick as a cat, his mother snatched the key out of his hand. "Better me," she whispered. "Don't want to risk Dulcey's daddy." She stepped out of Chase's reach and climbed the steps.

The key clicked, and Brigid moved sideways against the wall as she turned the knob and pushed the door open, letting it squeak inward into blank darkness.

Carrie held her breath for seconds that seemed like minutes. Then Brigid Mason stepped around the door frame and into the house, while the other three hurried up the steps behind her. When they were all through the door, Carrie shut it as quietly as she could.

Tracy's voice said, "Dulcey?" sounding loud in the silence, and only silence answered her.

"Tracy, go turn on a light," Chase said, "and tell us how the house's laid out."

"Two bedrooms, bathroom on the left. A kitchen, right. We're in the main room now. There's no cellar, solid rock under the house. Loft's above us."

She switched on a lamp, revealing a large room that was clean, but full of male clutter. Most of the furniture was old and worn, but there were a few newer pieces, including a recliner and a television set.

Carrie drew a quick, involuntary breath. There was also a glass-front case in the room, with a collection of deadly looking knives displayed against its cloth backing.

Tracy noticed what Carrie was looking at and said, "Farel collected 'em," but she took no time to say more. She was already turning on a light in the kitchen, and Chase and his mother had disappeared in the direction of the bedrooms.

Carrie looked closely at the knife collection, then, seeing a plain wood stairway at the side of the room, she climbed up to take a look. The stairs led to an empty loft with a large rag rug on the floor. In the center of the rug sat a cloth doll with staring button eyes, a child's plastic tea set, and building blocks stacked in a small wagon pulled by two painted horses. A child was meant to be here. Carrie could imagine what fun a four-year-old would find in this high-up hidey hole. Maybe Tracy had known what she was talking about, and Farel really hadn't meant Dulcey any harm.

But now the toys were silent, alone, and arranged way too neatly.

Carrie heard footsteps below and looked over the railing. Chase was back in the room, carrying a blue hair ribbon. Tracy followed him, her face drawn and frightened. "She was here," was all Chase said.

Tracy spoke, her voice shaky, almost too weak to carry. "I tied that ribbon myself. There were two of them. They match her performance dress."

"There are toys up here," Carrie said as she started down the steps, "but I don't think she had time to play with them."

"Back door ain't locked," Brigid said, appearing from the hall, "but the whole house is empty. Did everyone look in closets, under beds 'n' such?"

No one spoke, but they were nodding as she went on, holding up a red plastic cylinder. "I found a flash-light."

Suddenly all of them lifted their heads as they heard the sound of a motor beginning its uphill struggle on the front lane. Chase moved first, switching off the lamp. "This way," he said as Tracy grabbed Carrie's hand and pulled her toward the back door, following Chase and Brigid.

Car lights were appearing as the four crossed the clearing and, with the house shielding them from the sight of anyone in the car, crashed into the shelter of the trees. Tracy still had Carrie's hand, pulling her along as they raced into the woods. As soon as they were hidden by trees and underbrush, they moved in a circle to where they could see the front of the house. The noise of the car stopped as the porch came into their view, and they froze into silence.

"Front door's still unlocked," hissed Tracy, turning toward Chase.

"No matter," whispered Brigid, "back door allus was."

Carrie paid no attention to them. She was busy watching the man who got out of the car. His face was in shadow, but he was tall, and Carrie had glimpsed a red and white checked shirt when the car's dome light flashed on. She wondered if anyone else in the group recognized the driver of the car. If they did, no one said anything.

They were very still as the man walked slowly up the steps, and it was easy to hear the thunk of his boots on the boards. He carried a tote bag in his left hand.

A barred owl called, this time a real one, Carrie hoped.

The man reached for the door knob and, when the door opened easily, hesitated. His right hand went to the back of his waist. He has a gun tucked in his belt, Carrie thought, and saw the glint of moonlight on metal before he disappeared inside the house.

Tracy gasped, and Carrie put out an arm and hugged the young woman against her side. She could feel the warmth of Tracy's body as the two of them drew together, silent and tense. Brigid's breath was making short puffs only inches away, and Carrie sensed the electric alertness in Chase's body, just behind her.

They waited as a flashlight flickered back and forth through the uncurtained windows. What was the man searching for? Carrie wondered if they had missed finding something important.

Suddenly the man's feet thudded on the boards as, tote bag in hand, he hurried out, leaped over the steps, and catapulted into his car.

Chase's exclamation, "What th . . . ," was choked into silence as flickering light, then a roar of flame, beat against the horrified faces of the four watchers. The visitor's car came to life, turned, and rocketed away from the burning house.

Tracy's scream was drowned by the noise of the fire as both Brigid and Carrie held her, fighting against her struggle to run toward the house.

"Dulcey's not in there! No one's in there! You saw that yourself," shouted Brigid over the noise of the fire as the three of them huddled around Tracy and began, as one body, to pull her away toward the back lane.

I forgot about fingerprints, Carrie thought as she stumbled through the darkness, but it sure isn't going to matter now.

# Chapter VII

They plunged through the woods, half-carrying Tracy, forcing her to move with them. Chase was walking in front of Carrie, and the branches he shoved aside whipped back against her body and face. One cracked across her lips, and she tasted blood.

Even after they reached the lane, Carrie was gasping breath, moving in a black hole of pain and fear for a missing child.

They were almost to the van when she felt Tracy go limp and start to slump. Pulled by Tracy's weight, Carrie began to topple after her, but at the last moment her arm slid free. Unsupported, Tracy folded silently to the ground and lay there, motionless as a rag doll.

Chase continued on to the van, ignoring all three women. After he had unlocked the doors, his sharp voice ordered, "Get in. Momma, in the front, you—Carrie—in back."

When the two women were seated, Chase returned for Tracy and, lifting her across the back seat, put her head in Carrie's lap. He moved slowly, carefully, his eyes shadowed and sorrowful. It's as if, Carrie thought, he's grieving for a dead wife rather than carrying a living one.

Tears stung Carrie's own eyes as she laid her hand on Tracy's forehead, thinking of the moment in the dressmaker's shop when the sobbing young woman had said, "I laid my hand on his forehead like Momma

89

would when we were kids." It was a natural thing to do. Tracy was breathing evenly, strongly, and her temperature felt normal—a good sign.

"Perhaps this is not so bad," Carrie said, more to herself than to Brigid Mason, who had turned in the front seat and was watching them. "How much is any human supposed to endure? Tracy seems so young, so vulnerable. For now, at least, maybe the nightmare things are shut out."

Carrie had stood up under some pretty awful human challenges but didn't know how well she could have made it through this kind of hell. If it had been twenty-five years ago and the missing child was Rob . . .

She shut her eyes in silent prayer, thinking of God's tender love for everyone and especially for Dulcey Mason. As Carrie was praying, Chase got in the driver's seat, and he and his mother began talking in low tones, but Carrie paid no attention to them. She had begun stroking Tracy's hair and face, speaking the words of the 91st Psalm to her very softly.

She was up to, "For he shall give his angels charge over thee," when Chase and his mother fell silent.

"I see yer a prayin' woman," Brigid said, turning to look at her again. "That's good, we can sure use the Lord's he'p about now. I hope He's watching over Dulcey and she's not too scared."

"He *is* with her," Carrie said and went back to low-voiced repetition of the words that had comforted and helped her so many times.

Tracy stirred, whispered, "Dulcey," once, then was

quiet as Carrie finished: "With long life will I satisfy him, and shew him my salvation." After a short pause, she returned to the beginning and said again, "He that dwelleth in the secret place of the most High shall abide under the shadow of the almighty." As she spoke, she was aware that Chase had started the van and they were moving.

When the Psalm ended for the second time, Carrie shut her eyes for a moment, then raised her head and looked toward Brigid and Chase.

Keeping her voice as low as possible, she asked, "Shouldn't we call the fire department? Could the fire spread?"

"Won't be enough left to save," Chase said, " 'n' the woods are too damp to catch. Fire truck'll come anyway. Neighbors across the valley'll have seen the flames, 'n' besides, the sheriff'll be headed this way soon enough."

Accenting his words, flashing lights appeared around the curve ahead of them. A fire engine and water truck passed, leading a long, winding line of volunteer fire department members in their trucks and cars.

"I hope they don't think anyone was in that house," Carrie said. "We could tell them no one was."

"Why should they take our word?" Chase asked. " 'N' reporting it'd just make trouble for us. They'll have to search through what's left anyhow. Besides, they'll see there's no car there. Farel's car's in the employee parking lot. I saw it myself when we went

91

to the van tonight. I looked through the windows to see if . . . maybe Dulcey . . . I didn't see anything inside except a blanket on the back seat. Car was locked, but the blanket was too flat for Dulcey to be under it."

"Best keep quiet fer now," Brigid said. "It's time we all got some rest. Soon as we're home, I'll brew up some of my special feverfew tea. That'll help. Nothin' more we can do, 'lest we talk to Sheriff Wylie . . ."

"*No*," her son said.

"Well, then . . ."

Carrie spoke up. "According to the note, the kidnappers will be in touch with you tomorrow evening, most likely to ask for ransom. It sounded like money was all they wanted, unless there's some other reason you know about?"

Neither Brigid nor Chase said anything, so she went on. "If we haven't made progress soon, you simply must tell the sheriff about the kidnapping—if he's the one that would have jurisdiction. He or the police would likely call in the FBI, wouldn't they? That'd bring us expert help."

"Sheriff has jurisdiction at the Folk Center grounds," Chase said.

"But Dulcey was taken from your home."

"I'm out in Stone County," Brigid said, "on Harmony Road, north o'town. Besides, I figure Police Chief Bolen only takes the city law job 'cause he likes the uniform, and on account of he's related to mosta the city council. There's lots of Bolen kin. 'N' he's

92

related to the Teals on his wife's side, way back at least."

She snorted, dismissing the police chief.

"Sheriff Wylie, then." Carrie paused to watch Tracy's face and quiet breathing for a moment before she asked, "Did either of you get a good enough look at the car or man at Farel's to identify them?"

Chase and Brigid were both silent.

I'll bet they saw the man as clearly as I did, Carrie thought, or at least his shirt.

"Don't know much about cars," Brigid said finally, "but it was old, wasn't it? Rattled a lot. Didn't see any license plate."

"I saw one," Carrie said, "but it was smudged with dirt, and there was mud or tape masking the light above it. It wasn't an Arkansas plate. White and blue, but no red."

"Missouri, maybe," Chase said as they started down Mountain View's main street.

"That's what I thought." Carrie wanted to ask if Bobby Lee Logan would be driving a car with a Missouri plate, but decided she should keep some information to herself—for now, at least—so all she said was, "Can you drop me off somewhere near the Folk Center Lodge? I hope it's not much out of your way. I don't think I could make it up that hill on foot tonight."

Chase nodded and turned off on the road they had come down earlier in the evening.

Carrie continued, thinking aloud. "As soon as I can

get out tomorrow I'll try to find Margaret Culpeper, and, whether you tell the sheriff or not, I will tell her I know there's a child missing. Why would she find it necessary to say anything more about that to me if I don't tell her how true her prophecy is? It could encourage her to talk to me if she knows a child has been kidnapped."

"I think she knows already," replied Brigid as the van turned up the hill toward the Folk Center.

"I wasn't kidding when I mentioned to be careful there," Chase said. "Family is quirky . . . real strange, maybe even dangerous. Lots of rumors around that family for years. People don't mess with 'em."

"Well, since I was born a Culpeper, I have an advantage," Carrie said. "I may not be a real relative, but why not act as if I am? Why can't I have a few peculiar quirks myself? Besides, I have a friend coming here tomorrow who can help. He's a neighbor from back home, a good man, and a very smart one. He can go with me." She didn't add that her friend was a former homicide detective.

"Lady," Brigid said, "I think there's things we haven't heard about you yet, like how you knew about the feud, or, uh, the *trouble* 'tween Teals and Masons. That goes years back, so I bet your folks was from here onc't upon a time. Beats me how else you'd-a figured out the Masons would be looked at purty close if anything happened to a Teal—how we'd need someone to speak fer us 'n' say where we was. Even Tracy. Mebbe especially Tracy. Teals treat her like she's some kinda poison since she married my Chase. She had to run off to marry him. That tuk backbone. She mebbe seems young, but she's still got backbone, 'n' don't you fergit it."

So, Carrie thought, there really are bad feelings between Tracy's family and the Masons, but that still shouldn't mean murder, not these days.

As if she'd picked up Carrie's thoughts, Brigid continued, "Farel now . . . well, I don't hold with killin'. He thought like a Teal, though, not like Tracy." She looked over the back of the seat at her daughter-in-law. "Poor little flower, she just give out. They's limits to what anyone can take. Poor, purty little flower."

Chase broke in. "Farel was trouble, Momma. Nothin' but trouble for us, for himself . . . for anyone."

Carrie thought she felt Tracy twitch, but decided it had been her imagination, or the bounce of the van over a bump in the road.

Chase continued, "And he started this whole mess when he took Dulcey, don't forget."

His voice faded into silence as they passed the drive to the administration building and restaurant. It was obvious the sheriff had arrived. There were flashing lights in the parking lot, all the security lights were now on, and a crowd of people stood clustered around the gate to the craft grounds.

"Well, that's that," said Brigid as they continued on the road to the motel units. "Carrie, call my house tomorrow morning. I'm in the phone book, B. E. Mason. We'll make plans then. I hope Chase 'n' Tracy

95

kin get some good rest, since I reckon we won't hear nothin' from those skunks got Dulcey 'til tomorrow night. Now, will you be all right? Sorry I can't give you some of my herb tea."

"Oh, I'll be fine," Carrie said as Chase stopped the van.

Brigid Mason got out and came around to take Carrie's place in the back seat. Tracy stirred as Carrie lifted her head to slide out, but she didn't open her eyes. Brigid slipped carefully under Carrie's hands until, once more, the young woman lay safely cradled in a lap.

"Goodnight then," Carrie said. "I'll call tomorrow morning. And, for now, I'll respect your wish to be silent about the kidnapping, but if the sheriff. . . ."

"We'd best go on," said Chase, interrupting her. "Most folks here don't know what we drive, but there's a few that might. We wanta get out of sight."

The door shut in her face, and the van sped toward the main road.

As soon as she was in her room, Carrie looked at the clock. She'd lost all track of time and had forgotten to look at her watch when they had the lights on at Farel's. Was it only half past midnight? It seemed like it must be near morning.

She kicked off the hated shoes and stuck her aching feet into slippers. Now, one more thing to do before a hot shower and bed. She picked up the phone, punched in a number, and waited to hear the low

96

rumble of a familiar voice.

"Henry, I am sorry to wake you, but we have big difficulties here, and I need to ask a couple of favors . . ."

Carrie decided to skip the shower. She could manage no more than a quick face washing, and it wasn't until she was standing in front of the bathroom mirror that she realized her face looked like she'd fallen head-first into a bed of brambles. What on earth would Henry say when he saw her this time? Here she was again—scraped, bruised, and muddy. And, once again, she was smack dab in the middle of murder!

She stared at her reflection in the mirror. Well, she could wash, but as for the rest, Henry would just have to get used to it.

She took off her filthy clothes and let them fall in a heap on the floor. Before 1:30, Carrie McCrite was sound asleep.

## Chapter VIII

A fire engine raced through the night, its siren a jerky jangle of irritating noise. Carrie ran toward it, stumbled, then ran again. She *had* to reach the fire engine, but it was going too fast, going away. She had to tell them something, what was it? The bells were so loud . . . tell them . . . fire!

Then she was aware that she was no longer running. She was lying down, and the ground was soft. She couldn't feel any rocks.

She opened her eyes. The noise didn't stop, though

97

the fire engine was gone and she was in her motel bed-room.

Carrie blinked and turned her head to stare at the telephone by her bed. It rang once, twice and, thank goodness, was silent. Bright sunlight filtered through the draperies, illuminating the telephone—and her travel clock.

Oh, oh. Oh, *no*. 8:30? She was sure she'd set the alarm last night or, it had been this morning, hadn't it? Yes, she had set it for seven, there were important things to do. She must have turned the thing off without waking.

Then it all came back—the child, the dead man, the fire. She sat up slowly, pushed her pillow against the headboard, leaned back, and thought about a little girl who had spent the night with strangers. She shut her eyes again, listening in the silence for ideas about what action to take today. She already had plans, but were they the best she could do?

For a moment she thought about what it would be like if she hadn't followed the Masons last night. She could lie in bed peacefully, looking forward to three carefree days with Henry and the Stacks. No dark shadows. No worries. She wouldn't be planning for anything but a good time.

She shoved the dreams aside and began thinking about Dulcey Mason and Farel Teal. Once again, Carrie McCrite had become part of the darkness of murder and, this time, kidnapping. She guessed that meant she was supposed to help. That was why she had followed the Masons last night. Probably, she thought, that's even why I'm here. Eyes still shut, she forced herself to pray about following God's direction and about loving her neighbors, every one of them.

At first it wasn't easy. She was just beginning to feel a familiar peace when the brrrring noise began again.

Carrie sighed and this time she reached for the phone.

Beth sounded testy. "Oh, did I wake you up, your royal highness? For goodness sake, I thought you got up with the chickens. You said to meet you here at eight. Too bad, it's almost nine and I've eaten. Got to get on the road. I did keep calling. I was beginning to worry."

Good glory! She and Beth had planned to meet at the Folk Center's Iron Skillet restaurant for breakfast before Beth started home to Spavinaw County.

"Oh, Beth, I am so sorry. I was out with the Masons later than I expected last night and . . ."

Oops, she'd already opened her mouth and said too much. Now she was in for it with questions from Beth, especially after her actions at the dinner last night. Following the Masons like she did would have seemed downright weird to anyone who took much time to think about it, and, spending time with the Masons, with such famous people, how could she explain why they'd even noticed her?

Fortunately Beth wasn't much of a thinker.

"Well, you've missed all the excitement and seeing every cop in Stone County here this morning.

99

Someone, a man, was actually killed here last night. Right here in the craft grounds! Everyone's talking about it." Now Beth sounded like she was gloating.

"How awful, who was killed?"

"Oh, no—not going to tell you one word more about it now. Get dressed, Carrie. I'll eat another biscuit and wait for you here. But hurry, I do need to start for home."

That was Beth. She had an exciting story and exclusive news to share, so she would delay her trip.

"I'll be there in thirty minutes."

She almost made it. The big schoolroom clock in the restaurant lobby said 9:35 when Carrie hurried past the hostess. She nodded at the young woman and pointed toward the window table where Beth was waving a hand with a half-eaten biscuit in it. Beth's face broke into a grin, but then, probably thinking grins weren't appropriate in a restaurant so near the scene of a murder, she frowned and stared at her biscuit as if considering where to take the next bite.

The dining room was unusually crowded for this late hour. People at most of the tables seemed to be lingering over empty plates and coffee cups, talking.

"Gosh, can you imagine . . . a murder?" Beth said as Carrie dropped into a chair facing the window wall. "I don't suppose you saw or heard anything when you were with the Masons, did you? The body was found last night in the dressmaker's shop. You know—the very place I bought that cute sunbonnet for my granddaughter Megan last year. It was a man named Terry

Teal. I heard he was actually Tracy Teal's uncle!"

"Farel Teal, her cousin," Carrie said without thinking. Her mind had flashed back to her first glimpse of the man lying on the floor of the dressmaker's shop.

"Huh?"

"Oh, um, I think a man out there said he was her cousin," mumbled Carrie, turning quickly toward the waitress who had come to take her order. "Special country breakfast with ham, eggs over medium, coffee."

Beth went on, changing the subject. "You must have been out awfully late if you slept through phone bells. So, before I'll tell you about the murder, you have to tell me all about the rich and famous."

Carrie had known Beth would ask such a question and had been thinking about her answer while she was walking up the hill to the restaurant.

"Yes, I was with the Masons for quite a while. They wanted to unwind after the performance and invited me to drive around the area with them. We, um, saw the night view of the town from that mountain to the south. I did set my alarm clock when I went to bed, but must have turned it off without really waking up, because I don't remember hearing it. I haven't pulled that trick since I was in college. Back then I had to keep my alarm clock clear across the room so I'd have to get out of bed to turn it off. Should have done that last night, though I haven't needed to in over forty years. And I didn't hear the phone until the last time

101

you called, but I admit I did have the volume turned down. When I got here, its ring was so noisy it made me jump."

Beth gave her a wicked grin. "You need a man in bed with you to wake you up. Oh, hey, I'm just kidding," she continued, as Carrie ducked her chin and glared at Beth over her glasses.

"Now, Carrie, tell me what the Masons are like, really. Don't skip a thing."

"They're regular folks. I mean, talented of course, but—except maybe for Chase—they don't seem to be affected much by the fact they're famous. In fact, Tracy seems very shy and almost overwhelmed by the world around her.

"Chase's mother has a wonderful way of talking, though sometimes it's hard to follow what she's saying. I think we hit it off well, in spite of the fact we're from cultures that are more different than I would have thought. She talks about things like second sight and characters from tall tales as if she takes them seriously . . . as if they're part of normal, everyday life. But you'd like Brigid Mason. I do."

"Bet I would too," Beth said and then changed the subject. "I wish we could have heard Dulcey Mason sing. A few weeks ago I saw a picture of her in a magazine. She was playing a miniature dulcimer, and the article said she really plays it. She's about the same age as Megan, but has long, dark hair and big, dark eyes with lashes out to here. Not as cute as Megan— she's too skinny. Maybe you got to see her last night?"

Carrie ignored Beth's question. "Now, you tell *me,* what are people saying about the death of Farel Teal? What on earth happened?"

Beth repeated a description of the scene in the dressmaker's shop that was basically true, if you discounted what were probably her own embellishments and those of the people who had passed the story on to her. She explained that a park ranger had found the body in the brightly lit shop after someone discovered several breaker switches were off and turned them back on.

"And," Beth said, lowering her voice and leaning toward Carrie, "when the ranger called the sheriff's office he found out some mysterious woman had already reported the murder and the sheriff was on his way. Isn't that exciting? A mystery woman! Wonder who she is? Maybe she's the murderer and reported the body because she was full of remorse at what happened! Otherwise, why did she just hang up?"

"I wouldn't know," Carrie said, avoiding Beth's gaze by looking out the window at the Folk Center's bird feeders.

Just then the waitress brought a full plate and a basket of biscuits. Carrie filled her mouth quickly so she'd be spared any need to say more about the mysterious caller.

Beth didn't seem to notice the lack of manners, but leaned still closer and continued as if she were now revealing inside secrets known only to her. "No clues yet about who the woman caller was, though they say she made the call from the auditorium building. *But* Adam Yost, you know him, that tall, handsome man"—Beth stopped to giggle—"who directs publicity for Parks and Tourism, says he was out walking late last night and actually saw them carry out the body. Right then he overheard some friend of Terry—uh, no, Farris, did you say?—Teal, raising a fuss with the sheriff about a family feud, just like Hatfield and McCoy stuff, I guess. Anyway, this man, the friend of whatchamacallit Teal, was carrying on ve-ry loudly and saying awful things about Chase Mason. You see, the Masons are supposed to be on one side of the feud and Teals on the other. But Adam couldn't explain it when I pointed out there mustn't be too big a feud, because Chase Mason is *married* to a Teal!" Beth sat back and smiled, obviously waiting for Carrie to praise her insight.

Carrie swallowed a mouthful of egg. "My, my. You must be right, of course."

Beth plunged on. "Anyway, Adam said he heard the man say that this Teal was furious at Chase Mason for something-or-other, but things never got out of hand, because everyone here is related to either Teals or Masons, including the police chief, so there were just *scads* of people who might get involved, and it could probably end up in an all-out Stone County war, and no one wanted that much serious trouble."

"My, my," Carrie said again.

"So, Teal was furious at Chase Mason for some reason or other, like I said, but he held back. Then something changed. Adam didn't hear the man say what, but anyway, something is different now.

"Then, after Adam left and I came in here, I asked the hostess if she knew anything about it, and she said years back some Mason dog, I mean a real dog, four legs, killed some Teal chickens and when the Masons wouldn't pay for the chickens, a man from the Teal family came with a gun to make them pay, but the Masons weren't home, so instead he stole their hog. I know it sounds silly," Beth said, noticing the incredulous look on Carrie's face, "but maybe that stuff on 'Beverly Hillbillies' was true after all! The hostess did seem very sure of her story.

"So, anyway, after that, no one would speak to the other side, and everyone in the area began taking sides, and it went from bad to worse. I don't know that any person has exactly been killed over it though. Well, not until now."

"When did this chicken killing and hog stealing take place?"

"Right after the Civil War, according to the hostess."

"Beth, that was over a hundred and forty years ago! Why on earth would it cause a murder now?"

"Well . . . I don't know . . ."

There was silence while Carrie watched a squirrel raiding the bird feeder outside the restaurant window. An agitated titmouse bobbed up and down on the roof of the feeder, snatching an occasional seed when the squirrel paused to look around. That little bird can't fight someone so much bigger than himself, she thought, but he's managing to get breakfast because he takes advantage of the options open to him.

She looked back at Beth, who was busy putting Apple Chunky on Carrie's last biscuit. "Did Adam hear the man—the friend of Farel Teal's—say who might have killed Farel?"

"Well, no, but he must have meant Chase Mason, so I guess it doesn't matter that he's married to a Teal, after all. Gee, this must be hard on that poor, sweet Tracy."

"But remember, Chase has an alibi for the whole evening."

"Carrie, if you know something, you should tell the sheriff. Did you see something last night you haven't told me about? How do you know Chase has an alibi?"

"Because I'm his alibi! I was with all three Masons after the show."

"Oh." Beth's face drooped. "Yes. Well, then . . . must have been that woman who called."

A twinge of doubt flew into Carrie's head. Was she really sure? Well, of course she was. She'd already thought it through. Chase and his mother had been together, and Tracy was just too tiny to have killed her cousin.

She asked another question. "Has anyone said anything about what the sheriff is doing? Did they find fingerprints?"

Beth looked sulky. "No one said anything about fingerprints, but then, the sheriff isn't reporting to *me*."

106

"Anything else you heard?"

Beth suddenly remembered more gossip, and she brightened. "Well! The hostess said there are several Masons in and around Mountain View who could be suspects, including Chase's two uncles and their families, and most of them are musical in some way. They take part in performances over at the auditorium, so there were Masons here during rehearsals last night. There are plenty of suspects to choose from if it can't be Chase Mason."

"But, Beth, I think there has to be more of a reason than a hog that was stolen over a hundred years ago . . . or even a hog that was stolen yesterday."

"Can't tell about these hillbillies."

Carrie humphed in exasperation and said aloud, as much to herself as Beth, "The Masons I met may have a few different ways, but they aren't killers."

"You know as well as I do, Carrie, that nice-seeming people can be murderers."

Carrie stared out the window again. Yes, she did know that, all too well, and Beth had no idea how much knowing it could hurt.*

The twinge of doubt wouldn't go away. After all, she had just met the Masons last night and certainly sensed a lot of unhappiness hidden behind Chase and Tracy's performance smiles. She was betting its cause was much older than the recent kidnapping of their daughter, so . . . maybe a feud . . .

"Something else I just remembered, Carrie. I overheard the waitress who was helping the people at that

*As told in *A Valley to Die For*    107

table in back of us tell them she was a Teal relation, and she thinks music is what caused the murder. They asked her to say more, but she wouldn't."

Carrie didn't reply, but she was thinking, *music?* And Ben Yokum had said someone was a "bad un." Who had he been talking about? Had he meant Chase Mason—or Farel Teal?

Beth picked up her purse. "Well, I'd better get on the road. Call me as soon as you get back home and tell me all the latest news about this. Promise to pay attention, now, and get all the details you can. Since Henry knows about cop stuff, I bet he'll find out even more than you do!"

"I promise to pay attention, and I know Henry will too," Carrie said.

Beth looked down at her bill. "I owe $6.50. How much tip should I leave?"

# Chapter IX

After Beth left, Carrie sat quietly, glad to be alone at the table. She was looking through the restaurant's window wall into the hilltop forest, but her mind wasn't conscious of landscape. Instead, she was thinking of words from the third chapter of Proverbs: "Trust in the Lord with all thine heart; and lean not unto thine own understanding. In all thy ways acknowledge him, and he shall direct thy paths."

It was hard to sit still, waiting for direction. Everything inside her wanted to be up and moving, taking action. Henry would be here this afternoon, and she hoped to have a progress report ready for him by then.

Once, when talking about police work, Henry had told her a well-thought-out action plan was of primary importance in any investigation, and the action plan must begin with clear thinking. After he'd explained this to her, she'd added something to his formula— prayer and listening for God's direction. Right now, though, she had to admit sitting and thinking, even praying, felt a lot like doing nothing.

Last November Henry had also told her that painstaking research was at least fifty percent of police work, and the other half was paper work. He'd smiled down at her then, and she'd wondered a bit about the paper work, but, if police work was like other professions, well, of course there would be a lot of paper work.

Last November. That was when she and Henry had faced life-threatening danger together. And, sadly, clearer thinking on her part would have kept them out of danger, though Henry never said anything about that. He didn't have to. Every time she saw the scar on his forehead, she remembered . . .

She lifted her chin. There was no point dwelling on regrets. After all, the real result of last November had been their friendship. And, probably because of that friendship, Henry had continued talking to her about detective work, had even said that, if he were still a police officer, he'd welcome her as his partner.

Carrie had known he meant it. The dear man was

incapable of lying about anything that mattered. She'd wondered if strict veracity had ever hampered his police work. Probably not, because he'd reached the top rank in his division before retiring.

So, for whatever reason, after last November he'd continued sharing information about the science and art of crime solving with her. She'd decided he was doing it partly for her entertainment, but also because he knew many of the skills he talked about were helpful in everyday life. She supposed by then he'd come to know her well enough to realize that logical thinking, an ability to grasp details, and patience had never been Carrie Culpeper McCrite's strong points.

But now, after several minutes of quiet reflection, Carrie was ready. It was time for action.

Pushing aside her reflective mood, she stood and went to pay the bill. She asked the cashier if the craft grounds had opened this morning as scheduled and received an affirmative answer. Good. She could get in the area for a very careful look-around, and . . . who knew what she might overhear if she was quiet, unobtrusive, and listened carefully. She was still way behind Henry in the organized mind department, but could at least prove to him that she'd paid attention to what he'd said, even though they'd both thought his tutoring would be applied in her work and her life at home, rather than to any continued crime solving.

Carrie left the restaurant and headed downhill toward her room. The first thing on her action list was a call to Brigid Mason.

The number was easy to find in the Mountain View phone book, and Brigid answered before the first ring was finished.

"Brigid, it's Carrie, I . . ."

"Carrie! Thank goodness it's you. I've been lookin' for your call."

"How are all of you doing? Is there any news?"

In answer, words from the other end of the line began tumbling out in Brigid's colorful language, her voice dropping so low that they were doubly difficult to understand.

"Law, yes, 'least I guess you'd say it's news. This phone's been ringin' off the wall. That dang Bobbie Lee Logan can't keep his mouth shut. He was Farel's best friend and now he's jes spilling his innards all over the place. He doesn't care who-all he hurts. He's gone and tol' the sheriff a bunch of lies, 'n' he's even hintin' that Dulcey is really Farel's daughter, of all the hurtful things, 'n' some folks prob'ly believe him, too. So far I've kep Chase and Tracy from hearin' what's goin' on, but somehow I gotta get 'em away from here. Ever'one knows where I live. It's too dang open to the public."

Brigid stopped to take a breath, but before Carrie could comment, she went on. "What if reporters find out what Bobby Lee is sayin'? It'll be in those big black headlines at all the grocery check-outs in the country.

"The sheriff's been here. He stayed pretty gentle 'n' didn't say too much, jes asked about what we did all

111

the time last night. Tracy stayed in bed, 'n' Chase 'n' me never let on that she had found Farel, 'n' he never asked, so we didn't lie neither. But now that Bobby Lee is raising such a fuss, I don't know. I tol' the sheriff that Tracy wasn't well—grievin' for her cousin—and Dulcey was sick, and both of 'em was asleep, and so far he's inclined to leave that alone."

Brigid paused again before asking, "Has he talked to you yet? I tol' him you was with us, sorta like our hostess."

"I haven't heard from him," said Carrie. "Have you heard from the kidnappers?"

"Nope, nary a word, but that note did say t'night. I got my brother's grandson to go look in the bird box as if he was just playin', and he sez it's empty. Box opens at the side 'n' Tommy sez all that's inside is a few dead wasps."

'Did you get any sleep?"

"Oh, I dozed, but mosta the time I was watchin' over one or t'other of the kids. An' since dawn ever-body 'n' his cousin's been calling sayin' they wanted to he'p, but most of 'em's jes curious, if truth be known. It makes me wild."

"Brigid, can't someone come to be with you? Glory, I wish I had a car right now."

Carrie was thinking she sure would be glad when Henry—and his car—arrived.

"Oh, yeah, my two brothers and their wives 'n' some other kin who don't hafta to be at work or school are here, sorta hangin' around to discourage company.

112

"I had to tell my family about Dulcey. Well, they wanted to go out right then and beat the woods in ever' direction from Farel's house, but how'd we know that would do any good? It's too much space to cover without us knowing somethin' particular, but Carrie, there is the Culpepers . . ."

"Yes, I haven't forgotten, and I have a plan about them."

There was a silence, then Brigid said, "Oh me, now I kin see another TV truck out there. Law, Carrie, what next? Stuff's gonna bust out all over the place. Wish I could ship Chase and Tracy to the moon, I can't hold off the whole dang world much longer. Famous is fine when things go good, but let somethin' bad happen and all tarnation breaks loose. Famous ain't so fine then. Folks're likely to find out Dulcey's gone any time and . . . what then . . . ?"

"Tracy now, she cried a lot durin' the night, and Chase, he paced the floor. Tracy's gone to sleep at last, but Chase is still pacin'. If Tracy stays asleep I'm gonna let Nell or Sarah answer this phone and rest a bit myself."

Carrie's thoughts were forming rapidly and clearly now. "Brigid, can you trust your family? They'll keep secrets?"

Brigid snorted. "O' course. That's part of bein' family, ain't it?"

"Then I have an idea we might try. I think I can get Chase and Tracy out of there and hide them here at the Folk Center, though I can't make my plan work until

113

this afternoon. Will they come back here if I promise to hide them? And how much can you change their looks? I'll send one set of different clothing for each of them . . . older, heavier people's clothing, but perhaps you could find jackets and another change of clothing around there, something in older styles they'd never wear. Maybe a change of hair style or color too—whatever you can manage. Here's what I have in mind . . ."

Brigid interrupted. "The Folk Center? How's that gonna work? Why, they'd be right in the midst o' things. It's hardly gettin' 'em away."

"You know they won't go far away until Dulcey's found. And who would ever think they'd be here? They should be willing to come here because it is near all that's going on and nearest where we'll find out something about Dulcey. And," she added gently, "you need rest too. If they're gone, maybe the reporters will leave you alone.

"Think about it, then ask them if they'll come. I have friends arriving this afternoon, and they have room reservations. No one here knows what my friends look like. Some of them can double up with me, and we'll put Chase and Tracy in one of the rooms under my friends' names—that is if they're willing to stay out of sight. We can bring in food and tell the housekeeping staff not to bother with the room."

"Well . . . mebbe . . . guess it could work. They might be willin', 'n' you're right, they'd never go away while Dulcey's missin'."

There was a pause, then Brigid said, "Yes, they'll come. I'll see to it. Prob'ly all I'll have to do is show 'em the reporters gettin' thick around here. But, how're we gonna get 'em there, even with a disguise? Oh . . . wait a minnit . . ."

The phone dropped, then Carrie heard Brigid's voice from a distance: "Nell, you go stop 'em! Herb's gonna shove that fella with the TV camera . . . you go on out there 'n' yell at the both of 'em."

The voice came close again. "Gotta go, Carrie. No tellin' what Herb might do. Call me back in a coupla hours. If you can't get in on the phone, do ya mind to keep tryin'? 'N', well, th-thanks for all this." Brigid Mason's voice wavered and, at last, she stopped talking.

"I want to help, and don't worry, I'll keep calling until I get you."

Carrie put the phone down. She felt a bit like pacing the floor herself. First she had involved Henry in this mess, and now she was planning to do the same to Eleanor and Jason. But what choice did she have? The Masons needed all the help the four of them could give.

She looked at the clock. Eleven. Henry had said he'd arrive by early afternoon, so there was time for the next part in her action plan, a thorough look around the craft grounds.

She put on old jeans and a grey sweatshirt. After glancing in the mirror at her flying grey curls, she found a scarf she often tied at the neck of her blue dress and put it on her head. She wanted to appear as plain and unnoticeable as possible, and the hats she had with her didn't fit with plain and unnoticeable at all.

She put on the park department badge that would let her into the craft area without paying, then took it off and dropped it back on the table. It had her name on it, and she'd stand out because almost everyone from the convention was now headed home.

When Carrie arrived at the administration building, it was alive with activity. Workers were setting up for the classes that would begin tomorrow morning, and the desk attendant was busy telling a bearded man in overalls where the woodcarver's equipment should be put. The attendant reached for Carrie's entrance fee and stamped the back of her hand without looking away from the workman. Carrie walked out the door quietly, grateful for anonymity.

There were a number of tourists on the concrete walkways in the craft area, but, other than two people trying to see in the windows of the darkened dress-maker's shop, no one acted as if they were aware of the murder; or at least they weren't letting it disturb the planned routine for opening day. Probably most of the people here had just arrived for the weekend and had no idea what had happened last night. Since it looked like all the craft shops other than the dress-maker's were open, tourists would take little notice of one shop that was locked.

Carrie wandered along the walkways, not really sure

what she was looking for or what she might learn. She had watched most of the craft workers before and had no interest now in seeing anyone weave or make pottery or operate the old presses in the print shop.

There were several people clustered under the long shed ahead of her, and she heard the sound of the bellows that heated the fire in the blacksmith's forge. She walked up to the group standing along the railing that separated spectators from the heavy equipment and hot fire. Peering around a tall man who smelled of too much cologne, she caught a glimpse of the blacksmith. It was Bobby Lee Logan. He held up a knife.

She stared for just an instant too long before she started to duck behind the tall man. Only her head was visible when Bobby Lee looked around. She saw his eyes make note of her presence before they swung past her and down the row of spectators.

He continued his spiel without a break, explaining that the knife blade was hand forged from a discarded automobile spring, not made by stock reduction like many blades.

"This knife," he said, as his eyes raked back along the row of spectators and stopped on Carrie, "has a blade sharp enough to cut a gnat's eyebrow."

Well, since Bobby Lee had seen her, why not stand her ground and make the best of it? Why not see if he'd talk with her? Perhaps she could bluff him into saying something helpful. He was certainly spilling words enough to the sheriff. And she would be in no danger here since there were lots of people around.

She almost laughed, thinking she was being melo-dramatic, but sobered again as she remembered the fire, the view of the man in the checked shirt, and why she needed to talk with Bobby Lee.

The demonstration finished. A few people asked questions, then the crowd moved on. Carrie was alone. She walked forward, stopping when she reached the railing, and could feel heat from the forge throbbing against her face.

Bobby Lee ignored her as long as he could. He straightened the heavy tools on his work table, then checked the fire. Finally he looked over at her, picked up the knife, and swaggered to the railing.

"Can I help you?" His tone was insolent.

"That's a handsome knife," Carrie said, as she looked at the double-edged blade. "Is it for sale?"

"Two hundred dollars," he told her. "Polished bone handle. And what do you want with a knife like this?"

"I have a friend who would like one," she said. "I suppose you have others you could show me?"

She paused for a moment, still looking at the knife, then said, "Did you make some of the knives in Farel Teal's collection?"

She raised her eyes to his face, which was now stony, and went on. "I saw that knife at Farel Teal's house last night. He had quite a collection in a display case on the wall. I might have known you couldn't let those beautiful knives be destroyed in the fire. You should be careful about showing them, though. There are others who will remember them as well as I do."

118

For a moment, Bobby Lee Logan didn't answer. He just stared at her, running his finger along the flat side of the knife blade as if caressing it. Finally he said, "We make lotsa knives like this here at the forge."

Looking around and seeing that there were still several people in the area, she swallowed, then spoke, forming her words clearly and softly. "But I don't suppose any of them have that unusual dark stripe at the base of the bone handle."

She stared into his cold blue eyes, tried not to blink, and continued in a voice that was almost a whisper, "Why did you set fire to Farel's house?"

She heard the hiss as Bobby Lee took a quick breath through clenched teeth. The blue eyes studied her face.

"Who says I did?"

"I was there."

"Oh, sure, some little old lady like you out tramping in the country at night."

The comment made her boil, but she brushed her anger aside and said, "I wasn't alone. There were three other people with me, and they saw the same things I did."

His eyes said he didn't believe her.

"You were still wearing your red and white checked shirt. You carried a bag with something inflammable in it. What? A bottle of gasoline? Paint thinner? It doesn't matter. Investigators will find out what you used. You spilled the liquid in several rooms, then took time to pack Farel's knife collection and put it in

119

your bag because you couldn't bear for that to be destroyed. After you set the fire, you ran out the front door, leaping clear over the steps and driving off in your car with the Missouri license plate. Isn't that about the way it happened?"

Now the look on Bobby Lee's face told Carrie she had guessed right. He said, "Well, if that's so, why aren't you telling Sheriff Wylie? Why are you talking to me?"

"Sheriff Wylie's first question to you would be, 'Why did you do it?' not, 'Tell me all about your friend, Farel Teal.' That's what my question is. I want to know why Farel Teal died and why he kidnapped Dulcey Mason, not why you set fire to that house—unless it has something to do with Dulcey. And, I'll tell you this, Bobby Lee, I care about that child, though I've never even seen her. She's the child you're telling some folks is Farel Teal's daughter, so maybe you care about her too. Farel took her from her parents, but then he was killed, and she was taken by others, probably by whoever killed him. I'm more interested in getting her safely home than I am in telling the sheriff about an arsonist right now. Or . . . are you worse than that? Did *you* kill Farel Teal? *Do you have Dulcey Mason?*"

For a moment her resolve faltered as she watched the fury gather in Bobby Lee's face. But then she realized his anger was meant for someone else. It wasn't directed at her. He acted as if she weren't there.

There was a long silence. Three people came into

the shed. Seeing that nothing was happening and the blacksmith was paying no attention to them, they moved on down the walkway.

"*Why,* Bobby Lee? Why are you trying to hurt the Masons? Where is Dulcey?"

"Is it really true about Dulcey?"

"Yes. Didn't you know Farel had kidnapped her?"

"I know you're lyin'. Farel wouldn't . . ."

"Oh, yes," she said, "he would. Farel took her out of Brigid Mason's yard yesterday afternoon. Why? Was it really for the ransom money? I hear he needed to get out of town, out of the state. Then others took Dulcey away from him. A kidnap note he didn't write was found by his body. Dulcey could be in great danger. I'm not going to argue with you about this. I want to hear what you know and I want to hear it right now. It may help us figure out who has Dulcey. It may help us save her life."

"Dulcey . . . Tracy's little girl . . ."

Suddenly Bobby Lee turned back into the black-smith's shop, unlocked a cabinet door, put the knife inside, and snapped the lock shut. Then he picked up a soot-smudged sign and rested it on an easel next to the railing. It said, "Gone to lunch. Back at . . ." Bobby Lee set the cardboard clock dial at 1:00 and vaulted over the railing. Before Carrie could protest, he had her by the arm and was pulling her down the concrete walk.

# Chapter X

"Stop," Carrie said. "You're hurting my arm."

Two people who were walking toward the herb garden turned to look at them, and Bobby Lee stopped.

He tightened his lips and glared at her. She glared back steadily, hoping she looked strong and calm.

Then Bobby Lee's face cleared, and he said, "You want something to eat or drink?"

She looked around. They were standing by the door to the craft area snack shop.

Carrie smiled up at him. "Why, yes, thank you. I'd like a Dr. Pepper, and why don't we have some popcorn?" She didn't reach for her purse, and after a moment, Bobby Lee left her alone on the sidewalk and went into the snack shop.

I could walk away right now if I wanted to, she thought, so I can't be in any danger.

When Bobby Lee bumped out the door he was holding a pop cup in each hand and had a popcorn sack under one arm. She took the popcorn.

"Did you get napkins?" she asked. "Well, never mind, I have tissues in my pocket."

They sat down facing each other at a nearby picnic table. Carrie carefully spread out two tissues and spilled small mountains of popcorn on each one. Bobby Lee began to laugh. He swore.

She glared at him.

"You don't like my language? Well, so what? You act like we're having a picnic. Can we get on with things? Tell me about Dulcey."

"No need. I've told you all I know. Dulcey has been kidnapped, twice it would seem. Now you tell me . . . why did Farel take her in the first place?"

"How would I know?"

"You say you were his best friend. Unless that's a lie, you must have some ideas about it. Tell me, for Dulcey's sake . . . for Tracy's."

For a moment he was still, saying nothing. Then he took a deep breath so his chest swelled, stretching his red braces and threatening the buttons on his sweat-stained chambray shirt. He flexed an arm and looked at the bulging muscles.

Carrie spoke carefully, keeping her teeth nearly closed so her words came out with a slight hiss. "You listen to me, Bobby Lee Logan. Dulcey Mason is in great danger and you sit here and act cute, like some kind of juvenile delinquent who thinks he's tough. Well, it won't work. You aren't tough, you're weaker than water . . . afraid to speak the truth. So, I'm going to Sheriff Wylie and tell him who set that fire. I will also tell him I think you killed Farel Teal. He may already be thinking that Bobby Lee Logan has spent an awful lot of time talking about what everyone else has done and said nothing about what he might have been doing. Sheriff Wylie may be thinking about Bobby Lee Logan right now."

Bobby Lee's arm came up in a swift arc, and he

hurled his pop cup against the board fence next to the picnic pavilion. The cup smashed, spraying ice and pop over picnic tables and one small boy who had wandered in.

The child began to scream. Carrie got up to check on him and saw that he wasn't even wet. He was, in fact, enjoying her attention. She left him to his unconvincing sobs, put the pop cup in the trash, and sat down again, watching the fury fade out of Bobby Lee's face.

Someone in the background collected the child, and his wailing died away.

Carrie waited.

"Chase Mason is a thief." His voice was low and steady.

He looked at her, testing her reaction. As she watched him she was thinking, I'm not afraid of a child with a bad attitude, Bobby Lee, and that's just how you act. You have an awful temper, but you don't frighten me, not really. You probably aren't as old as my own son, but you're acting much, much younger . . . . six or seven, maybe.

Finally his eyes drifted sideways. He looked off into some unknown distance and began to talk in a soft voice that didn't sound like it belonged to him.

"Farel, me, and Tracy, we grew up together, were always together. In fact, mosta the kids called us 'the triplets.' We played together, did our homework together, fought with and for each other—you name it. Shoot, we even learned a trade together."

124

Bobby Lee laughed, but the laugh was empty of humor. The sound of it sent a ripple down Carrie's backbone.

He continued, his eyes still looking into the unseen distance. "One of the things my dad did was black-smithin' and we all learned the trade. Tracy too. She's a wiry little gal, stronger than she looks. She could make a knife like the one you saw . . . did, in fact, make several of them, though she couldn't do some of the heavier work. Farel had two knives she made for him in his collection. There was only one there last night. I have it now."

Carrie nodded. She had noticed the missing knife.

"We made throwing knives, and we practiced with them. We could split apples, hit circles drawn on the side of the barn, stuff like that. Tracy was better at it than Farel or me. She could aim better. She has a good eye and could throw where she looked, straight as an arrow; but," Bobby Lee's chest swelled again, "not as hard as Farel or me, of course."

He paused for a moment and smiled—a real smile—then went on. "You should have seen what we did to the pun'kin at Farel's house one Halloween. His sister had just carved it and put it on that stump in the front yard. We used it for throwing practice, and there wasn't enough pun'kin to pray over when we got through. We were sure in trouble for that one. I wasn't allowed to go to town on weekends for a month.

"Well. When Farel and me were seniors in high school, things began to change. Tracy didn't act like

125

she could see it, maybe because she was a year younger, but I could. Farel was in love with her, and it was pretty hard on him. 'Course he was her cousin . . . but I wasn't." His voice dropped to a whisper. "I wasn't, and I loved her too."

He shook his head. Carrie didn't know if it was in simple regret or because he was trying to shake off unhappy memories.

"Farel and me used to play around makin' up songs for Tracy. One he wrote was special, a song he called 'Lying to Strangers.' It was the prettiest song he'd ever wrote. It was about how people loved each other and couldn't tell it to the outside world, a real sad song. The three of us used to sit in a clearing in the woods and sing it together, but we never sang it in public. It was our private song, you know. Can you see that? Our special song."

He looked at Carrie and, slowly, she nodded.

"Our special song, and we never sang it before anyone else. I wish to God now that we had.

"Then, one night, Tracy met Chase Mason at a performance in the auditorium. Farel and I weren't even here that night. We'd gone off to some big deal event in Harrison. It was such a big deal I don't even remember what it was, do you believe that? They began performing together, and she hardly spent time with us anymore, and when she did, she was kind of . . . distant . . . you know? Before we understood what was happening, she'd run off to marry him, and the two of them were singing our special song. Oh, they

126

changed it some, but it was still our private, special song."

Bobby Lee's face grew hard again, and the pain and fury returned to his voice.

"They told people everywhere that the two of them had written the song, *our special, private song,* and since few had ever heard us sing it, we had no way to prove different.

"Have you heard it?" he asked.

She nodded.

"So has most everyone else in the world by now. Well, like I said, they changed it a bit, but it's still our song, the song Farel wrote for *her!*

"Farel, he wouldn't do anything about it at first because he still loved Tracy, y'see, and that was the saddest thing I ever knew. It was tearing him apart. He didn't care about life anymore. Tracy and Mason had gone off to Branson. Her part of the family, as well as Farel's sisters, had already moved away. There was just Farel and his dad. His dad had debts, was about to lose the farm. That man never was smart about money, and neither was Farel for that matter. After his dad died, Farel got in with some bad folks who promised money . . ."

Bobby Lee lifted his chin and said, defensively, "Well, what would anyone expect? All the good had gone out of his life, the way he saw things. All he'd had left was his dad. He had me, too, of course, but he didn't want anything to do with me at that time. I don't know why. I guess Tracy had been the glue that held the three of us together. Maybe he was ashamed or something. I just don't know, I don't know."

Again, Carrie nodded and hoped Bobby Lee didn't realize she felt like crying.

"And after Farel's dad died, y'see, he needed to go over papers in his safe deposit box. Farel found things put there from Tracy's folks too, found out he and Tracy weren't related at all. She was adopted. He could have married her."

Carrie remembered Tracy's words, "Uncle Teddy died last year."

She asked Bobby Lee, "You're sure about this?"

"Yes, Farel came to me. He showed me the papers."

"And that was just last year?"

"Yes."

"In that case you made up the story about Dulcey being Farel's child. It isn't true, is it? You made it up after you learned Farel was dead."

"Well, so what. Anything to hurt that scum Mason!"

"Did Farel tell Tracy they weren't related by blood?"

"Yes. He called her, then went to see her about six months ago when Mason was off in Nashville making some special recording deals. I'm not sure what happened, but whatever did happen made Farel worse. He came home tore to pieces. After that all he could think about was leaving the state, going maybe to Dallas, trying to start over. By then we were friends again, and I encouraged him to get away from here—thought it was a good idea. But he didn't have money, and he

128

still owed for special care his dad had needed at the last. Of course he'd inherited the house and land, but there wasn't much to that house . . . you saw it, and the land had already been put up for his dad's debts. It's poor land anyway."

"Was Farel still in with the bad folks you mentioned?"

"Yes, he had to have money to live on, and they had a pretty tight hold on him anyway. You're smart enough to know how that goes. But he swore to me he wanted to get out of that and just leave here, leave it all behind, if he could find enough money for a new start.

"You see? That song is worth money, big money. If Farel took Dulcey, it was probably to get Chase to admit he stole that song, or at least force him to pay royalty for using it. And, he wouldn'a hurt Dulcey. They got along like real kin . . . *like* father and daughter. Tracy used to let Dulcey spend some time with Farel when they were in town on a visit. Chase didn't like it, but what could he say? Farel was Tracy's kin, remember?"

Anger hit her. "Even if Tracy and Chase did steal that song, anyone who would use an innocent child in a scheme like Farel's is despicable. And, look at the result."

She wasn't sure Bobby Lee understood despicable, but he sure understood her tone.

"Farel wouldn'a let anyone touch Dulcey or hurt her. He wouldn'a!"

"But what happened then? Don't you have any idea who took Dulcey?"

He looked at the table top. "Nah. Nothin' more than what I said. I never saw Farel yesterday."

They sat in silence, eating popcorn. She could hear him chewing. It sounded so ordinary. Two people sitting in a picnic pavilion sharing popcorn. It was such an ordinary thing to do.

She said, "What was in his house that you wanted to destroy? And how did you know Farel wouldn't ever need that house, or what was in it, again?"

"I overheard your 911 phone call. I had a bad feeling about it and went to the dressmaker's shop. When I said I never saw Farel yesterday, I meant I never saw him *alive*."

"What in that house needed to be destroyed?"

"If you can't figure it out, I'm not saying. If I told you more now, I'd have to make it up, because I will never talk to anyone about it. Not ever. Farel's dead. What's past in his life is dead too. I saw to that. It's over."

"No, it isn't, Bobby Lee. Someone must pay for Farel's murder. Unless you killed him yourself, you must agree to that. And what about Dulcey? Who has her? Are you sure you don't have any idea about that? Can't you help?"

He got to his feet and stood over her, so big that his body shaded hers. "I'd look in the hills behind here if I was you. A family lives there. Stays to themselves. You just ask around. Look in the hills. I can't say more. I like my life too much. I've even got a special girl now. I may just get married some day. Anyway, I can't say more."

"Well, Bobby Lee, for the sake of your special girl, I hope you learn to handle that temper of yours. If you don't, there's good in your life that may not last either."

"Yeh, mebbe, but I didn't kill Farel. I'm sure you know that now. As far as someone paying for his murder? That's on Mason's ticket. I figure the two of them had a face-off and Farel lost. But maybe it's better left to settle in the dust of these hills. How'd you like it if Dulcey's daddy was a killer? As for temper, well, Chase Mason's got one too."

Carrie didn't respond for a moment. Then she said, "And there is nothing more you'll tell me?"

"You just think about what I said. I'm gonna eat lunch now and go back to work. Lots of tourists today. If you want to buy a knife you can come see me at the blacksmith's shop. If two hundred dollars is too much, I have some cheaper. If you want anything else of me, forget it. We never had this conversation—you've been asking about having a knife made, and now, you're outa my life. I wish you luck in finding Dulcey, I do."

She watched Bobby Lee Logan stride out of the pavilion and disappear among the people on the sidewalk, then turned back to the picnic table, rested her elbows on it, and put her chin in her hands. She sat silently for a few minutes, ignoring the sounds behind

131

her as tourists began to line up for the snack shop lunch buffet.

Suddenly she remembered Bobby Lee Logan's voice saying, "She has a good eye . . . could throw . . . straight as an arrow."

Carrie jerked her head up and pounded her fist on the table, bouncing popcorn in all directions.

"Whoa there, my girl," said a rumbling male voice.

Carrie got up so fast she almost fell backwards over the picnic bench. She turned and held out her hands, but Henry ignored them. In a minute she was leaning over the bench with her face mashed against his chest. The bench began to topple, but fortunately it had no place to topple to. It, like Carrie, was caught against Henry's massive form.

The hug lasted a long time. Then Henry moved back, set the bench firmly in place, and said, "Well, it sounds like we're putting broken things back together again. So, what's the plan, Detective McCrite?"

She couldn't help it. She began to laugh.

## Chapter XI

"I get the idea," said Henry, studying her face, "that wood carving and herb growing are no longer our main interests here. I brought the things you asked for, but what are we going to do with that stuff?"

"Have you eaten lunch yet?"

"No."

"Have you checked in?"

132

"No. I meant to, but I took a wrong turn and ended up out front instead. I came in to ask directions and decided to see if the lady at the information desk knew where you were. She remembered that you had gone through into the craft area an hour or so ago."

So much for trying to remain anonymous, Carrie thought. I might as well have worn my badge and saved the entrance fee.

"Well," she said, "it's lunchtime, and we need privacy so I can tell you all that's been happening. If we keep our voices down, I think the restaurant across the way is the best place. Food's great, and I don't want to take time to drive into town. Is that okay?"

"Sure, lead the way. But shouldn't I go check in before we eat?"

"Um, no, let's talk first, we may need to change our plans a bit." To avoid further discussion about room arrangements until Henry fully understood what was going on, she asked, "How's FatCat?"

"Happy at Shirley and Roger's. Probably stretched out on the back of their couch enjoying the sun from that south window. I took her down there this morning." He hesitated, looking at her sideways as he opened the entry door to the administration building. "While she was at my house, I let her sleep with me so she wouldn't be too lonely."

"Lonely, phooey! That cat loves attention and doesn't care where she gets it as you know quite well. She's just as happy with you or with Shirley and Roger as she is with me . . . probably even happier,

133

since you spoil her, and I make her follow house rules, or at least *my* house rules. No sleeping on human beds, and especially no getting on a bed when I'm in it. She purrs too loudly for one thing. Sounds like a motor scooter with a bad muffler. When her motor goes on, I wake up."

"Purr doesn't bother me, it's kind of soothing, and of course she misses you. Besides, *you* weren't in my bed. She knew that as well as I did, so we didn't break your rules."

"Hmpf," said Carrie, not looking at him as she led the way into the dining room and asked the hostess for her favorite window table.

She pointed Henry into a chair facing the windows so he could see the forested hilltop and bird feeders. As soon as they were both seated, he asked, "What happened to your face?"

Surprised, she touched her scraped cheek. "I thought my make-up pretty much covered it. Beth and I had breakfast together and she didn't notice or comment."

"Does that mean I'm supposed to notice and comment, or I'm not? Even after one failed marriage, which should have taught me something, and all these years around women, I'm not sure I understand."

"What if I were a man?"

"I'd probably say, 'Hey, who've you been fighting with?'"

"Hmmm. I'm curious then, a male friend or me . . . which one would you have more sympathy for over a scratched face?"

134

"Is this one of your trick questions? I'd have more sympathy for you, of course, make of that whatever you will. I don't want you hurt, and I don't want this discussion, either, so it stops here. Now, how *did* your face get scratched?"

She laced her fingers together and looked down at them, realizing that, after all, Henry's concerns about her welfare always touched and comforted her. She thought of how the Bible frequently mentions God comforting His children. Perhaps Henry's concern was one way the promised comfort was being shown. She'd have to think more about it, but, for now, she guessed she should show she was grateful.

Still, it was hard to say anything aloud. Finally she managed, "I do appreciate the concern."

The words sounded stiff and formal, but it was too late to call them back or substitute the softer phrase, "I'm glad you care," which was how she'd answered him inside her head.

"My scraped face is part of the whole story, so I'll fit it in at the right place, but, first things first. Here comes the waitress. I can recommend several things . . ."

After they'd ordered, specifying separate checks, Henry leaned forward in his chair. "I'm listening," he said.

Speaking as quickly as she could, she began telling him everything that had happened since the time— was it only yesterday afternoon?—when she had seen the woman in the woods. Henry's face remained almost expressionless as he listened, but the familiar line between his widely spaced brown eyes deepened as she got to the part about the murder of Farel Teal and the probable second kidnapping. She described everything she'd noticed in the dressmaker's shop, hoping she was doing a good job, hoping he would now know how carefully she had listened to his advice about observing and remembering. Surely his years of experience in the criminal investigation division of the Kansas City Police Department would help bring some enlightenment to this terrible mess.

He held up a hand. "Tell me what you thought when you looked at those scissors and the wound."

Ahhh. She waited a minute before answering, not because she had no opinion, but because she was savoring the awareness that he wasn't treating her like a squeamish female who must be protected from thinking about such dreadful details.

"The scissors aren't what killed Farel Teal."

"I agree. Knife, maybe. Very sharp, wide, double-edged blade. But why the substitution?"

She shook her head, warning him as the waitress came to put bowls of bean soup and a plate of corn-bread on the table, then walked away. Carrie pushed the dishes of Peach and Apple Chunky nearer his plate and said, "Because the knife, maybe even the fact a knife was used, could help identify the killer. I'm sure I know where the knife came from, and you'll see why in a minute." She returned to her recitation, pausing at intervals to take bites of food and see if Henry had questions. But he was silent, listening while he ate.

After she had described Farel's house, the knife display case and its contents, the fire, the rush back to the car and to town, Henry said, "I wish I had been with you, Cara."

She smiled up at him, then began to speak more slowly, choosing words carefully.

"Henry, something is really bothering me. I thought in the beginning that, because she's so tiny, and he was so big and strong, there was no way Tracy could have stabbed Farel from the front."

He nodded. "He'd have seen her coming at him, and if he's tall, she'd need to reach up, making her movements even more evident."

"Well, what about throwing the knife?"

"Throwing . . . ?"

She told Henry about Bobby Lee and what he'd said, then waited.

"Hm, I suppose it would be possible. If the knife hit him just right, it could kill. Even a good, forceful thrower would have to be lucky for the blow to hit like that, missing the ribs. But, the motive?"

"I don't know, but if it was about Dulcey . . . oh, glory, Henry, I hate to think of it."

He frowned. "I know." He tilted his bowl to finish the last bite. "Where are the Masons now?"

She returned to her story, ending with an explanation of what was going on at Brigid's house and why there was a need to get Tracy and Chase away from the public eye. Then she took a deep breath and rushed on, telling him her plan for concealing the young

137

couple over the weekend. When she had finished, Henry sat quietly for a moment, then said, "Fine, good idea. Dessert?"

"Not for me. Eating cornbread drowned in sweet peaches is plenty. But, there's berry cobbler . . ."

When Henry had ordered blackberry cobbler with ice cream, Carrie spoke again, "Of course Eleanor could move in with me, and you and Jason could room together, but I think it would be best if both a man and woman were close to Chase and Tracy most of the time. Jason and Eleanor can stay with them and see if they say anything that puts light on this mess while you and I try to locate Dulcey. Henry, we *must* find her, that's the important thing, no matter who killed Farel. Or, do you think Chase and Tracy should just pay the ransom, if that's what the kidnappers want, and get Dulcey back that way?"

"Sometimes that works. Sometimes it doesn't. If the parents seem willing to pay once, why not twice . . . or more? It's always a gamble, a gamble with a child's life. And you should have told the sheriff—you know that. Surely you don't think we can save that child by ourselves?"

"I wanted to call in the sheriff, but the Masons wouldn't allow it, and I really can't blame them. Besides, you and I don't know anything about law enforcement in this county. How sophisticated are they, how would they handle something as delicate as this? And we have special advantages the sheriff could never have, especially for approaching the Culpepers.

I'm a pudgy, innocent-looking older woman whose name just happens to be Culpeper. The way you'll be dressed will help you fit in too, and no Culpeper here except Margaret has ever seen either of us."

He answered slowly, thinking aloud. "Umm. We won't look at all like the law, and that woman's name is Culpeper . . ."

"Yes. We'll find where the Culpepers live and talk with Margaret. Remember what the Masons told me? Law enforcement won't go near them. We can. I want to learn the meaning of that strange story about a beast taking a child."

She smiled up at him. "Henry, I feel just like you do. I don't want *you* hurt either, but it seems to me that the two of us, looking like what we are, plain folks, will be perfectly safe."

"Hmmm . . . yes."

She knew she was winning him over. He was looking at her thoughtfully and had reached out to put his hand over hers when a pair of voices said, "Hi," in unison.

"Thought we'd find you two together where the food is," said Jason Stack as he dropped into the chair across from Henry, and Eleanor came around to accept Carrie's hug.

"You're early," Carrie said. "We weren't expecting you until later this afternoon. I'm glad you're here, though. Have you eaten?"

Eleanor nodded. "I wanted to stop over in Eureka Springs, so we decided to leave a day early and spend

139

last night there. It's a good place to shop for the grandchildren's birthdays. There's this little store on Spring Street where they sell handmade wooden toys, and . . ."

"Yes, yes," interrupted Jason. "We came, we shopped, we left. Eleanor went shopping first thing this morning, and it took her, praise the Lord, less time than I thought. That's why we're early. We've eaten, but from the looks of the left-overs, or lack of them, I wish we'd waited."

"Hate to tell you," Carrie said, "but they sell lots of wonderful toys here in the craft area, as well as at the gift shop next to it. You can even watch toys being made. Maybe you'll want to stock up for Christmas now.

"But, I'm glad you're early, and I hope you're in the mood for adventure. Quite a bit has happened here. A man has been murdered, a child has been kidnapped, and all four of us are in a position to be of real help."

"My word," Jason said, "you're at it again. Maybe those books Eleanor reads aren't so far-fetched. Whoever said retirement was supposed to be dull didn't have a friend like Carrie McCrite. Think I'll write a book myself, *Carrie McCrite, Senior Detective*, or . . ."

"Stop it, Jason," Eleanor said. "You're babbling, and I'm sure this is not a joking matter." She turned to Carrie. "So, how are we going to help? We're listening. *Both* of us are listening."

So Carrie began her story again, a shortened version

140

this time. She finished by telling them about the need to hide Chase and Tracy.

"But our plan for that won't work without you, as you'll soon see."

"Of course we'll help," Eleanor said, sounding eager. "This is awful, those poor children, and their little girl. So, what's the plan?"

"The room reserved for Henry is right next to yours in a duplex cabin, with locking doors between. All the rooms have two beds. So, I thought we could put the Masons in Henry's room, calling them Mr. and Mrs. Henry King. That way you two can get to know them, talk with them, bring in food, and so on. Henry will share my room."

Jason smirked and opened his mouth to say something, but Eleanor put her hand on his arm and said, "Splendid. So how do we get them here?"

Carrie gave a bare outline of her plan, and after Eleanor and Jason had agreed to their part, said, "Let's meet in my room after you check in. I'll call Brigid Mason and make arrangements with her. Go ahead and check in under your own name, but sign up for Mr. and Mrs. Henry King too. You might tell the people at the desk they're your newly wed daughter and son-in-law who will be joining you here this evening. Get their key too. We'll have to be sure the housekeeping staff doesn't go in the room while Chase and Tracy are there, and I thought saying they're newlyweds would make that seem less unusual. We can straighten the charges out later. I'm sure the Masons will pay their part. Henry will check in as Herman Culpeper."

"Not McCrite?" said Jason, winking towards Henry.

"No, there's a family here named Culpeper that may be involved with the kidnapping. The woman I saw in the woods is one of them. Since my maiden name is Culpeper I can assume a family relationship, say I'm Carrie Culpeper McCrite, a widow, and this is my brother, Herman. The two of us will call on the Mountain View Culpepers this afternoon while you pick up Chase and Tracy and see what we can find out.

"So, shall we get started? Come to my room, number 149, as soon as you've checked in and unloaded your things. Turn right at the shed with pop machines in it. And . . . thanks, both of you. You can still back out if you want. Some parts of this might be unpleasant, or even a little dangerous. You could miss some of your classes too."

"They'll have them again next year," said Jason. "Now, let's get busy and see if we can help save that little girl."

As she and Henry came down the path toward her motel room, Carrie could see a white card stuck in the door. She pulled it loose and read the name, "Ryerson T. Wylie, Sheriff." In red ink, a note on the back instructed her to call Sheriff Wylie's office immediately.

She handed the card to Henry and said, "I can't talk to the man now. I'd have to lie, and I'm not sure I

142

should do that—lying to a sheriff. It could get me in trouble, couldn't it? And what if he sees you, asks your name, wants to look at your driver's license or something? What am I going to do?"

"Don't worry about it," Henry said. "You don't need to call right away. He's got enough to keep him busy for the present. I am wondering if he understood the significance of that wound and what he's discovered since then. Are you sure he doesn't know the Mason child has been kidnapped?"

"If he does, he's being quiet about it, which is good. But I don't see how he could possibly know unless Bobby Lee rushed to tell him after our talk this morning. I don't think Bobby Lee knew it until I told him. I think he was honestly shocked, but Bobby Lee Logan is very good at lying, especially to outsiders like me. Oh, Henry, I'm confused. I don't really know who is telling the truth about anything, including Chase, Tracy, and Aunt Brigid."

"So we'll act on the facts we can confirm," he said. "First thing to do is call the Masons and work out your plans with Brigid before Eleanor and Jason get here. While you're doing that, I'll check in and bring my things from the car.

"Carrie, I do have my gun. After you called last night, I thought . . ." He didn't finish. Instead he turned and headed down the path toward the parking lot.

She stood still, looking at Henry's back as he walked away. He had only carried a hand gun once since leaving police work, and that had been to protect her and his daughter, Susan. Refusal to carry a gun was one reason Henry had left the Kansas City Police Department. It began with one more teenager high on drugs. The boy had a gun and was robbing a convenience store near Henry's home. Henry, just off duty, was coming in the store to pay for gas.

He heard shots and saw the cashier, a man he knew well, fall behind the counter. Yelling obscenities, the teenager had turned his gun toward Henry, but Henry shot first.

"The kid died right there, and I still can't remember whether or not I shot to kill," he had told Carrie.

A week after that, Henry went to see the dead boy's mother. He wouldn't talk about what had happened during that visit, but Carrie knew he stopped carrying his gun then. Three months after the visit, he resigned from the police department.

Six months later his wife, Irena, the only child of a wealthy Kansas City family, left him. Being the wife of a police detective had earned sympathy and attention from her family and friends throughout their marriage. Henry said that when he quit police work, Irena lost her only reason for staying married to him.

Just last November he had confided to Carrie, "She could no longer say, 'my husband, Police Major Henry King,' at social events. She has plenty of her own money. I guess being married to an ex-police officer who was selling real estate didn't interest her at all."

Carrie sighed, turned away from the door, and went to the telephone. She was sorry for Henry, but glad Irena had left him after twenty-five years of an unhappy and childless marriage. And she was very glad that Henry's search for the daughter he'd never seen, born after a brief encounter with a woman he'd met at adult night school, had brought him to the Ozarks.

Brigid Mason's line was busy, but when Carrie dialed a second time, the phone rang. A strange voice answered. "Ah-low?"

"May I speak to Brigid Mason, please?"

"Is no spik angless. Is bad nuumbeer."

"Tell her Carrie Culpeper. Please."

"Ah."

There was a short silence, then Brigid's voice said, "Carrie? Whew! We're tryin' to fool callers. This gets more worrisome by the minit."

"What's happened?"

"Reporters. Now another TV station has made it here. Herb 'n' the rest are keepin' them outside the fence so far, but they make such a crowd it's gettin' harder all the time. We got cameras poked at us from all over.

"Besides that, the sheriff called. He was curious if Dulcey felt better. I'm afeerd he has an idea she's been taken, else why would he ask if she was still here? God forgive me, I keep sayin' she is. After all, he kin hardly want to question her, 'n' Chase won't let me tell she's kidnapped."

145

"Brigid, have you talked with Chase and Tracy about hiding at the Folk Center?"

"Yup, 'n' now that they see they can't get out to that bird box nor anywheres else, they'll come with you gladly. I don't know how you're gonna fix it up, but we're sure game to try. I did change their looks, much as I could. Got their stuff packed, too. We're ready."

"Good. Now, here's what we're going to do . . ."

## Chapter XII

Carrie was finishing her conversation with Brigid as Henry came into the room. He carried the two L. L. Bean travel bags his daughter Susan and her husband had given him for Christmas, and, arms loaded, he stopped just inside the door, staring at the nearest bed.

"Oops," she said, noticing what he was looking at. "I've been using the extra bed to organize brochures by county and location within each county. That's the way we display them at the information center. The bed was such a nice flat area, and I . . . didn't know you'd be sleeping in it. It'll only take me a minute to move them."

She grabbed a brochure box and started to sweep a stack into it.

"Wait! If they're organized, let's keep them that way. Do you have any rubber bands?"

She reached in her briefcase and held up a sandwich bag with rubber bands in it.

"Good. Just a minute."

He went into the bathroom and came back with the extra roll of toilet paper. "Here, I'll lay a piece of this between each different type of brochure, then you can use the rubber bands to keep them together by county. That way they'll be easy to separate and put in your racks when you get home—though you may have to do some explaining about your little white dividers!"

Both of them were laughing as he began tearing off squares, and they went to work.

Carrie was filling the last brochure box when someone's knuckles banged against the door.

She jerked her head up in alarm. "I didn't expect Eleanor and Jason this quickly. They usually travel with lots of stuff. It would take them some time to unload . . . so, could that be the sheriff?"

"Guess it could be," Henry said, as he waved his arm toward the bathroom. "You might . . ." But she was already moving in that direction.

She pushed the bathroom door closed and reached in the tub enclosure to turn on the water. Surely the sheriff wouldn't stand around and wait for her to take a very long shower.

In a minute the bathroom door opened and Henry's face came into view around its edge. He hadn't knocked. Good heavens!

"The Stacks are here," was all he said.

Both Eleanor and Jason gave her a curious look when she came into the room fully clothed. She supposed they'd heard the shower running, but, instead of explaining, she asked, "Did everything go okay?"

147

"No problems," Jason said. "I have keys to both rooms in the unit—143, A and B.

"Couldn't be better," she said. "It's as secluded as any of the cabins. Chase and Tracy should be able to get in and out when they need to."

She handed Jason a piece of paper. "Brigid gave me directions to her house. She said it will be easy to find with all the reporters hanging around.

"You'll need to wear the most concealing clothing you have with you. Eleanor, that pantsuit's fine. Jason, do you have plain slacks and a loose jacket or windbreaker? The clothes you wear going into the house will be what Chase and Tracy wear coming out, so take a change of clothing, and make it as different in style from what you wear in as you can. I imagine you brought sun hats? Good. They'll cover most of your hair or . . . whatever," she amended as Jason ran a hand over the bare skin on top of his head. "Put your change of clothing in this black bag of Henry's. It can be your medical bag. You're going to play doctor."

Jason started to laugh, and Eleanor poked him in the side. The laugh subsided, but he winked at Henry. Carrie continued. "Brigid is letting her kinfolk know you're coming, and they'll block out a way through what she says is a gaggle of reporters and cameras. The relatives will tell the reporters you're the Masons' doctors from Branson and you've been asked to come and check on Dulcey and Tracy. People believe stars do odd things and can afford anything, so there should be no question that you've come all the way here to take care of your important patients for what are being reported to the press as minor problems—Dulcey's cold and Tracy's distress over the death of her cousin. They may suspect your presence here means the problems are bigger than stated but, for now, who cares? And since you have an Arkansas license plate on your car, the relatives will say you flew to a small airport near here and rented a car.

"Reporters are undoubtedly going to try and reach you for an interview, so getting in and out will be crucial times. The relatives will do the best they can to keep everyone back. Obviously you can't talk to anyone. Family members will take care of answering questions. I can guess they're leaning heavily on their hillbilly image to create quite a show for the media, so that helps as a distraction.

"Keep the car windows rolled up and the doors locked. Wear your sunglasses. I wish we could wait until dark for this, but we can't, because the note telling what the kidnappers are demanding is supposed to be in the bird box after the show begins tonight, and Chase and Tracy will want to be here by then.

"Remember, at whatever distance, there will be cameras pointing at you. The hats and sunglasses should keep you from being identified—you don't want your kids or others to recognize you on TV and wonder what's going on."

"Don't want them to wonder why we're playing doctor?" Jason said, making no attempt to conceal his smirk.

Carrie glared at him, then went on, enunciating each word carefully. "Pretending to be medical professionals. This is no joke. Chase and Tracy are very, very famous, as Henry can tell you, and that's why they need to go into hiding until Dulcey is safely back with them.

"You'll have to make up your own script to fit whatever happens when you get to the house. Drive the car as close to the front entry as you can. Brigid says reporters are all around the house, even in her nearest neighbor's yard, so, since the front door has bushes around it, she thought that would be the best to use. The car itself can also help shield all of you.

"When you get inside, change clothes, then give Chase and Tracy what you had on, including sunglasses and hats. The clothing may have to be padded here and there—both of them are slender, though your heights are similar.

"You'll need to kill some time there to make the visit plausible, but eventually Chase and Tracy will come back out in your clothes, carrying your bag with their own clothing in it, and get in the front of the car. Chase will have to be the one driving the car out. We can only hope this will fool reporters and anyone else who may be watching. The fact Dulcey won't be with them will help.

"How you two get back in the car is up to you. Perhaps you can rush out as if you were part of the Mason clan asking for a lift somewhere. You'll have to figure out what to do about that after you get there. If all their

150

things won't fit in this bag of Henry's, pack them in sacks or whatever Brigid has.

"Follow your best instincts, but that's the outline of the plot. Any suggestions? See any way to make it work better?"

Jason, serious now, said, "It would be natural for medical professionals to resist having their pictures splashed across the tabloids, so if the photographers are too aggressive, we could hold something up to shield our faces. Eleanor can use her purse, and I'll have this bag. And, just in case, we can each carry a magazine or newspaper."

"Good idea. As far as running interference, Brigid says there are at least a dozen relatives there right now, including several large men, who will help.

"Now, after the four of you are safely away, see if you can get Chase and Tracy to talk about anything at all, but especially the kidnapping and murder. Maybe something helpful that we haven't learned so far will come out. I'm sure they aren't telling the whole truth about any of this mess. There are also undercurrents of an even deeper problem between them. Maybe you can find out what it is, especially if you have a chance to talk with either or both of them alone. The problem could have something to do with the fact that Farel Teal was supposedly in love with Tracy, but I don't know how much Chase knows about that. In any case, I'm sure they're not being honest with each other, or anyone else. Something's very wrong there.

"Eleanor, they might respond to cozy mothering,

and Jason, you can use the diplomatic skills you practiced during labor negotiations at your plant up north. Maybe they'll confide in you, especially since you're obviously giving up a vacation to help them out.

"Neither of them has slept much since yesterday, so they may just want to nap after you get them back here. Assure them they can do nothing until time for one of them to go look in the bird box tonight."

Henry spoke up. "I have a thought about that. Since it's fairly certain the kidnappers won't know either Jason or me, we could go to the auditorium early, as if we wanted to be sure and get tickets for the evening show. It will be a pleasant evening, so, after we pretend to buy tickets, we could hang around outside as if waiting for the rest of our group, but instead, we'd keep watch on the bird box.

"It will be easy for the kidnapper's messenger to approach the drop-off box. Regular tourists wouldn't pay much attention to anyone working in the area . . . maybe pretending to clean out a bird house to get it ready for spring. I'm sure the kidnappers are counting on that.

"I think Carrie should be there with us tonight if Eleanor doesn't need her, because she might recognize the person who puts the note in the box. I doubt we can keep Chase or Tracy from going early too, and it's even more likely they'd recognize the messenger. But because many people, including the messenger, might also recognize them, they'd need to be out of sight. How well do you know the area, Carrie? Any easy hiding places?"

"Yes . . . hmmm, bushes that I think are big enough. The craft shop porch. And there's a wooded area on the opposite side of the parking lot."

"Okay," Henry said. "Guess we're all ready for our afternoon's work. We'll meet back here before supper."

Eleanor asked, "What, exactly, did you say you two are going to do while we're getting Chase and Tracy?"

"Dress up and go visit relatives we've never met," said Carrie.

As soon as Eleanor and Jason had left, Henry opened his big soft-sided bag and began laying out women's clothing.

"Hope this is what you wanted. I have my overalls and flannel shirt. Our heavy boots are in the car."

"Yes, this is fine," she said, "so shall we get dressed and go calling?"

For a minute she stood still, staring at Henry's back while he rummaged about in his suitcase.

"Uh, the bathroom is pretty small," she said, beginning to feel flustered, "so let's get everything ready and I'll face this way on this side and you face toward the door."

"Sure," Henry said. "Are there any hangers left? I'd like to hang a couple of things."

Oh goodness, Carrie thought, this is awful.

She wasn't thinking about hangers, there were plenty of those. Hangers weren't the problem at all.

153

She pointed at the clothes rack, waited until Henry's back was turned again, then rushed to get out of her jeans and sweatshirt and into the clothes Henry had brought for her. She almost ripped her print cotton skirt as she yanked it on, covering bare flesh as quickly as she could.

She wished she'd planned to dress in the bathroom, crowded or not, but it was too late now. His half of the room was nearest the bathroom door.

She'd done this. It was her own fault. She'd acted without thinking. She'd never been one to stare at herself in the mirror, but she did know what the body she'd see there was like . . . rumply in spots, pudgy, too. If only . . . well, there had been that exercise class in town . . . maybe if she'd enrolled in that . . .

She was reaching for the long-sleeved blouse she usually wore for gardening when she sensed something behind her. Henry's hand touched her bare arm. She jerked back in confusion, turned toward him, and gasped.

He was naked to the waist. There were two ugly scars. And . . . rumply places.

She raised her eyes to his face.

"Oh, Cara, I'm so used to the scars I didn't think. Sometimes police work gives you body decorations you hadn't planned on. I didn't mean to startle you."

"No . . . no. I . . ." She stared at him, she couldn't help it. Then she remembered that, except for a bra, she too was bare to the waist. She put her hand up and looked around for her blouse.

154

Henry picked it up off the floor and handed it to her.

"What I wanted to tell you, Ms. McCrite, is that I think this is something we might have had fantasies about when we were young. Can you imagine . . . ?"

He hesitated, looking at her face with some kind of gentle appeal in his eyes. But his eyes weren't sad. Not at all. They were twinkly.

She could feel it coming. The sides of her mouth wiggled, then a real smile began, and spread.

She said, "Yes. Yes, I can. Mother and Daddy should see me now. In a motel room. Half naked . . . with a man. And . . . we're not, um, related."

"The secret is safe with me," he said, putting out a hand to touch her cheek—oh, so lightly.

After a moment she stepped back, in no hurry now, and pulled her blouse over her head.

"Move aside, sir," she said. "We have a long hike ahead of us. Before we leave, I'd better visit the bathroom."

## Chapter XIII

When they were finished dressing, Carrie looked both of them over critically. Perhaps she should have asked Henry not to shave this morning, but she hadn't thought of that. Otherwise, with his faded shirt, overalls, and heavy boots, he looked like many of the older men she saw around Mountain View's central square. Her own cotton skirt flapped above socks and battered hiking boots, and her blouse and sun hat seemed acceptable. She was almost a younger caricature of the woman she'd seen in the woods—the woman Brigid had called Mad Margaret Culpeper.

Yes, the two of them would do. She picked up her walking stick, then stopped. Henry had his back to her, but she could tell he was sliding his gun under his overalls. A sudden fizz of fear rippled down her backbone. "I don't think you'll need a gun. Surely . . ."

He smiled down at her. "I know. From what you said, this is just a reclusive family, not used to seeing or welcoming strangers. If I thought they were more than that I wouldn't be headed there and certainly wouldn't want you going. Still, we aren't a hundred percent sure what we'll meet. We don't have much information other than your brief encounter with a very peculiar woman and what Brigid said about the Culpeper family. So, it's best to be cautious . . . and prepared."

"But . . ."

He held up a hand. "I agree this is something we need to investigate. If there's a possibility the woman you saw knows anything about the kidnapping of Dulcey Mason, we should try and find out what it is. I also agree that calling the sheriff and storming the place could be counterproductive, at least until we know more about what's really going on and who might be involved. If the Culpepers are kidnappers, an aggressive approach might cause harm to the child. Anyway, your bizarre conversation in the woods wouldn't provide sufficient reason for a judge or any

156

law enforcement officer to authorize an intrusive approach to the Culpeper homestead. But two supposed relatives should be able to make that approach, especially on foot, without causing suspicion. Your plan is a good one. But I'll carry the gun anyway. There are too many unknowns."

Carrie was thinking about Chase's warning to take someone with a gun when she went to visit Mad Margaret. She hadn't told Henry about that. Should she? Surely there was no need. Dressed as they were, two innocent looking older people, well, Henry was right, the most suspicious Culpeper couldn't possibly see any harm in them.

Then she remembered Farel Teal, and the fizz down her backbone turned into a chill, almost shaking loose the calm façade she was preserving for Henry. For the first time she felt real doubt about their venture.

But she had been so positive this was the right thing to do. She mustn't let fear change that conviction. Nothing would stop them now. They must think only of Dulcey Mason.

She murmured a simple prayer to herself. "Lead me, guide me, keep all of us safe and busy doing Your will." Then, head up, she marched out of the room.

"We'll plan what to say while we're walking," she said as Henry locked the door, and they headed for the path.

The main trail was easy to follow, and warm sun glittered through the tiny chartreuse tree leaves. Spring breathed innocence and charm, making their discussion about strategy for saving a kidnapped child seem oddly dissonant.

Henry agreed that Carrie should do most of the talking. He would be the silent, alert male. They couldn't plan much more than that, since neither of them had a clue as to what they'd be facing when they found the Culpeper homestead.

"I guess it's okay not to know exactly what we're going to talk about if we can keep our background information straight," she said. "Remember, our family moved to Oklahoma from somewhere around here at the start of World War II. They went to Tulsa to get jobs at the bomber plant. It was an awful place for people used to being outdoors, a mile-long building with concrete floors and no windows. But the pay was good, and our parents never came back. They couldn't afford to. No jobs to be had here then. About all they could have done was farm."

"Is it true? Was your family from the Ozarks?"

"No, they were from Indiana, but that won't matter. Surely we know enough to make the story work."

"All right, but what if Margaret remembers those times and knows no relatives left?"

"Can't help it. Besides, we won't be *positive* they were from Stone County. I think we just need a basic story ready, and I couldn't give details that are fact-based any further back than the 1940's. As you've pointed out to me more than once, I don't mind lying for a good cause, but I've learned not to over-extend and get caught in too many details I have to make up. At least I've read and heard enough about World War II times in Tulsa to be on firm ground if she asks questions we aren't prepared for. And, besides, she wasn't born a Culpeper—at least I assume she wasn't—so she might not know that much about what her husband's extended family was doing way back then. If she challenges me, I can always say, 'Well, my pappy told me that's what happened.'"

"And I'm retired now," Henry said. "No need to say from what. In fact—especially if their own family business could be shady in some way—it's best *not* to say. They won't expect me to reveal too many secrets that might get me crosswise of the law."

Carrie smiled to herself. This was the first time Henry had let the fact she was using a lie as a means to an end go unchallenged. Not only did he avoid lying himself, he didn't like it when she lied. But now he seemed to be getting into the spirit of their play-acting.

"Another question, Carrie. Why did we come here to Mountain View right now, and why haven't we, or our parents, been back before? It isn't that far."

"Oh, um, I guess we came back to find our roots before all the old folks here were gone," she said.

"And why didn't we come back before now?"

"Ah . . . uh, well . . ."

"How about this? Our parents had promised to send money back here to help the folks out, but after they learned how much more it costs to live in the city, they

159

couldn't spare a lot. Accusations flew back and forth, no one here in the Ozarks understood, and eventually someone sent a letter saying our family wasn't welcome back home. Does that story work?"

"Sounds good to me." She didn't say aloud what she was thinking . . . See, Henry, lying can be okay when it's for a worthwhile cause.

They stopped talking after they had branched off the main path in the direction Carrie had seen Margaret Culpeper go the evening before. It was rough hiking, and both of them were concentrating on avoiding rocks and fallen branches. They were also aware that ears could be listening anywhere around them.

The path headed downhill at first, and then they were following a stream, listening to its hollow-sounding gurgle as it bounced over rocks and tiny waterfalls. Carrie could only assume this was the direction Mad Margaret had come and that she had been heading toward home. Now she was sorry she hadn't asked Brigid for more information about the Culpeper homestead.

The creek banks were lush with spring greenery, and there were several places where Carrie wanted to stop and look at wildflowers, but she didn't. They had more important things to do.

After they had followed the stream for some time, Carrie's confidence began to waver. The mysterious woman could have turned off anywhere, though there had been no evidence of any foot traffic leaving the path, no disturbed underbrush or flattened leaves.

During the five years she had lived in the woods, Carrie had become adept at reading signs on the forest floor. Her friend JoAnne Harrington had been an expert at it, and after JoAnne's murder, Carrie inherited her books on the subject. Before JoAnne died, the two women had spent many enjoyable Saturday mornings together, puzzling over marks left in their woods by both animals and humans. Carrie still continued those Saturday hikes when weather permitted—sometimes alone, sometimes with Henry.

And now Henry was evidently trusting Carrie to lead the way. He followed her closely, saying nothing.

Finally she stopped and pointed. There was a faint trail leading up the hill to their right. The path they were on continued ahead of them.

"What next?" Henry asked, speaking softly in her ear.

"Let's go a bit farther along the main trail and see where it leads," she said. "We can try this other path if nothing opens up soon. I think we must be near the place where national forest land begins."

"Carry on then," he said.

In a short time it was obvious where the valley trail led. They came to another branch of the stream, a fence, a locked gate, and, behind it, a sewage treatment plant.

"Well," Carrie said, "they sure don't live here. This must be the treatment plant for the Folk Center. Maybe that fence on the other side is the boundary between the state park and the national forest."

"I think the fence is just to keep unwanted intruders from coming near the treatment plant," Henry said. "See, there's a gravel road over there and another gate."

"So it looks like we go back to that side trail and up the hill."

As soon as they turned onto the faint hill path, Carrie wished she had forgotten about dressing like Margaret Culpeper. How did the woman manage this tangle in a skirt? Anything but tough jeans would be a problem.

She tried to sweep branches and brambles out of the way with her walking stick while she held her skirt up with the other hand, but that left the bare skin above her socks to catch loose brambles. Phooey! Had Margaret, wearing a skirt even longer than hers, really come up this path?

When they reached the top of the ridge, they stopped to catch their breath and survey the area.

"There must be a road if anyone really lives around here," Henry said. "They'd have to own vehicles of some sort."

They did. Not long after starting down the other side of the ridge, Carrie and Henry came to a rusted out truck body, three old cars without tires, a wrecked delivery van, a lop-sided tractor, and numerous metal parts that had once belonged to deceased internal combustion engines.

"I don't think this is their main entrance," she said.

A dog began to bark, then several dogs, and in a moment they came to a clearing—clear, that is, of anything but weeds, stumps, and the most wildly varied assortment of junk that Carrie had ever seen. There were two weathered board and batten houses at opposite sides of the clearing, several sheds in assorted sizes, a wire pen holding four dogs, and two fairly new trucks. An old chicken house stood at the edge of the woods, just to their left. It was almost completely covered in brambles and looked like it was about to fall in on itself.

Carrie stared at the chicken house, which was certainly a picturesque sight. It had heavy plastic over its crumbling roof and seemed to glow from within— probably an odd effect of sun through plastic. Now she wished she'd brought her camera to take "family" pictures, as well as photographs of the old chicken house, which would have made a unique addition to her Ozarks album. And why didn't they just repair the roof if they wanted to save the ridiculous-looking structure? But then, the whole building looked like it might fall over at any moment. Why cover it in plastic at all?

Henry's low rumbling voice startled her. "Quit looking at that chicken house. Don't look around, period," he said.

She was turning to ask him why on earth not when she heard a hound baying and looked toward the sound instead. A fifth dog was loose and running toward them, teeth first.

"Hello?" Carrie shouted as she watched the dog and wondered if they should turn and run. Oh, why was she always getting into messes like this when Henry was around? She wasn't even sure now that this was the Culpeper place.

The hound came closer, and his bark changed to a low, threatening rumble. Poised for flight, she looked over at Henry to see if he was ready to run too. In astonishment she saw that he was hunkered down next to a rusty cattle feed container and had his hand out, palm up. The dog slowed, came close, sniffed. After a pause, his tail lifted and wagged. He sniffed again, then ducked his head under Henry's hand, inviting the scratching fingers.

Suddenly Carrie sensed noise and movement at the far edge of the clearing, and she jerked her head around toward the larger of the two houses. Its entry door was creaking open. A white-haired string bean of a man wearing overalls like Henry's slid out through the partially opened door, and it creaked shut behind him. The man ambled over to lean against a porch pillar that wobbled when his shoulder touched it. He looked relaxed, but he held a shotgun in his right hand. His facial features were so nearly a masculine copy of Margaret Culpeper's that Carrie was sure they were, after all, at the right place.

Henry stood and went forward a few steps with the hound at his heels. He stopped between an old swinging easel gasoline sign that read "Ethyl 25¢" and a bottomless laundry tub. "Hello there," he said.

"Hello," echoed Carrie, keeping her eyes on the shotgun. "I'm Carrie Culpeper and this is my brother, Herman. We're from Tulsa, Oklahoma, and I think we're relatives of yours. I met Margaret in the woods yesterday, and now I've brought Herman here to meet her, and . . . the rest of the family."

The man called the hound, waited until it was sitting by his side, then stared at Carrie and Henry with shrewd eyes that belied any image of hillbilly lassitude. Finally he said, "Kin? From Tulsa? Don't recall kin there. Ma never mentioned you, nor talked of seeing strangers yesterday."

"Don't know you either," Carrie said, "but we heard a long time ago that we had kin here. S'posed that would be you. Margaret might know where the family tie-in is."

The man didn't move.

"Does she live over there?" She pointed to the smaller house. "Is she home? Could we go knock?"

His eyes, as sharp as his mother's, were still assessing, alert. "Walk all the way here? By yerself? No one came along to show the way?" Now he was looking around the clearing, obviously checking the entire area.

She shook her head.

"Where'd you walk from?"

"Folk Center. We're staying there. Margaret came this way along the path yesterday," she waved her arm toward the valley behind them, "and I thought probably that path would lead to her house. Guess I

165

should have phoned first . . ."

No reply.

He's evaluating us as if we were federal agents and he was a moonshiner, she thought. Surely they didn't make moonshine here. Were people still doing that? Without thinking, she began to look around the clearing again and was stopped by Henry's low warning rumble, "Hunh-uh."

"No matter about the phone," the man was saying. "Ma's usually at home. I'll go see if she wants to meet you. Sometimes she naps this time o' day." He came down the porch steps and headed toward the other house, leaving Carrie and Henry waiting among the junk.

But he never turned his back on them. And he hadn't put down the shotgun.

## Chapter XIV

Carrie took a step toward Margaret Culpeper's house, planning to follow the man who was just now reaching the front porch, but Henry's hand closed tightly on her arm. "Let's stay here until someone invites us to come," he murmured.

"Ouch," she said, then hated the comment, which had been spoken more in impatience than pain. Still, she thought his hold on her arm had been firmer than necessary.

Oh, dear, this was bizarre, like being inside an unpleasant dream. Henry was acting bossy, which

166

meant that he was worried, and of course his worry was now worrying her.

But why was he so worried? True, the Culpepers hadn't exactly welcomed them, but she and Henry weren't expecting hugs and an invitation to dinner. They expected people who were reclusive and strange. She already knew Mad Margaret was strange.

And, after all, Henry had easily charmed that dog, and the man hadn't ordered it to attack them when it ended up being friendly. They were getting along fine. They would *be* fine.

She looked up at Henry and said, "Sorry. It didn't really hurt." He nodded briefly but kept his eyes on the front door of Margaret's house.

Now Carrie's spine was fizzing again. Henry looked absolutely rigid, and he was being so fussy about not looking around. Was it because they were exposed and vulnerable in this open clearing? Why hadn't she noticed that before?

Anyone could shoot . . . oh, stop, stop it! Her imagination was running wild, her thoughts churning back and forth in a good-bad bounce.

No! This might be an unusual family, but there was absolutely no reason she and Henry would be seen as a threat. They were just what they looked like, harmless senior citizens, come to call.

She stared at Margaret's house and concentrated on seeing the details there, since it was in her line of sight and she couldn't be accused of looking around. Both this house and the larger one were typical Ozarks cabins. Each had a roofed porch extending clear across the front and a central entry door opening off the porch. Margaret's porch displayed two rockers and a small table. There was an enormous brass doorbell on the wall by the front door. Or was it a dinner bell?

Like all the buildings in the clearing, the cabin's vertical board and batten walls had weathered to a soft grey. Carrie would have found it impossible to guess the age of the buildings or of anything else she had seen in the clearing so far, but all of it looked old— and that included Margaret's son, who had now been out of sight in his mother's house for a very long time.

Carrie began an attempt to see what she could of the clearing without turning her head, swiveling only her eyes back and forth. The frames of her glasses were in the way, and trying to see beyond their edge made her feel dizzy, so she stopped.

What on earth was wrong with looking around? There were such interesting things here, and much of the junk could be of real value. The copper wash boiler right in front of her was like one she'd seen in an antique shop with a high-dollar price tag attached. And that brass bedstead over there . . . why couldn't she look at it? There was no harm in wash boilers or bedsteads. And why not look at the chicken house if she wanted to? She wished Henry would explain, but he was silent, thoughtful, his eyes riveted on the porch.

More time passed. Carrie was getting very tired of standing still, and she had begun to break the monotony by balancing on one foot and then the other when the cabin's front door finally opened. Margaret Culpeper came out on the porch. She was dressed in a dark, enveloping garment, and her tightly-bunned white hair caught the sunlight as she came to stand at the top of the steps, giving her an angelic halo that, Carrie thought, might be far from what she deserved.

As Margaret peered down at them, her son came out behind her, and this time he chose to lean on the wall next to the brass bell. During the long wait Carrie had noticed that the bell's pull rope led inside the house where visitors couldn't reach it. Well, maybe it really was to call the family to dinner . . . or something. She almost laughed. Folks like this didn't have any use for doorbells. It was plain they didn't expect visitors.

Margaret broke the silence. "Well, come on then, come closer," she said, sounding impatient. "Micah sez ye're kin, thet right? Ye've come to talk?"

"Yes," Carrie answered, walking toward the porch and glancing at the copper wash boiler out of the corner of her eye as she walked around it. "Our name is Culpeper, spelled like yours, with two p's. I'm Carrie. This is my brother, Herman. We're from Tulsa. Our folks left the Ozarks in 1941. They never came back, but now that we're getting up in years, Herman and I wanted to visit any relatives we might have here. We thought you would be family and could tell us more about the rest of our relatives in this area."

Carrie halted at the foot of the porch and looked up into Margaret's face, which showed more suspicion than welcome. Her son—Micah, she had called him—certainly remained wary. Though he was lounging against the wall and still looked relaxed, his deeply lined face was alert and cold, as if he were daring them to make a false move.

Carrie felt nervous sweat trickling down the valley between her breasts. "Well, you see, our folks never came back here, because . . . um, well, we think there was some kind of family disagreement a long time ago, but they—that is, our parents—are gone now, and since probably the ones who lived here then"—she looked into Margaret's ancient, wrinkled face—"ah, most of those who lived here back then may be gone too, well, ur, why would anyone still be angry at anyone, all these years later, I mean?"

She knew she was babbling, and she felt like a fool, especially since Henry was next to her, the strong, silent male hanging on her every word. He must be wishing he'd done the talking. But, my goodness, how could anyone act normal when they were faced by a stranger with a shotgun?

"Ah," said Margaret, still studying Carrie, "I remember ye from the woods." Then, suddenly, her lips lifted in a smile which, somehow, didn't seem quite genuine, but she stood aside and waved an arm toward the door. "Well, here ye aire then, come in, come in."

The sudden change in mood startled Carrie, and by now she'd decided she didn't want to go inside that house at all. She wanted to go back to the Folk Center, get on with her weekend, and forget this stupid involvement in something that really had nothing to do with her. But it was too late. Micah was opening the door for them.

Carrie, with Henry right behind her, his hand now a light touch on her elbow, crossed the porch—and passed through a time warp.

People used to live like this, she thought, but today? Was it real? This was like living in a stage set.

The few pieces of furniture in the log-paneled room were made of hand-hewn wood, though they were far from being crude. The five rush-seat chairs and rocker that faced the large stone fireplace were padded with hand-stitched, tufted quilting. There was a braided circular rug on the floor, its riotous colors gaudy and cheerful among the wood tones. Carrie realized the rug, at least, wasn't an antique. The bright fabric pieces had the look of polyester.

The room was spotless.

Margaret Culpeper indicated that Henry was to sit in the rocker and pointed out another chair for Carrie before she herself sat on a low stool between the front wall and the fireplace. Micah Culpeper still chose to stand. He had come inside and was leaning on the wall again. Carrie wished he'd either sit or leave. How could she really talk with Margaret if he kept standing there like a guard?

In spite of Micah's wary presence and Henry's warning, Carrie couldn't help looking around. There was a curtained-off rectangle against the back wall that probably held a bed. A table with a mountain dulcimer on it stood by the bed curtain, and Carrie thought of the music she'd heard in the woods.

Next on the wall was a door to what might be a kitchen or bathroom, and she wondered if the home had indoor plumbing, a kitchen stove, or refrigeration. She hadn't seen any outhouses in the clearing, but she hadn't seen electric wires or propane tanks either. Was the wiring underground?

Ah, yes, there was an electric outlet on the wall, but nothing was plugged into it. The lamps in the room were plain, no-nonsense, and had full oil bowls and glass chimneys. All the chimneys were clean except for the one sitting on the table next to Carrie's chair, which had a light coat of soot. It had probably been used this morning when Margaret ate breakfast at this table.

There was the acid smell of burnt things in the room—lamp oil and wood.

"Will ye have tea?" asked Margaret when they were seated. "Make hit from yarbs I collec' in the woods and from my garden patch. Most of 'em's native here."

Carrie hesitated and was surprised when Henry leaned forward in the rocker and said, "Yes, that would be most kind."

He, at least, wasn't afraid of being poisoned in this house.

Margaret rose easily and went to take three white cups from a cupboard next to the stone fireplace. Then she seemed to remember her son. "Ye can go on, Micah. We'll set and chat a while. I'll ring the bell if I need ye."

Carrie looked around again as Micah slipped out the door and saw that the rope to the porch bell hung right beside Margaret's stool. So it was a warning bell, to be rung in emergencies.

Suddenly, the thought of the gun concealed inside Henry's overalls was a comfort, and the very fact its presence made her feel safer was in itself unsettling. She usually wanted nothing to do with guns. To be honest, right now she wanted nothing to do with the Mountain View Culpepers either. But she couldn't forget Dulcey Mason—or her family.

She sighed, and both Margaret and Henry looked at her. She made no explanation. She couldn't, in fact, think of anything to say, so she just sat there, watching Margaret make her "yarb" tea. Hadn't she meant herb?

Their hostess opened a tin canister and spooned a combination of what looked like stem chunks and dried leaves into a heavy pottery tea pot. Then she lifted a kettle from a grate that squatted over burning coals in the fireplace and filled the pot with steaming water. After putting the kettle back on the grate, she sat again, looking at Carrie as if she expected her to open the conversation.

But what should she say? So much depended on this conversation.

Finally Margaret broke the silence.

173

"Ye be Culpepers?"

Carrie gulped. Well, of course, that was what she should be talking about. She and Henry had worked it all out, but now, in this out-of-time place, everything was topsy-turvy and all their careful plans had gone completely out of her head.

"Um, yes, and when I mentioned why we were here to a woman at the Folk Center she told me about you, and I thought we should come see if there was a family connection."

While the tea brewed, Carrie chattered on about the bomber plant jobs and life in Tulsa for an imaginary Culpeper family. Margaret said nothing and most of the time stared into space, only occasionally glancing over at Carrie with what—and Carrie thought she must be imagining it—looked like amusement.

"And then I saw you in the woods, out on the path, yesterday," she gestured in that direction with her arm, "and I thought you must live this way."

Margaret was definitely smiling as she interrupted Carrie. "Ah, Tulsey, ye say? Well, now, don't rightly know. Not many from thet time left. They's jes my husband, gone more'n twenty year now, 'n' his two sisters, both widered and livin' together over Timbo way. Puraps they'd recall other kin. Robert E. niver did say—thet's my husband, Robert E. Lee Culpeper. Culpepers come here from Kaintuck durin' the war. Think they wuz leavin' to keep from goin' to the fightin', truth be told. My boys calls 'em draft-dodgers, though I don't think they know thet fer a fact."

174

"Well," Carrie said, "maybe my family came here then too, then went on to Oklahoma shortly after. I guess that would be possible."

Margaret gave her a strange look. "No, I reckon not, it bein' the War 'tween the States we're speakin' of, o'course."

Henry cleared his throat, and Carrie was sure he was covering up a laugh. She didn't look at him, but kept her eyes on Margaret, saying only, "Oh, ah, yes, of course."

Margaret went on. "They's bin a lot of Culpepers here in past years, 'n' now they's quite a few in jes our bunch—me and my four sons. Three of the boys married. I got grandkids, great-grandkids, three great-greats."

She paused, reflecting for a moment, then said, "Any more Culpepers over yer way?"

Good, Carrie thought, our story is going to work. She doesn't know all the history. "Well," she said, "not so many. I have a son with his father's name and Hen . . . Herman has a married daughter who lives in Kansas City now. But, since our family came from around here, we probably are kin."

"Ah," Margaret said, nodding her head as she got up to strain a pale gold liquid from the tea pot into the three cups. She handed a cup to Henry, set one on the table next to Carrie, and returned to her own low stool by the fireplace holding the third cup. She sipped before she put the cup down on the bench beside her.

Carrie lifted her cup, tasted cautiously, found that

175

the tea—whatever "yarbs" it was made from—was delicious. She had seen no sugar, but the liquid was slightly sweet. The aroma spoke of lemon balm. She wondered if the brew included ginseng and glanced at Henry. He was sipping slowly, his eyes on their hostess.

Margaret picked up her cup again and held it near her mouth, breathing in the fragrance of the hot liquid as Carrie herself had done.

"They's more. They's what ye really come fer," said Margaret in a matter of fact way from behind her cup.

Carrie almost dropped her own cup. "Oh, I, well . . ."

The dark eyes were on Carrie's face, calm and serious. "Ye didn't dress in thet get-up 'n' come here jest about bein' kin, though ye may be kin fer truth. Ye come here fer another reason. Now tell me what thet is a'fore I ring the bell." Her free hand went to the rope.

Carrie spoke quickly. "The gowerow. Did you know when you told me about the gowerow that a child had been kidnapped from Mountain View?"

Margaret said nothing, just continued looking at Carrie with those deep, dark, eyes.

"You said the gowerow had taken a child. We wanted to find out if it was this child."

Margaret snorted. "Thet were funnin' fer the tourists. Pure funnin'. Ye shouldn'a took it serious." She gazed toward the ceiling.

Carrie went on, speaking gently, a prayer in the back of her thoughts. "This child is a little girl, and her parents are wild with worry. Her mother has done almost nothing but cry since she learned the child was taken by strangers. The father paces the floor, day and night."

Margaret said nothing for a moment. Then she drained her cup, set it aside, and stood, the rope still in her hand. "Nothin' to me. Time fer ye to go. Hit's bin a nice visit."

Henry's voice broke in. "Could you wait? At least let me finish this delicious tea. And tell us about the gowerow. We've never heard that story before."

Margaret hesitated. Then, nodding her head so slightly it could have been a tic, she sat, looked at the ceiling again, and began to hum—a slow, tuneless roll of sound that awakened the chills along Carrie's backbone.

That confirmed it. The name "Mad Margaret" was accurate. If Henry wanted to stay, well, they'd have to stay, but Carrie would have said, "Let's get out of here," had she been given the opportunity. Mad Margaret couldn't tell them anything about Dulcey's kidnapping. She was just a crazy old woman. The gowerow comment must have been coincidence.

At least a minute of tuneless humming passed before Margaret began to chant words in the same tone, "Hoohoo, gowerow, don't scare me, three little young-uns in the apple tree. Hoohoo, gowerow, go away, we're comin' down, 'n' steal no apples today."

The strange song trailed off, and Margaret was silent again, her eyes closed. She acted like she had for-

177

gotten them. Had she fallen asleep?

Carrie looked over at Henry. He was sitting forward in his chair, listening, alert.

He said, his voice low and measured, the rhythm almost a copy of Margaret's chant. "And who is the gowerow?"

Silence, then the hum began again, though Margaret's eyes remained closed.

Henry repeated, "Who is the gowerow?"

More of the humming, then, "Big, ugly beast. Said to be mixed razorback hawg 'n' swamp 'gator. Thet's a dragonlike thing. Eats kids, 'specially bad-uns. Grown folks too." Margaret opened her eyes. "See," she snapped, "foolishness. Who'd take thet fer true? Jest foolin' tourists."

She rang the bell.

The clang made Carrie jerk with shock, and she stood, eager to leave. Then something stopped her. She turned to Margaret and, not really thinking about her words, said, "So you know nothing about the kidnapping of Tracy Teal's little girl?"

Margaret's eyes widened in a paralyzing stare. She whirled at Carrie, grabbing her by the arm and shaking her as if she were a child being punished.

"Tracy? Thet young-un is Tracy's?"

Carrie froze, unable to move. "Yes, y-yes. I . . ."

"Sit! Ye *sit!* I'll do the talkin'. Keep still, both o' ye. Quick now, woman, *sit!*"

Margaret's grip tightened on Carrie's arm, and she shoved her down in the chair. Henry, who had started to get up, sat too, just as the back door opened and a stranger—a younger version of Micah—strode into the room.

This time the gun was an automatic pistol.

Carrie stared at it, held, oh-so-casually, in the man's right hand, simple dark barrel pointing at the floor.

An image she'd never forget floated inside her head. She saw Farel Teal in candlelight, stains that looked black marking his chest, draining down the side of his shirt, pooling on the floor. A knife wound.

The Culpepers liked carrying guns. Did they carry knives too?

## Chapter XV

Margaret ignored the gun and bobbed her head, welcoming her son.

"There ye be, Zeph. These here folks aire Carrie and Herman Culpeper, from Tulsey, Oklahoma, third cuzins of Robert E. Knowed ye'd want to say 'howdy' to some o' yer pap's kin, come to call.

"Carrie and Herman, this here's my youngest son, name of Zephaniah Lee Culpeper. Call him Zeph."

Henry stood, smiled, and held a hand out to the startled Zeph, who suddenly seemed unable to figure out what to do with the gun he was holding. He finally shifted it to his left hand, wiped his right hand on his jeans as if he'd been touching something dirty, and shook hands with Henry. Then he nodded toward Carrie, who smiled and nodded in return but said nothing.

Margaret laughed, and, looking at Carrie and Henry, she now pointed toward the gun and said, "Sometimes, as ye kin see, we use the bell to signal trouble. Zeph wouldn'a kenned what I wanted, so he come prepared. These days ye need be wary out here in the forest. Lots o' strangers up to no good—thet right, Zeph?"

Again he nodded, looking at his mother rather than at Carrie or Henry. He still hadn't said anything.

"Guess ye'll be off to work then? I wanted ye to make the acquaintance o' these folks a'fore leavin', thet's all. Micah met 'em when they come. Guess Hab's still away? Well—mebbe they'll meet 'nother time."

Zephaniah Culpeper nodded at Carrie and Henry once more and finally spoke. "Pleased to meet you now. Uh, Ma, want anything else before I go?"

"No, son, things is fine, 'cept mebbe ye could check in town 'n' see when my radio'll be fixed. I shore do miss hit, been gone a long time. Oh . . . and when did ye say Hab's expected?"

"Sometime tonight. He was planning to get groceries and some fried chicken on the way through town for him and Micah and for . . ."—he stopped just a second too long before going on, and Carrie wondered about the pause—". . . and for you too, if you want."

"No, thankee, son, I got plenty, but I hope Hab remembers to get more milk fer the big house. Ah, well, now, ye run along, don't want t' make ye late."

Zephaniah Culpeper bounced his head toward his mother's guests one last time, said, "I'll check on your radio, Ma," and disappeared through the back door.

"He drives a bus fer the shows," Margaret told them. "Brings folks up from the Folk Center parkin' lot and takes 'em back down after the shows finish." Then she was silent, her head turned slightly toward the window. Everything in her manner suggested that she was waiting for something to happen.

Carrie still didn't speak. She hadn't a clue to what was coming next and hoped Margaret would be the one to open the conversation. Henry remained quiet too. All that could be heard in the room were soft hisses and cracks from the fireplace and an occasional swish of indrawn breath. Once, Carrie heard her own sigh.

Then, at last, there was the noise of a truck engine starting and the fading sound of a motor as it left the clearing. Silence returned, and Carrie thought, what now?

Finally, Margaret Culpeper began to speak, quietly and very slowly, almost in a sing-song. Her eyes were turned toward the ceiling as if she saw someone or something there.

"I got four sons. All near by. Micah's over in the big house, as ye seen. His wife Lee Ellen's there too, though she's away now, helpin' a sister who's doin' poorly. Since Micah 'n' Lee Ellen's chillern is growed long ago 'n' all live away, they tuk in Zeph when his wife Mary left him.

"Then they's the twins, Habbakuk 'n' Nahum. Both lives nearby, Nahum in a house jes over the hill, 'n' Hab 'n' his fam'ly not a mile distant t' other way."

Margaret paused and as Carrie watched, something sad and secret flowed over the old woman. It deepened the creases around her eyes and softened the look of her entire body. Even more quietly than before, she went on.

"I once had a daughter, name of Elizabeth. She come when I were over forty, not a good time fer me to be havin' a baby. She struggled to live fer a long piece, then she were sometimes sickly, growin' up. I tuk good care of her, even if Robert E. 'n' the boys did think she were a bother. Oh, they niver said hit, but, y'see, all Culpepers mus' work. Culpepers don't approve of folks thet need to be cared fer—not even thur own kin.

"Elizabeth weren't 'special purty 'n' niver had purties to fix up in, but she done good at school. She were good at poetry 'n' thinkin' up music. Oh, my, she loved music—she had the purty things in her head. She made music all the time."

Margaret looked at Henry. "I'll play her last tune fer ye now. Bring me thet dulcimer and the pick too, young man—hit's the little bitty triangle piece on the table."

Henry jumped, and Carrie knew why. Margaret's hypnotic voice had been weaving a spell, and the sudden break sliced into that spell, scattering the magic. After a minute he got up and, without saying

182

anything, put the dulcimer in Margaret's hands before easing back into his chair.

She shut her eyes, strummed across the strings, and tightened two of them, picking softly while turning the screws. Then, after another silence, she began to play.

It was as if the melody were being called from a dream by someone awakened after a long sleep. It hesitated, then swelled quietly, gently, filling all the air and space in the room, filling Carrie's heart, and it was the music that Carrie had expected. It was Chase and Tracy's theme song, "Lying to Strangers."

Henry, however, wasn't prepared. She heard the not quite soundless hiss of his breath as he recognized the tune.

After a bit, Margaret began to speak, her words keeping time to the music:

"In woodland flower, in bird and tree, there's love and beauty all kin see. But in her heart a love is hid that she kin see—and only she.

"Fer love come a stranger, 'n' she loved a stranger . . ."

Margaret stopped. Her eyes were closed, but tears seeped under the lids, draining down her cheeks, dripping into darker dots on her dark dress.

Carrie whispered, "Beautiful," but the word caught in her throat and she wasn't sure Margaret had heard.

Now the dulcimer lay silent in Margaret's lap as she continued with her story.

"Elizabeth niver had many friends. She daren't to bring young-uns home, see, 'n' town folks didn't want a Culpeper playin' with thur chillern. She weren't

183

asked to parties nur other affairs the young folks had. So she found her friends in the woods. I seen deer walk right up to her, rabbits sit on her lap. She got to spendin' all her time in the woods after school, 'n' when she were growed 'n' had nowheres to go, she had her music and her times in the woods."

Margaret raised her arm and waved it in a wide, circular sweep. "It were out there she met the stranger."

Then she opened her eyes, still full of tears, and looked, first at Carrie, then Henry, as if she were pleading with them to understand something.

"I didn't ken fer a long time, but then she come to me to say she were goin' to have the stranger's chile. I couldn't think whut to do . . . it were a turrible time. Ye see, Robert E. had strong notions 'bout that sort o' thing. We all did.

"Elizabeth 'n' I kep' the secret as long as we could, but come time we couldn't hide whut happened anymore—the chile inside her were growin' too big. Fer once I defied Robert E., stood my ground 'n' wouldn't put her out as he said should be done. So, Robert E., he went to stay with Micah, his wife Lee Ellen, 'n' the boys in the big house. Elizabeth and I stayed here. None of 'em had anythin' to do with us, nary Robert E. nur the boys. Thet's why Elizabeth 'n' I were alone here when her time come. T'were hard, hard . . ."

Margaret was staring into the air, into a past she alone could see, and her face showed the grief she found there.

"A time before I'd learned the father. He were

184

yearnin' t' see Elizabeth, 'n' he come to us in the woods one day. But, though he said he loved her, he weren't inclined toward marriage. Might o' even had a wife somewheres, I don't know. Elizabeth thought if I tol' the men to make him wed her, they jes might rather kill him, 'n' she coulda bin right 'bout thet."

Margaret paused, still staring into space, ignoring the tears flowing down the creases in her cheeks.

"My Elizabeth died a few days after her baby come . . . a girl . . . born right there." She pointed toward the curtained bed.

"A week after Elizabeth passed, the baby's daddy claimed his chile 'n' tuk her away—though I'd-a kep her.

"The baby goin' wuz fine with Robert E. and my boys. They didn't want no extra girl chile, though," she repeated softly, "I'd-a kep her. The men, they niver asked whut had happened to the baby, nur who had her, 'n' they didn't know I'd seen the daddy.

"The daddy's sister 'n' her man raised Elizabeth's chile as thur own 'n' the daddy disappeared, who knows where. Hit were said he went to Californee, meanin' ta get a job 'n' send fur his chile. I niver heer'd of him agin—then 'til now. So, my Elizabeth's baby were raised by her daddy's kin 'n' grew up as theirs. I'm most certain she don't know her real mama, nur thet she's a Culpeper—then 'til now."

Carrie, sure of the answer before she asked the question, said, "Who is Elizabeth's child? Who adopted her?"

185

"Teals. My granddaughter is called Tracy Teal. But her real mama, Elizabeth Margaret Culpeper, is buried on the hillside, yonder."

For a few moments the silence in the room seemed to be crying in Carrie's ears. She didn't dare look at Henry. He must be thinking of his own daughter, Susan, whose beginning had not been so very different from Tracy's. But Susan's daddy had returned. Henry had come back to his child.

Now Carrie realized she was crying and dug in her pocket for a tissue.

When she was able to speak, she asked, "Who knows this?"

"Wal, some few. I don't think no one tol' Tracy, nur would I want 'em to. We ain't . . . well, she's a fine, famous lady now . . . I heerd her sing once on my radio . . . a voice like Elizabeth's. No, they's too much time 'n' life 'tween us now."

Carrie leaned forward. "But who else may know? It could be important, Margaret."

"My own boys 'n' Micah's Lee Ellen knows 'bout Elizabeth's baby bein' born o' course, but they's all closemouthed. Need to be, ye see. My Elizabeth, she niver wed, so I reckon they niver tole no one 'bout any baby. Not them. Their pa said Elizabeth's death were a jedgement on her.

"I niver said nothin' 'bout where the baby went to any of 'em, 'n' Robert E., he died a short space after. Micah 'n' Hab's wed, as I said, but I doubt anyone but Lee Ellen knows the story, 'n' most Teals has died or

186

moved away from here now."

Margaret shut her eyes once more, and, once more, tears crept from under the parchment lids. "Elizabeth's name's not bin mentioned in this fam'ly fer many-a-year, 'cept she's nigh me . . ." She put her hand over her heart. "She's allus nigh me here."

Margaret opened her eyes to look at the ceiling again, but Carrie could tell her thoughts were back in the present when she said, "If ye hafta know more, they's a boy Tracy growed up with, name o' Farel Teal. Purhaps he kin tell ye more. He's still 'round here, I know 'cuz my boys does business with him. Maybe he . . . but why's hit matter now? What matters is Tracy's chile. We must git her back with her momma, 'n' "—she sat up and turned toward Carrie—"we gotta think o' how to do hit a'fore Hab comes back."

Now, why did Hab matter . . . ?

Then, all at once, Carrie thought she understood. Dulcey Mason *had* been taken from Farel by a Culpeper, and *Margaret knew all about it.* The only thing she hadn't known was the identity of the child.

But she must have known about the kidnapping all along. Had she condoned it, or even taken part? Was she only concerned now because she had learned who the child was?

Maybe, just maybe, if she'd had so little power to help her own daughter, she also had no power now to help her great granddaughter.

So, it didn't really matter what Margaret Culpeper

herself thought of the kidnapping. It was obvious the men in this family called the tunes.

Still, there was the gowerow story. Why had she told it? And . . . who killed Farel? Margaret didn't seem to know about his death, and she certainly couldn't have heard news about it on her radio.

Swallowing her own anguish, as well as sorrow for the pain they were awakening in this woman, Carrie said, "Farel Teal cannot help us now. He's dead. He was murdered last night. Farel had kidnapped Tracy's little girl, then we think she was taken by the person who killed him."

She was watching Margaret closely, and what passed over her face this time wasn't sorrow. It was fear.

"No! They couldn'a kilt Farel, no, no, they couldn'a. Oh, no, oh, no . . ."

For a moment, no one said anything. Then Margaret turned toward Henry. "Who aire ye? Not a Culpeper. Law man? How do ye fit in here?"

"No," said Henry, "I'm not a Culpeper, nor law, and"—he glanced at Carrie—"we're sorry for the lie. My real name is Henry King, and I'm a good friend, though not a brother, of this lady. Our main concern all along has been for the child. The gowerow story brought us here. We had to find out . . ."

"Ahhh," Margaret said. "Didn't ken 'zactly why I spoke like thet to . . ."—she waved a hand—". . . to Carrie here. Now mebbe I do ken, jes mebbe I do."

Once more the room filled with silence.

Carrie's thoughts were wandering, detached—as if they could take in no more worry or fear. Instead of thinking about Dulcey Mason, she was thinking about Margaret's manner of speech, realizing that some of it seemed to be based on medieval English. She knew many hill settlers had come to the United States from the British Isles and, partly because of isolation, there were still pockets of the old language patterns in both the Appalachians and the Ozarks, though they were fast fading. Margaret's conversation was a mixture of old English and modern hill speech.

Suddenly, in the silence, Carrie heard a creak behind the door in the room's back wall.

Margaret Culpeper held up a warning hand.

No, there sure wasn't anything wrong with her hearing.

"Wal, then," said Margaret, "seems as if 'n yer grandpa 'n' Robert E.'s pa wuz cuzins. Now, thet's sumpin' I'm mighty glad to know. Robert E. allus did hanker after findin' whut happened to thet part o' the fam'ly. Too bad he ain't here to meet ye. Now, I recall . . ."

The door in the back wall opened, and Micah Culpeper, without any gun visible this time, stepped into the room.

Carrie wondered how much he had overheard and was sure his mother wondered too. She seemed relaxed, however, as she greeted her eldest son, who must be, Carrie decided, at least seventy-five years old.

"Howdy, Micah," Margaret said. "Turns out these folks is long-lost cuzins o' Robert E. We're havin' a fine time tryin' to match up old family stories."

Carrie was deciding no Culpeper male ever smiled. Micah's eyes were as icy as they had been when Carrie and Henry first arrived in the clearing. She hoped it wasn't because he'd heard any of the conversation about his sister Elizabeth or the kidnapped child.

"Yer pa woulda bin glad to learn whut happened with the Culpepers who went over to Oklahoma . . ."

Margaret paused, studying her son.

"Did ye need somethin', 'er aire ye come to sit and chat with us a spell?"

"Ma, I think it's time I escorted these . . . cousins . . . to the path. I wouldn't want them to lose their way. It's getting late, and I'll need your help over at the house before long."

"My gracious, how time does go on! Well, thankee fer the courtesy, son, but no need to bother. I'll guide Carrie 'n' Herman to the path as soon as we finish our chat. I ain't gone out yet t'day, 'n' I'd like the air. Ye kin go on back to yer house, son. I'll take care of ever' thin' here."

## Chapter XVI

Micah turned to leave, and Margaret went back to her monologue about long-dead relatives. As soon as the door had shut behind her eldest son, she stood and

190

walked to the window overlooking the clearing, but her voice kept rolling on.

As far as Carrie was concerned, the woman might as well have been speaking Greek. The heavy dialect was becoming increasingly difficult to follow, and, since Carrie knew nothing of the people or events Margaret was talking about, there were no familiar islands to help make sense out of the sea of words.

It was hard for Carrie to quell the impatience that was fizzing inside her. For garden seed, why didn't the woman just shut up and get on with telling them what all this was leading to?

Finally the drone of voice sounds stopped.

"Micah's gone in his house," Margaret said, turning to face them. "We're safe to talk."

Still, she remained standing by the window, glancing out every few moments as she began speaking again. This time Carrie, now ashamed of her impatience, understood each word perfectly. In fact, the first four words Margaret spoke made Carrie want to leap out of her chair with a whoop of joy and rush to hug her, then Henry. But instead she sat, quiet as a statue. She was afraid to move—to do anything at all—that might stop this new flow of words.

"The chile is here," is what Margaret said.

*Their quest had succeeded!*

"She's over in the big house. I don't fer certain know how Zeph got her, but he tol me he see'd her asleep all by herself in a car at the worker's parking lot. It's hard to think she'd be left alone like thet, but

191

he said she truly were. Zeph said he kenned right off she belonged to some famous music stars, though he niver tol' thur name to me. He reckoned she were worth money, big money, so he tuk her. Hit were easy as slippin' in a fresh cow pie, he said. No one were watchin' over her, no one in the lot anywheres. He picked her up sleepin' 'n' brought her to Micah's house—jes like thet."

Margaret paused, reflecting. "He'd a knowed Farel's car, if 'n thet's where she were. But he said nuthin, *nuthin,* 'bout Farel Teal, nur ever meetin' him last night. He tol' me he found a chile's paint set with paper 'n' color-brush things thur with her. She'd been playin' with hit, waitin' by herself a'fore she fell asleep, I su'pose. Anyways, Zeph made a ransom note outa thet paint set 'n' left hit in the car.

"I didn't hear 'bout the chile bein' here 'til this mornin'. When Zeph come to tell me whut he'd done, he asked me t' help care fer her til the ransom were paid, so I went over with a doll Elizabeth had when she were little 'n' a toy bear she'd made fer her baby a'fore it come. I'd kep ol' teddy bear, 'cuz it were meant fer Elizabeth's chile 'n' were all I had o' hers. But, I thought mebbe this chile . . . she had to be wantin' her mama, so I tuk her the doll 'n' ol' bear.

"When I got there she were frozen quiet; looked at me with them big, dark eyes. I sat near, gave her the doll 'n' bear. She hugged ol' bear 'n' by and by leaned agin' me. I asked her name. She said somethin' too soft to hear 'n' put a thumb in her mouth. I niver thought o' Tracy. Why should I?"

Now Margaret lifted her chin and spoke defiantly. "I know my boys wouldn'a hurt her, jes usin' her to get money.

"See, Robert E. before 'n' the boys now—all 'cept Nahum, o'course—likes money, 'n' the boys' wives sure does too. Hits like a sickness inside 'em, and hit shames me. All they see in this chile is money. But they wouldn'a hurt her!"

Margaret paused for a minute before she continued. "I bin thinkin' 'bout gettin' her back t' her mama. The boys'll be powerful mad, but cain't he'p it. If they find out hit's me tuk her, they'd hardly mess with me anyways, 'n' I think I kin fix it so they don't ken. Now, here's whut we mus' do.

"Micah 'n' Hab's set fer a Little Rock run tonight, 'n' Zeph'll be over at the Folk Center, drivin' the bus 'til late. Hit's good thur women aire gone, as I'm to stay with the chile while all the men's away.

"Should be clear here by 'bout nine, ever' one gone. Thet's when I kin bring the chile down to you at Nahum's house. He's differnt. He ain't in on the others' do'ins. Dulcey'll be safe at Nahum's fer a short piece, 'n' you kin meet me thur to pick her up.

"Now then, I'll go git my shawl 'n' walkin' stick. We'd best leave a'fore Micah gets itchy 'n' comes back over here to see whut's keepin' us."

In bonnet and shawl, Margaret led the way across the clearing. It was easy to see why the intruding briars

193

and weedy undergrowth didn't bother her. She had halted a moment on the porch steps to twist the fabric of her long skirt in a rope-like coil, and now she held it above her knees with her left hand. The prickly brush along the path didn't seem to catch on her tightly woven cotton stockings, and she swept heavier branches out of her way with her walking stick as Carrie had done coming up.

At the edge of the clearing, Carrie looked back and, once more, saw Micah Culpeper leaning against his porch pillar watching them. This time, though, the shotgun was held loosely in his left hand. Thank goodness he was making no attempt to come with them. For a moment she wondered if he might follow, but then decided if his mother wasn't worrying about that, she wouldn't either.

Margaret reached the top of the ridge in record time, and, as soon as they were over the edge and the clearing was out of sight, she cut sideways, leaving the path. In a few moments they came to another path, marked only by compressed leaves and patches of bright green moss. Margaret followed this at an angle down the hillside, while Carrie and Henry raced to keep up with her.

They came to the sewage treatment plant fence, and Margaret veered right, heading deeper into the woods behind the plant. Then, suddenly, they were in a tiny clearing where someone had been preparing a garden plot. Carrie heard a quick hiss of breath from Henry, and she glanced up at his face. His expression was grim. What on earth was the matter?

Margaret seemed not to have heard him, and she plunged back into thick woods on the other side of the garden patch. In a minute they came to the small stream that flowed toward the treatment plant.

Margaret never hesitated or even paused to catch her breath. There was no doubt she knew exactly where she was going.

Finally the forest opened up again, and they were in a larger clearing, one that was as clean as if the forest floor had been swept. A carpet of wildflowers—pink-striped spring beauty and tiny bluet—covered the ground. The yellow cottage in the center of the clearing looked like something out of a fairy tale.

Now, for the first time, Margaret paused. She called, "Nahum? Hit's Ma. Brung comp'ny."

A tall, pale man, very like his brothers, came out of the house. His almost colorless hair and beard were neatly combed, his jeans and shirt clean and pressed. His movements were slow, and when he walked across the porch his body rocked slightly sideways, favoring a shortened right leg and twisted foot.

Margaret met her son at the steps, put her arm around him, and turned toward Carrie and Henry. "This here's Nahum. Nahum, meet Carrie and Henry, friends of mine 'n' yers. We got a story t' tell ye, 'n' we need yer help tonight."

She told him a shortened version of Dulcey's kidnapping, and, finally, the identity of the child. Nahum, who seemed more unlike his brothers with every passing moment, smiled sweetly and said, in a voice full of emotion, "Oh, Ma, oh, Ma," when she got to the part where Carrie and Henry had told her who the little girl was.

"Hit's a blessin'," he told his mother. "We'll go to meet Tracy. She's our kin. We should meet her. She should know who we aire."

"We'll see, son, we'll see."

Carrie and Henry stood by, unnoticed during this exchange, and Carrie wondered at the fact Margaret was trusting this one son with her secrets, and with Tracy's. Yes, indeed he was different from his brothers. She also noticed that, while the two Culpeper men she'd met so far spoke conventional English, Nahum's speech sounded more like his mother's, and she wondered why.

Now, Nahum put his cheek against the top of his mother's head, and Carrie looked away, turning toward Henry. She was embarrassed to be seeing such a strong and private affection, but when she looked up into Henry's face, she saw that he was watching the two intently, and, for the first time since they'd left their room at the Folk Center Lodge, he looked happy.

As Nahum raised his head, Henry moved forward, stopping just short of the steps, and looked up at the pale man on the porch. "We'll be here when your mother says," he told Nahum. "You're very kind to help us."

The responding smile lit Nahum's whole face. "She's my kin too. Of course I'll help."

196

Margaret stepped off the porch and walked to Carrie. "I'm gonna stay here with Nahum a bit," she said. "I read the Bible aloud to him—some ever day. He's like his pa in thet he cain't read fer hisself. But if 'n ye go straight thur a short piece," she pointed, "ye'll come out on the sewerage plant road. Head towards the sunset on thet 'n' ye'll find yer way back easy enough. Ye kin drive it tonight if 'n ye wish, but don't come too close. Best leave the car at the fork. Ye'll see. Come when the moon's there." She pointed. "Thet'll be about 9:30."

Margaret leaned toward Carrie as if she were going to embrace her, but all she did was brush her cheek against Carrie's. The aged skin was so soft that the touch seemed more like a gentle breeze than human flesh. Carrie's natural reaction was to hug Margaret, and, when she did, she felt Margaret's hands brush the sides of her skirt. She said, "We'll be here. And . . . thank you. God speed."

When Henry reached Carrie's side, the two of them turned in the direction Margaret had indicated, leaving mother and son together on the porch of the yellow house in the forest.

Following Margaret's instructions, Carrie and Henry were soon on the main path leading to Dry Creek Lodge. After they were safely out of Margaret and Nahum's hearing, Carrie asked, "Did I dream all that?"

"No," Henry said, "I was there too, but in all my years of police work I never saw anything like this. In

197

fact, I doubt a regular police officer, or anyone who refused to let humanity inform logic, could have experienced what we just did. The whole thing moves me, and gives me hope. Now I believe we will be able to bring the child back safely and get her out of the way before the law moves in."

"The law? But think of Margaret and Nahum . . . we can't."

"Cara, at least two of Margaret's sons are involved in a kidnapping. You know that's a serious crime as well as I do. Would you want them to take someone else's child next week or next month? They need to be stopped.

"I hope the woman's right—they wouldn't hurt Dulcey, but just saw a chance to make extra money. They may have no idea Dulcey is their great-niece, though I think they do know. Why, otherwise, wouldn't they tell their mother the name of the family the child belongs to? They could even be exacting their form of retribution for the illegitimacy they believe tainted their family. It is convenient for them that Margaret's radio is broken, isn't it? She won't hear local news about Tracy and her family visiting here, or about Farel's death. His murder must fit in with this somehow. Margaret confirmed he'd been involved in the Culpepers' business."

"Oh?" Carrie said. "I wondered. Moonshine?"

"No, today's version of the same sort of thing. It's easy to see the signs. I think the Culpepers have a very well developed marijuana growing, production, and distribution business."

"Well, gracious, how can you tell that? I didn't see any of that stuff growing . . . though, come to think of it, I might not recognize the plants."

"Not quite time for cultivating plants outside. You noticed the old chicken house had light coming from inside?"

"Yes, of course. It looked odd, a glow from within. I wished I had my camera with me to take a picture of it."

"Good thing you didn't. We'd have been in big trouble. I'd bet the inside of the chicken house is full of grow lights and small marijuana plants. It's the right time of year for that. You told me neither the sheriff nor police chief ever sets foot on Culpeper property. Didn't you also say they can't decide whether it's the police or county sheriff who has jurisdiction there? Well, that may be the honest truth, and it may not. It may simply be convenience for everyone. And, the Culpepers probably make enough money to pay several people to look the other way."

"Henry!"

"It's true. These days a single marijuana plant can be worth a thousand dollars. It's my guess the forest is full of those little garden plots like we saw. Almost impossible to see from the air, but big enough for quite a few plants in each one. And they'd have water from the creek just at hand. The location's ideal. Who would normally walk into deep woods around a sewage plant? It's a natural deterrent."

199

"That's awful. Margaret's boys? I'd hate to hurt her."

"Carrie, she knows quite well what the family business is."

"What about Nahum? He seems so gentle and kind, very different from his brothers. And, there's his leg . . ."

"Probably injured, or broken and improperly set years ago. But he could certainly tend the growing marijuana plants."

"He can't read. How sad. Margaret said his father couldn't read either, though it seems like Nahum's the only one of her sons that doesn't. She said Elizabeth was good in school, too. I wonder if he . . ." She shook her head and changed the subject, deciding she'd think about Nahum's problems later.

"Henry, tell me this. If their, um, business makes so much money, why on earth does Zeph bother to go out to work driving that bus? It seems odd he'd choose that."

"Not really. Can you imagine what opportunities his job would provide for distribution of the family's merchandise without attracting attention? Very conveniently he would usually be working after dark and have long breaks to do what he wanted while the auditorium shows are going on. Besides, just for appearance's sake, someone in that family should have a legitimate job. Maybe the others did too, in past years."

She couldn't resist a laugh. "Margaret must be

nearly a hundred years old, her youngest son about our age. They'd probably all be eligible for Social Security."

She stopped laughing as she thought about Margaret and Nahum, because she realized now that she liked them both very much, no matter what their business was. "Henry, what can we do to protect Margaret and Nahum? I think they've suffered enough. I don't care what the family business is or even if Margaret herself started it!"

"I doubt, at her age, that the law would bother her. And Nahum does seem very different. His attitude of innocence would probably save him from trouble.

"But still, Cara, that's not our decision. We have to think of Dulcey's safety first, Farel's murder second, drug business third. When the child is safe, I can't promise I won't talk to someone. In case the law here is being bribed, I'd probably tell the Arkansas State Police."

"Oh, this gets worse and worse."

"Well, for now it's beside the point, except it makes the Culpeper place much more dangerous for us and for any outsider. Our Culpeper relationship story is what's saved us so far."

"Yes, it did work pretty well, didn't it?"

She'd been watching the creek bank as they walked and stopped now to look more closely at white blossoms bobbing next to the water. "See, Henry, bloodroot. How delicate the blooms are—they only last one day. I love the shape of the leaves, too. But then, all the wildflowers seem like miniature miracles to me."

She looked up at him and said, almost whispering, "Here's another miracle. Margaret talked to me about the gowerow *before* she knew about Dulcey . . ."

Henry smiled. "Yes, I know."

After walking a few steps in silence, she asked, "How much of this are we going to tell Chase and Tracy? I'd love to give them the good news, but what can we say? 'Hey, guess what, you have a whole family you didn't know existed whose business is drugs, and, surprise, your mean old uncles kidnapped your daughter, and your grandmother is going to help us save her.' They'd want to go with us, of course, and who knows how either of them would act, and . . . well, we can't tell them! We've got to do this alone, don't we? The two of us?"

"I wouldn't even let you come, Cara, but it does seem the danger tonight will be minimal. Nahum's house is close to the sewage plant road, and we don't need to go near anything else the Culpepers own."

"Thanks for the concern, Henry King, but you need me with you. I'm sure a grandmotherly type will be less frightening for Dulcey than big old you. Besides, you already know you couldn't keep me from coming along."

"Yes, I'm afraid I do know that. But you're right, we can't tell Chase or Tracy anything until this is all over, and maybe not the complete story, even then."

"I've got it! Let's just tell everyone that Margaret thinks she might be able to help and is checking her country grapevine . . . or something like that. That's kind of hopeful, isn't it? Oh, this is so awful for Tracy. I keep thinking how I'd feel if it were my child . . . if it were Rob."

"Or my Susan or Johnny," Henry added.

They walked in silence again. Thinking about Rob, Susan, or Henry's baby grandson Johnny being kidnapped had made Carrie's eyes start to feel wet again. She reached in her skirt pocket, looking for a tissue.

What on earth? Then she remembered Margaret's hand near her pocket. She pulled out her own hand and opened it.

A blue hair ribbon, the mate to the one she'd seen in Farel's house, lay on her palm.

## Chapter XVII

This time the note stuck in the door to their room read, "Phone us, 143A."

"I'll be right over," Jason said as soon as he heard Carrie's voice. "Eleanor wants to stay here in case either Chase or Tracy needs her."

It was a subdued Jason who walked in the door this time. Henry already had his shoes off and was sitting on one bed with his back against the headboard, so Jason lowered himself into a rocking chair.

After letting Jason in, Carrie pulled off her own shoes, pushed the pillows on her bed up against the headboard, sat back, and waited.

Jason rubbed his hand back and forth across his

forehead. She was sure he didn't realize what he was doing or care that he was pushing the small amount of hair growing above his ears into bristly spikes.

He looked at her and sighed. "Have you told us all you know about this?"

"Yes," she said, not looking at Henry.

"Well, things are bad enough, God knows, but Eleanor and I agree there is something besides the kidnapping—an undercurrent of trouble between those two—just like you said there might be.

"After we had Chase and Tracy settled in their room, I brought soup and cornbread from the restaurant. Eleanor got them to eat, and they're both asleep now."

Jason held his hands up in frustration. "They aren't talking to each other at all and will barely speak to us beyond saying 'thank you.' They're wrapped inside two separate balls of misery. It's way beyond what you'd expect, even from parents whose child has been kidnapped. This is a time they'd need each other most, wouldn't you think? Are they blaming each other? Do they think their child is dead?"

After a pause, he continued, "Chase finally fell asleep on top of one of the beds, but Tracy couldn't settle down until Eleanor sat by her on the other bed, rubbing her back like she sometimes did for our daughters. Finally, Tracy fell asleep too. And that's it. That's all."

Henry asked, "I guess you got away from Brigid Mason's house without problems?"

"Oh, yes, that part was okay. It worked pretty much

like we planned. Chase and Tracy did look a lot like us after his mother was through with them. She knows how to do stage make-up. The clothing and Tracy's face stuff all went in that suitcase of yours and a big paper bag. Mrs. Mason packed some cookies she insisted on sending with us in a large priority mail box, then, after Chase and Tracy were in the car with their things, we rushed out with the box, hollering about getting to the post office before the mail went out.

"The reporters looked at us, of course, and there were video cameras, but the car was always between us and the reporters, and the windows were rolled up when we drove through the crowd. Fortunately none of them followed us. One possibility we hadn't thought of was that they might follow, planning to catch us for an interview at the post office. As it was, I doubt a single one of them suspected what we were really doing."

Carrie resisted the urge to ask what Brigid Mason's house was like. "Didn't Chase or Tracy say anything interesting at all?"

"No. That's what I mean, nothing. Tracy has been restless—mumbling something about Farel in her sleep, so Eleanor is staying close by. I'll hate to wake either of them to go to that bird box, but I don't think they'd forgive us if we went without them." He paused a moment before asking, "How long have they been married?"

Carrie shrugged and looked over at Henry, who said,

"They were singing as a married couple when I moved to Arkansas, so it can't be less than five years."

She said, "Dulcey is four. I suppose Tracy is somewhere around twenty-three. From what Bobby Lee Logan said, she hadn't been out of high school long when she married Chase. Why? Is it important?"

"Well, I guess we'd all react to the kidnapping of our child in different ways, but it's like those two are living in separate worlds, not a team at all, not partners, and I doubt it began with the kidnapping. It's like they're frozen apart and had been for some time before this happened."

"There've been rumors about troubles recently—temperament, that sort of thing," Henry said. "That's been going on for five or six months . . . long enough for a few tabloid-type magazines to pick up on it at least."

And, thought Carrie, it's been about that long since Farel went to tell Tracy they weren't blood relations and could have married.

Aloud, she said, "Brigid Mason did say Bobby Lee was telling people Dulcey was really Farel's daughter. I found out he made the story up simply because he doesn't like Chase. But it's a story Brigid didn't want her children to hear."

"Well, they heard it," Jason said, "or at least Chase did. While we were changing clothes, he turned the radio on. Some reporter mentioned it. He just laughed, but it wasn't the kind of laugh sound that people make when they really think something is funny. Know what I mean? Chase Mason didn't think that story was funny at all."

Carrie had pulled Dulcey's blue hair ribbon out of her pocket and was busy untying and re-tying it.

"What's that?" Jason asked.

"Oh!" She shoved the ribbon back in her pocket. "A piece of ribbon."

"A piece of ribbon? It's a girl's hair ribbon, isn't it? Is it Dulcey's?" Now Jason was leaning forward in the rocker. Carrie didn't dare look at Henry. She couldn't believe she'd been dumb enough to take Dulcey's hair bow out of her pocket. Now they'd have to trust Jason and Eleanor with more of the story than they'd planned. Otherwise, how could they explain the ribbon?

"So you did find out something?" Jason asked. "Good news?"

Carrie only nodded and stared at the quilt on her bed so, after a moment of silence, Henry began to give Jason an abridged version of their afternoon's adventure.

She sat there, feeling incredibly stupid and wondering what poor Henry would say when he got to the part of the story where the presence of the hair ribbon must be explained.

Henry was just finishing—"And then, when Carrie and I were on the path coming back here, we saw that hair bow"—when the phone rang.

By golly, he did the whole story without a single lie,

Carrie thought as Henry reached for the phone.

She watched him put the receiver against his ear. His hair was getting just long enough to wave over the tops of his ears. The hair was lighter there . . . like pure silver. She wondered what it would be like to touch his hair, to smooth the waves behind his ears . . .

With a start, she realized Henry was talking to her. He had his hand over the receiver's mouthpiece. "Sheriff," he repeated, speaking softly. "Wants to know if you're here. I think you'd better talk to him now."

"I can't! What would I say? I'm not as good at not lying as you are . . . that is, I don't want to tell him about Dulcey . . . what if he asks questions I can't answer without lying? You can't lie to a sheriff. What if he asks something about Chase and Tracy? Henry, I *can't* talk to him yet."

Henry smiled at her. "Yes, you can. I'm sure you won't have to say anything difficult about Dulcey or her parents. Sheriff Wylie has no idea you've talked with the Masons since last night, and I doubt he knows anything about the kidnapping. Even if he does, he probably won't be any more inclined to discuss it than you are. It's Farel's murder he's concerned with. Here. Talk to him." He held out the receiver.

So she had no choice. "This is Carrie McCrite," she said.

It began easily enough. The sheriff asked her to confirm that she had been with the Masons after the show the night before. Omitting the fact that she had not been with Tracy every moment following the performance, she answered his questions easily. He asked no questions about the dressmaker's shop, and she didn't mention that she and Tracy had been there.

He also said nothing about Dulcey or about the fire at Farel's house. Henry was right, this was going to be all right.

Then the drawling voice said, "I understand you got into some kind of a tussle last night."

"I . . . what?"

"Tussle. Mebbe tore your dress? Got dirty? Scratched your cheek? How'd all that happen?"

"Oh. Well, I . . . well, there certainly was no tussle. I tripped and fell when I was walking through the craft area." She started to say the lights had been off, then paused. She didn't have any idea when the security lights had gone out. The man was pretty sharp. He might know the answer already. She didn't. And had he seen the imprint of her fall in that square of garden? It wasn't near any path, so what would she have been doing there?

Had Bobby Lee Logan been the one who told the sheriff how she looked? What else had Bobby Lee said? She could feel her heartbeat throbbing in her ears. Could Sheriff Wylie think she had something to do with Farel's death?

"It was shadowy. I missed my footing, that's all."

"Ah, yes."

Now she spoke quickly, hoping to change the subject. "Sheriff Wylie, I'm with Parks and Tourism as

I'm sure you know. We're very concerned. Everyone is talking about the murder, and they're saying all sorts of things, mostly gossip, I assume. But we don't want this to mar the opening of the season here . . . don't want the tourists disturbed. I know you're keeping this as quiet as you can, but are you making any progress? Did you find fingerprints or something that could help? Any prospect of an arrest?"

Henry and Jason were both staring at her—in admiration, she hoped. After all, she hadn't lied. She just hoped the sheriff didn't know her job with Parks and Tourism was managing a highway information center in the far northwest corner of the state.

"Yes, ma'am, I understand. We're concerned too, and we've been workin' very hard. No one here got more than two, three hours' sleep last night. And fingerprints prob'ly won't be much help. Of course we have samples from all who are regularly in that shop, and Farel Teal's were on one of the display cases. But it's a public place, lots of tourists as well as workers, so all we can do is identify folks here, that's about it."

"I see."

"But, now that you confirm the Masons' alibi, our list of suspects has narrowed a bit."

"So you do have other suspects?"

"Oh, yes."

Henry and Jason were still staring, their faces carefully blank.

"How awful this must be for you, Sheriff Wylie. I'll bet you know all the people here at the Folk Center and in town. You'll probably know the killer, won't you? We heard about the scissors. Tell me, what kind of person would use scissors to kill someone? Must have been a spur-of-the minute thing since, I assume, the scissors came from inside the shop."

Her pounding pulse was slowing down. She tried to make her tone of voice say she was full of admiration for this big, strong male who was going to solve a terrible crime. She decided to ignore Henry's waving hand and whispered warning, "You're going too far."

After all, Henry was male too.

"Well, now, off the record, twasn't scissors did the killin'." She could imagine the sheriff puffing his chest out. "The killer just wanted us to think it was scissors. But, figurin' he . . . or she . . . didn't want us to know what the real weapon was, well, that in itself is a big help.

"Now, Miz McCrite, I can't say more than that, except don't worry. We'll catch the killer, and, in the meantime, we're keepin' things as quiet as we can so as not to bother the tourists. Since the famous ones, the Masons, are out of it, that will be easier."

"Were there fingerprints on the scissors?"

He hesitated, said, "No," and ended her questions by closing the conversation. "I thank you for your cooperation. I understand you'll be here through the weekend?"

"Yes, Sheriff, I will."

"Good, then. That's all I need for now. Thanks again."

She put the receiver down and said, "I'm willing to bet Bobby Lee Logan is his prime suspect. The sheriff did figure out the scissors weren't the murder weapon. There were lots of fingerprints everywhere because of the tourists and workers who have been in the place. They found Farel's on one of the display cases. There were no fingerprints on the scissors, as we already guessed.

"He didn't mention that the inside door knob and light switch had no fingerprints, but I know they didn't. I wiped those off myself. Tracy or I could have had fingerprints there, and I figured the killer didn't, since he left the door open and was probably the one who had put all the lights out of commission before he came to the shop. He would have known there was no reason to touch a light switch."

"Dangerous to surmise and wrong to destroy evidence," Henry said, then held up his hands as she started to speak. "I know, I know, couldn't help it since one or both of you had touched them. Actually I'm glad you remembered. I have no doubt you recall that I once left my fingerprints at a crime scene and, as a result, was almost arrested for murder."

He looked at his watch. "It's about time for supper. We'd better get something to eat and head toward the gift shop area to keep watch on that bird house."

Carrie changed back into her jeans and sweatshirt and went to sit with Eleanor while Henry and Jason drove into town for hamburgers. "Better bring six, no . . .

212

maybe seven, with slaw, beans, and fries, as well as drinks," instructed Eleanor. "A couple of cold sandwiches too, in case Tracy stays asleep for a while. And, don't forget the ketchup.

"I won't wake Chase until you come back, and I hope Tracy just keeps sleeping. I can stay with her while you go to see about the ransom note. I don't care if she screams like a cat at being left out. I wouldn't wake her for anything."

Eleanor had shut both doors between the two bedrooms so the four of them could talk freely, and after the men left, she told Carrie she had called Brigid Mason as soon as Chase and Tracy fell asleep.

"I wanted to tell her we arrived here without any problems and that both of them were sleeping. She said it was a good thing we got away when we did. Not many minutes later a reporter from the Little Rock daily and two television reporters complete with cameras came to the door. They insisted on an interview with Chase Mason and Tracy Teal. Brigid was glad she could say in all honesty that they weren't there. She told the reporters they had gone away to rest for a few days before returning to Branson and would speak with reporters when they were back home. She says since then the crowd outside her house has thinned considerably. She's heard no more from the sheriff. I promised I'd call her after you picked up the note, no matter how late it is.

"Now, tell me all about your trip to the Culpepers'."

Carrie rose from her rocking chair and headed for

213

the bathroom. "In a minute. First, while the men are gone, think I'll take a trip in here."

When she returned, Eleanor was knitting. She'd turned both rocking chairs around to face the windows that overlooked the forest. Nice, Carrie thought, much better than facing the door to the adjoining bedroom.

After they were settled, Carrie told Eleanor about some of their unusual experiences at the Culpepers', though she left out any mention of Tracy's relationship to the family, just as Henry had left it out of his account to Jason. She explained the plans for a rendezvous to pick up the child at Nahum's cabin that very night, while Eleanor's murmured comments, "How wonderful," and, "Thank God," blended softly under and around her story.

"But it isn't the time to talk about this to Chase or Tracy yet," Carrie cautioned. "We want to be sure we have the child safely back here before anyone but the four of us knows. We can't risk any awkward intrusion. Since Margaret Culpeper made all the plans and knows where everyone in her family will be, she's really the one in charge. We don't want to spoil anything, and, to be honest, I'm not sure Chase or Tracy can be trusted to keep cool heads now."

"Well, goodness knows I couldn't if it were one of our children," Eleanor said, "so, hard as it is, I agree it has to be secret until it's all over, safely over."

Then she said, "Carrie, let's be quiet for a minute. I want to pray."

"Me too," said Carrie, closing her eyes.

For quite a while after that they remained silent. The only sounds in the room were the squeak of the rocking chair as Carrie's foot pushed it back and forth, and the swish and click of Eleanor's knitting needles, completing the last rows of a sweater for one of her grandchildren. Once Carrie thought she heard the creak of the door behind them, but, when she looked around, the door was closed.

Finally she said, "Eleanor, do you think it's possible that Chase really isn't Dulcey's father and that he knows it?"

"Mmmm, maybe. Guess that could explain his odd behavior and the fact that, in the conversation you overheard, it sounded like he was more concerned over losing a performer than losing his child. But you said Tracy talked as if the original kidnapping of the child by Farel was no big concern, and Chase was the one who wanted to take some action right away. Neither of them has reacted in what I'd call a normal manner. Would you feel as Tracy did if you were in her place?"

"No, I would not. If even a close family member had taken Rob without my permission, I'd have been furious . . . and frantic."

"So would I," said Eleanor. "So, what if Tracy knew about that first kidnapping, maybe even helped arrange it, to . . . to . . . perhaps to make it easy for her cousin to extort money from her husband?"

"Ugh, when you put it that way, it sounds awful, but

215

it sure fits with the part of the Masons' conversation that I overheard. And if that is the case, then Tracy could be feeling a double load of guilt right now. Obviously the scheme backfired in a terrible way."

"Indeed it did," Eleanor said. "Let's see, we can imagine she promised Dulcey a good time spending the night with Cousin Farel, but it was to be a secret from Daddy. That would explain her initial lack of concern. She thought Dulcey would be perfectly safe, having a good time, in fact. And, you said all three Masons seemed to accept the idea that Farel needed money to get out of town. Bobby Lee confirmed that, didn't he, though he said Farel just wanted money for his song? So which is it? Money for ransom? Or money for a song?"

Carrie shook her head. "Both? Maybe Farel was going to tell Chase and Tracy later that Dulcey wouldn't be returned unless they admitted they did not write their theme song and agreed to pay him royalty for it. I don't suppose Tracy knew anything about that part of it, if indeed that was his real plan. After all, the story about a stolen song would hurt her career as much as Chase's."

And, Carrie was thinking, Farel didn't write that song either. Tracy's birth mother, Elizabeth Culpeper, wrote it. I suppose Farel heard Margaret playing and singing in the woods when he was a boy. How ever he heard the music, he always knew it wasn't his, though I don't suppose he told Bobby Lee that. He may have also realized that it was the Culpepers' sister who wrote the song he was going to ask royalty for. Sticky doings, indeed, if any of the Culpepers found out about his scheme.

"Carrie, Carrie! Hello, Carrie. You must be a million miles away!"

"Oh, sorry. I was thinking about something. I, uh, just remembered that Bobby Lee Logan told me Tracy can throw a knife accurately enough to split apples and hit targets in the center. Of course, right away, when we were still in the dressmaker's shop, I saw that she wasn't strong enough or tall enough to stab Farel when they were face-to-face. He would have stopped her easily with one hand. But could she have thrown a knife with enough force, and accurately enough, to kill him? Henry says it might be possible. Still, do you think she had enough motive to kill Farel? What if she thought he had given Dulcey to other people or . . . something like that? If someone was endangering or hurting your child, could you kill . . . if you had the skill and means?"

They looked at each other for a moment, then Eleanor's eyes dropped to her lap. "To protect my child?"

Neither rocker moved as the two women sat together in the silent room. Then Eleanor looked up, and the tears in her eyes echoed those now falling down Carrie's cheeks.

"Could you call it murder?" Eleanor asked. "If it was to save your own child, would it be murder?"

"Justifiable homicide?" said Carrie. "Maybe it

217

would be justifiable homicide. But what if the person didn't actually have a gun at your child's head, but was just . . . just . . . hurting the child in some way? Could you kill?"

Dear God, Carrie said to herself, oh, dear God. She looked out the window into the lights and shadows of the evening forest. She was way out of bounds. She had no right to have asked this question of Eleanor.

But now Eleanor said, steadily and quite calmly, "Oh, yes. I've known that since Tom was born. To save any of my children I could do it. I could, and I would."

The rocking chair began squeaking again, but Carrie had no idea she was pushing it back and forth. This gentle, motherly woman, if she . . . well, then . . .

But that was it. She was a mother. Carrie remembered a nature program she'd seen on AETN. There had been a mother bear and two cubs, and she still remembered what had happened when a male bear, much larger than the mother, got too close to the cubs. Stay away from bear cubs, the program had warned. Never get between a mother and her cubs.

It was true. When Rob was little, to save him—if there had been no other choice—she, too, could have attacked and probably could have killed.

Finally she said, "Of course it's possible Tracy had nothing to do with any of this, and I'm just imagining things."

They sat motionless, thinking their own thoughts, though Carrie was very conscious now of a sisterhood of shared understanding.

Then rocking and knitting sounds once more filled the room until the men knocked on the door and Carrie and Eleanor rose to help them. As Jason and Henry came in, floating in a heady aroma of onions and French fried potatoes, Carrie thought, once more, that she heard the creak of the door to the adjoining bedroom. She looked around. Maybe Chase and Tracy were awake after all and were coming to join them. But she was wrong. The door was still closed.

## Chapter XVIII

Henry and Jason pulled the room's largest table between the two beds and arranged chairs, then Carrie opened sacks and set out food. Eleanor went to awaken Chase. When she returned, shutting the doors softly behind her, she said he was alert the moment her fingers touched his shoulder. By signs they had agreed they wouldn't disturb Tracy, who was curled on her side, breathing evenly, and didn't stir when Eleanor bent to be sure she was all right.

Chase joined them in a few minutes, and Carrie had a hard time suppressing a gasp. He certainly did look different. Brigid had used some kind of hair color to put grey streaks in his dark hair. He hadn't shaved, and the shadowy growth of beard, together with hair combed back rather than to the side, gave him a menacing, much older look. He had changed out of Jason's clothing and wore pleat-front slacks, a dark shirt, and a baggy cardigan sweater. Possibly, Carrie decided, they were things that had once belonged to his father . . . or grandfather.

Though Chase's manner remained reserved, she noticed that some of his disdainful coldness began to fade while they were eating. It would be, she thought, difficult for anyone to remain aloof while eating from a communal heap of French fries and onion rings, especially when these were provided by people willing to go all out to help him.

After they'd eaten, Chase took the lead in planning for the evening's watch on the bird house. First he described the area and, with Carrie's help, drew a small map showing the location of possible hiding places.

"Since I'm agile, I should be closest," he said, pointing at the map, "so I'll sit in this corner of the gift shop porch."

Carrie and Henry exchanged glances at hearing Chase's cool assumption that none of them was capable of quick action. Carrie decided now was not the time to protest stereotypes about the super adult set, and Henry said, "We're not going to approach the messenger, Chase. This is the time to observe. We don't want anyone to know we're watching."

Carrie was having difficulty behaving as solemnly as the situation supposedly warranted. She was thinking that it really didn't matter about the kidnapper's note, since she and Henry would return Dulcey to her family not long after the note was left. Everyone here but Chase knew that.

Henry was still talking. "The important thing is to be able to identify the kidnapper and, if neither Carrie nor Chase knows who it is, be able to describe the person accurately later."

Carrie had already decided the messenger would be Zeph, since he was working in the area anyway and would only have to step down from his bus and make a quick trip to the bird house after the show began.

"Okay," said Chase in a monotone, "whatever. Your idea of Jason going in the auditorium to pretend he's buying tickets is good, because he can come back out and sit down right here." He indicated the location of the steps with a finger. "Like he's waiting for the rest of his group. Folks do that, especially when they know the show might sell out, or maybe they don't want to stand in line later."

He became more lively as he studied their map. "See, Jason, there are evergreen shrubs here . . . and here. You can sit on the steps behind one of those. You'll have to figure out how to sit so you can see the bird box, or at least see anyone who walks toward it."

He turned to Carrie and Henry. "And you're going to do . . . what?" he asked.

Carrie pointed. "The group of trees here? Lots of cedars among them, very concealing. Couldn't we pretend to be heading toward the campground and walk into those trees instead? It will be pretty dark by then, and I don't think anyone could see us. We'll just have to be careful and not make noises in the brush and leaves."

221

Chase nodded. "Okay."

Henry took over. "Jason can drive all of us to the handicapped parking at the top of the hill by the auditorium. Someone might recognize Carrie, but no one knows me. I'll limp and take Carrie's walking stick to use as a cane. If you stay in the dim light, Chase, I doubt you'll be recognized, especially if you don't get too close to anyone there. You can get out of the car with us and pretend to be helping me.

"Do any of you know if we can leave the car close by, since it doesn't have a handicapped permit? Is every space at the top of the hill reserved for that?"

Jason said, "I have the handicapped card from when I had my knee surgery last year. I'll clip it on. I don't often use it now, but it's valid."

"Okay," Henry said. "If they do ask you to move, you can drive down to the public lot and ride a bus back up. But it will be best if we can have the car nearby.

"After the three of us are out of the car, Chase, you might act like you're interested in what's in the craft shop windows. Go up on the porch. Act like you're trying to see in the windows if there's light there. Carrie and I will hang around the edge of the driveway by the woods. Since I'm supposed to have a game leg, I shouldn't move too much. Eventually we'll slip into those trees."

He checked his watch. "Sunset is about 6:30 . . . it's already getting dark, and I don't think we'll have any problems with the hiding part. But," he cautioned, "except for Jason, don't let bus drivers see you. They're at work every evening and would be used to normal activity, so they'd be most likely to notice anything that looks out of the norm. They'd know how people going to the shows behave."

He looked around the circle of solemn faces. "All of us will watch and remember as much as we can about the person who comes to the bird house. Since we'll be situated on three sides, we can probably do a good job.

"The important thing tonight is to find out who has Dulcey without alarming them. Chase, do not try to stop the messenger—that would definitely be alarming. Notice as much as you can, but stay in hiding. Leave the person alone."

Chase said nothing, but finally he nodded, and Henry went on. "Is there a light near the bird house? Either of you remember?"

Carrie said. "Yes, a post light at the edge of the drive. Anyone going to the bird house will have to pass it."

"Good. That'll help. Now, while you're waiting, study people and plan ways to judge physical characteristics. Compare heights in relation to landmarks—buildings and landscaping. Notice at what point a head is level with the third limb up on a tree, for example. Think about weight, notice hair color, and if hair is long or short. Also skin color, and by that I mean more than race . . . I mean what shade of light or dark. Practice detecting clothing colors. As it gets darker, see how browns, blues, and blacks vary in artificial light. Don't forget footwear and anything at all unusual that catches your eye. Think about that as you wait—use the time productively to intensify your ability to notice. Not only will it help with identification later, but it'll also help keep you from getting bored, and believe me, surveillance can be boring, even sleep-inducing. We've all got to stay alert.

"Jason, in case the person comes in a car, you might be able to get to your car—if you can keep it at the top—and follow when they leave. Maybe you can learn something about where they're going. But keep your doors locked, don't get too close, and don't get out of your car, no matter what. Better to lose them than put yourself in danger.

"Okay, that's it—our purpose now is only to notice as much as we can from our hiding places. It's my guess one or more of us will know the messenger. If not, being able to describe that person is our goal. We could well be asked to testify about it in court later."

Carrie wondered if the fact she and Henry were both sure the messenger would be Zephaniah and that they were going to have Dulcey back safely in—she looked at her watch—about three hours was coloring his instructions. If that weren't the case, would he have contacted the sheriff? She was glad that Chase hadn't questioned any of the plans. He might be wondering why she and Henry were taking a relatively passive role, but, if he was, he didn't comment. She just hoped the person would come to the blue bird house before the two of them had to leave for Nahum's.

"Now," Henry was saying, "after the messenger leaves, all of us will stay where we are for at least ten minutes. Then, Chase, you can slip off the edge of the porch and get the note. When you have it, start down the stairs toward the parking lot. Jason, pick up Chase at the foot of the stairs. If Jason has left in the car to follow someone, then I guess you'll have to walk back here, Chase, but be careful. We don't want you kidnapped too. Stay on the lighted road where there will be cars and people.

"Carrie and I won't be riding back in the car. We'll continue to stay out of sight. I'm taking a flashlight, and we'll walk to the lodge on the path below the auditorium. We may be late, so don't worry about us.

"As soon as you get back here, write down everything you can remember about the messenger. Then sleep if you can. There's nothing more we can do tonight. We'll make further plans tomorrow morning, depending on what the ransom note says. Okay, guess that's all. Any questions or concerns?"

No one said anything, so Henry went on, "Everyone wear dark jackets or sweaters." He looked at Carrie. "Dark hats covering grey hair. Okay, all of you get what you need, and we'll meet at the car in about ten minutes." He was almost out the door when he stopped and turned back. "Don't forget a potty stop. We'll be away from conveniences for a while."

"Hope Tracy stays asleep," Carrie whispered to Eleanor before she left to follow Henry.

"Don't worry, we'll be fine," Eleanor said, "and besides, someone has to stay at home and pray, though I know quite well you can pray fast and on your feet, Carrie McCrite. God goes with you, but be careful anyway."

The smile they exchanged made more talk unnecessary, and Carrie hurried out to catch up with Henry.

Back in the room, she put on her indigo denim jacket and hat. Henry had left her walking stick against the wall by his suitcase, and when she went to pick it up, he had the suitcase open and was lifting folded clothing, exposing his .38 and a flashlight. He picked up the flashlight, but left the gun, though he glanced at Carrie as his hand passed over it. Seeing her questioning look, he shook his head and said, "No, not around the child," and she nodded. Taking the gun acknowledged too much danger. Why should they need it?

Carrie wondered if Jason and Eleanor regretted not being able to attend the show in the auditorium tonight. Well, there was always tomorrow night, and for now, neither of them acted as if they minded the turn of events. Both, in fact, seemed enlivened by their involvement in the Masons' problems.

When they arrived at the auditorium, only a few people were around, talking in small groups or strolling on the sidewalks, enjoying the unusually warm evening. The craft shop had closed for the day, and everything there was dark.

Carrie and Chase helped Henry out of the car, and she took his arm as he limped beside her to the edge of the grove of trees across from the auditorium. They stopped to look around as if enjoying the evening along with everyone else. Carrie noticed that Chase was already out of sight. He'd gone to the darkened craft shop porch right away.

She and Henry stood together on the shadowy pavement while Jason parked the car, then they watched him head inside the auditorium. In a few moments he came back out and sat on the steps next to a large juniper.

Now the buses were making repeated trips from the parking lot, emptying out crowds of people who flocked toward the auditorium, intent only on finding a good seat for the coming entertainment. Carrie watched for Zephaniah, but light glare on the bus drivers' windows made identifying any individual impossible.

Eventually Henry slid out of sight into the forest, and in a few minutes Carrie joined him. He was standing close to the edge of the paved area with his back against a large oak tree trunk, but darkness and the cedar trees made it difficult for even Carrie to pick him out among the shadows. She stood beside him for a time, watching the people, her vision filtered by cedar branches.

She began noticing things as Henry had suggested. That man there—dark hair, needs a hair cut, tight jeans and shirt, tall, top of head at third branch on the cedar tree when he stands on the first auditorium step. In the artificial light his shirt looks yellow, but it's probably white.

The buses continued their runs, over and over. People milled about. She wondered where the term *milled* had come from. Time crawled. No one approached the bird house. Henry was right, surveillance could be boring.

She shifted, moving her weight back and forth between increasingly stressed feet, being careful not to rustle the leaves. Sitting was out of the question. The best thing to do was lean on something. For Henry, that meant leaning on a large tree. Other nearby trees were smaller or had low branches in the way, and she'd have to move several feet to reach the next clear trunk. No, she'd rather stay here, close to Henry, where it was either stand erect or . . .

She shifted her feet again. Henry reached out and pulled her in front of him. She leaned.

There was no protest from Henry, and as time passed, she became more and more conscious of each contour of his body, of the rise and fall of his chest, and even, she imagined, the thump of his heart. He was very nice to lean on. Their bodies fit together . . . quite . . . well.

The moon was lifting higher now, but the forest remained in shadow. Carrie could barely see Jason on the steps across from them.

Henry shifted, and his left arm came around her, settling at her waist. She wanted to tilt her head against his chest but couldn't watch the bird house if she did, so she kept her neck straight, her eyes alternately sweeping the area and looking toward the blue box.

Though she was trying to concentrate only on their mission and think about all she had heard and seen during the past twenty-four hours, she found she could not shut out intense awareness of Henry's warm body. He was holding her so closely that she was sure she must be moving with each breath he took. After several minutes his head ducked, and his cheek rested briefly against the top of her denim cap.

They stood together in their hiding place—watching, waiting, breathing—shifting position from time to time.

She was alert, tingling with excitement, and she didn't need to wonder if Henry was as aware of the feel of her body as she was of his. She did wonder, though, if she should be shocked by the way her body was reacting to the closeness of this man, or, for that matter, by how his body was reacting to hers. It was certainly nothing like any physical connection she had known with Amos McCrite. The two of them had made a son, of course, but . . . there had been no romance at all in Amos McCrite.

In spite of her concern for Dulcey and the Masons, a bubbling joy was taking hold of her. This was what being with a man could mean. How many years had it been? And now, and now . . . She sucked air involuntarily as Henry's other arm circled around her, resting higher than the one at her waist, his fingers little wands of fire just under her breast.

She thought again of how she looked when she stood, naked, in front of a mirror. Then she shoved that aside. Henry had seen her in her bra just hours ago, though she hadn't actually caught him looking, not really. Surely he knew what was under her clothing. In fact, now his strong hand was under her sweatshirt. He was surprisingly gentle, even hesitant, as he touched her.

All the tourists had gone into the auditorium, and the only sound Carrie could hear was the inner noise of two thumping hearts. Her thoughts were drifting into dreams of touching, and closeness to Henry, and . . .

The creak of the fence gate next to the auditorium wall was a harsh surprise. Both she and Henry tensed, body awareness faded, and their urgent mission demanded full attention once more.

Someone was going to the blue bird house. Long skirt. Female. Her back was toward them, and it didn't look familiar, but when she turned around toward the post light . . .

The bang of heels on wood echoed as Chase vaulted over the porch railing and met the shadow by the box. Henry swore as both he and Carrie ran toward Chase. By the time they reached him he had the arms of a girl pinned against the fence, and she was spitting out the most unique assortment of angry words Carrie had ever heard, terms in which *skunk* and *mule* figured largely, and the modifiers were full of color quite out of character for a mere child in pigtails. Carrie didn't know her name but recognized her as one of those who had been listening to Brigid Mason's story the night before.

After a second, Carrie decided they were lucky the girl wasn't screaming, considering the force Chase was applying to hold her. Since Henry looked like he was about to hit Chase, she reached out quickly, pulled Chase's arms away from the girl, glanced at the white envelope he was holding in his hand, and turned back toward his fire-breathing captive.

"I'm sorry this man frightened you," she said, "but what on earth are you doing out here? Looks like you're supposed to be getting ready for the show inside, so why are you here delivering messages?"

The girl looked Carrie over, taking in her grey curls, wrinkles, and ample curves. Then she glanced up at Henry and evidently decided he was no threat to her either. She sniffed toward Chase and stuck her nose in the air. "Sure, 'n' see if I ever do Ben favors again, no matter how ro-man-tic. See, he wanted me to deliver his love note."

"Love note?" Henry and Carrie said together. Then Carrie went on, more calmly, "Ben told you to put his love note in the bird house?"

"Well, it's not his, o'course," the girl said, with all the wisdom of a dozen years or so. "He's an old man, so couldn't be his, now could it! Said someone had asked him to put it in the box, but there was trouble with a stage set that needed fixin' quick, and he didn't have time to bring it out. Asked me to. What's the

231

harm in that? And what's this . . ." she indicated Chase, "son of a jackass doin' grabbin' me?"

Henry had moved in front of Chase and backed up, pushing the younger man away from the girl and using his body to shield him from her view. Carrie ignored both of them and continued with her questions.

"Did Ben say who the note came from?"

" 'Course not, it's a secret. *I* think it's from one of the boys in the show to his special girl. Mebbe his folks don't ap-prove of the girl. They's lotsa that goin' 'round. So, it's ro-man-tic, and I said I'd do it." She giggled, her good nature restored. "Lotsa cute boys in the show tonight."

She looked closely into Carrie's face again and seemed to read something there. Her own face became thoughtful, then she ducked her chin and said, more softly, "Wouldn't you'uv done the same? Helped?"

"Yes," Carrie said, "I would have, and I don't blame you a bit, but I'm afraid Ben was fooling you. I'll tell you a secret. The note is for me. I'm Ben's, uh, friend, and I was expecting to meet him here. This is my brother and my nephew. They wanted to meet Ben, that's all, since we're talking about—now don't you tell—getting married. Sorry my nephew was rough." She waved an arm in Chase's direction. "He some-times acts before he thinks.

"Now, I'd like to ask you to do a favor for me, since you know my secret. Just tell Ben you put his note in the box, nothing more. I'll send an answer, but I want to surprise him. Don't tell him you saw me. I want my answer to be romantic too, you see? Promise?" Carrie reached her right hand up, made a solemn "X" sign over her heart.

The girl's face showed skepticism, then delight. It was easy to tell the idea of romantic possibilities for grandparents was going to fill her head for days.

Wish she could have seen Henry and me just a few minutes ago, Carrie was thinking.

Now the girl crossed her heart just as solemnly as Carrie had, said, "Okay, secret, I won't say nothin'," and scooted toward the gate.

Chase opened the note, held it to the light to read, then shoved it in his pocket. "Gotta see Ben," he said.

"Not really a love note, I suppose?" asked Henry.

"Sure isn't," Chase said, as he turned to go through the gate to the back of the auditorium.

Jason had appeared, and the three of them followed Chase. As soon as they were all inside the fence, Henry caught Chase's arm. "Wait, man," he said, "and think! If you go inside that auditorium, all hell will break loose. In bright light you'll be recognized, especially if you storm in the place. You can't go after Ben now. You and Jason go back to the rooms. Carrie and I will talk to him."

Chase glared at Henry, who asked, "What does the note say?"

"$500,000, or we'll never see Dulcey again. Assorted bills, none larger than a hundred dollars, at least eighty percent used. Put the money in a black guitar case and leave it on the ground at the end of the

233

gift shop porch just after the evening show begins tomorrow night. If nothing goes wrong, Dulcey will be dropped off somewhere in the visitor parking lot after the show's over."

"That's clever of them," Henry said. "There will be so many cars coming and going then we'd have a very hard time watching for her to be dropped off. But how would you get that kind of money on a weekend?"

Carrie supposed Henry was just making conversation. None of this was going to matter anyway.

"Can't get it," Chase said. "I can't. Oh, we've got enough money, but our bank is in Branson. There's no way they'd wire funds on a Saturday. I doubt I could get it even if I went there. And, I don't think Ma has . . . well, how could she? How come these folks don't know that? Who carries that kind of money in their pockets?" He started to laugh, a bitter, hollow sound. "Do kidnappers take checks these days? How about credit cards? What do they expect me to do?" He stopped and slumped against the wall, suddenly looking, Carrie thought, as young and vulnerable as Tracy had earlier.

"It comes down to this," Chase said. "I can't pay the ransom tomorrow night, and they're too stupid to know that."

# Chapter XIX

Henry finally persuaded Chase to go back to the lodge with Jason, insisting he and Carrie must be the ones to talk with Ben.

As soon as their car was out of sight, he handed Carrie her walking stick and said, "We'd better not take time to get my car. I think we can intersect the path to the sewage treatment plant over there, somewhere below the auditorium."

"What about Ben?" Carrie asked.

"Do you know him?"

"I know who he is. Chase called him Ben Yokum—like L'il Abner. Said he used to live somewhere in the Ozarks, went to California, came back here not long ago. Evidently he's a stage hand and general handyman for the Folk Center. He was smoking out back of the auditorium when I went looking for the Masons last night. Pruney-faced man, possibly around our age, never seems to smile. I don't think Brigid and Chase know him well. They're certainly not friends. I suppose they see him as a stage hand and pay little attention to him otherwise."

"Would Ben Yokum resent that?"

"I have no idea, but that's not enough reason to kidnap a child, is it? I suppose the Culpepers could have paid him to take Dulcey. He'd have had access to her if she was in Farel's car. He didn't like Farel. I don't think he likes Chase much either, come to think of it."

"So he might be involved?"

"Well, he did have the note. I guess, rather than wondering if the Masons know him, it's more to the point to wonder what his relationship with the Culpepers might be. I wish I'd asked Chase more about him."

"We'll have to leave him for later anyway," Henry said. "Our rendezvous with Margaret Culpeper and Dulcey Mason is at the top of the agenda now."

For the first part of their downhill hike through the woods, the lights around the auditorium and the moon helped guide their way, and Henry didn't take out his flashlight. Then the forest got heavier, and the glow from the post lamps faded. Henry turned on the flashlight, startling a cottontail, whose gleaming eyes exposed its location before the sudden leap and dash into deeper forest did.

After about ten minutes of crashing noisily through leaves and underbrush, they intersected the path and turned left, reaching the sewage treatment plant and its one mercury vapor security light when they had gone only a few hundred yards.

For a moment they stood at the edge of the forest, keeping out of the eerie light. Finally Henry said, "I hate to use the flashlight now, it's too noticeable. Let's go around to the road that leads from the gate on the other side. The lighter gravel there may make it possible for us to follow it to the fork without using additional light."

"But won't it seem even more suspicious not to have a flashlight if someone does see us?" Carrie asked. "We wouldn't be out for a walk without light."

"Oh, maybe we would," Henry said. "If we hear anything, woman, prepare for a passionate love scene. We wouldn't want a flashlight for that, would we?"

"Nope," she said and wondered what he would really do if they did hear someone. She didn't mind trying to imagine it.

The light gravel on the road was easy to follow in the moonlight, and in a short time they were at the road fork Margaret had described. They stopped, looking around, seeing nothing, until Carrie finally pointed her walking stick to a faint path leading into the woods.

She went first, taking Henry's hand and sliding each foot forward in turn, holding it just above the ground to feel the way without disturbing leaves and brush. It was impossible to be completely quiet, and their progress was slow. The moon was almost in the 9:30 position Margaret had indicated when they came to the edge of the clearing.

There was one dim light in the cottage. Candle, or lamp turned low, Carrie thought. By its light it was easy to see that the front door was open, though a screen door kept out any early insects that might be around.

"What now?" she whispered.

"Let's listen for a while," he said in her ear.

All they heard were forest sounds, increasing in a

breeze that had begun to blow, bouncing leaves before it. No sound came from the house.

Finally Henry said, "Stay here, out of sight. I'll circle around toward the path from Margaret's. Maybe I'll see them coming. I don't think they've arrived—wouldn't Margaret and Nahum be talking? I'll meet you right here if I'm alone, or you'll see the three of us come in the clearing. Don't go any closer until I'm back. You'll be safe, hidden here."

She nodded, keeping her eye on the door. "You be careful too. Maybe you can stay hidden in the woods next to the path since the breeze is stirring leaves anyway."

After a quick squeeze of her hand, Henry was gone.

This time Carrie found a tree to lean on, cold and hard. She waited and heard no sounds from the house. Nothing.

Then, wood scraped on wood. A chair moving? A man came to the door. Nahum. He said, "Anyone here yet?"

Carrie hesitated, didn't speak. He must be alone. Should she answer?

Again, Nahum's voice, "Are you there?" In a moment he turned back, and the doorway was empty.

Maybe he was supposed to signal Margaret somehow when they had arrived. Maybe they were waiting, too.

She shifted her weight back and forth, wondering what to do. If Nahum came to the door again . . .

And he did. Again the shadowed figure said, "Are

you there?" It was enough. Carrie walked into the clearing.

He held the screen door open as she went up the steps and into the dim light. The front door shut.

Oh, no, no, no!

A woman lay on the floor. Silvery stuff—tape—wrapped her wrists and ankles and covered her eyes and mouth. An empty, twisted tape roll sat on the floor by her.

The blond hair was shorter now. Brigid must have cut it as part of the disguise, curled it. But there was no mistaking who the woman was. Dulcey Mason was not going home to her mother. Her mother was here.

Carrie whirled, facing Nahum—but not Nahum. No limp. Why hadn't she noticed? Hard eyes, hard hands holding her, shoving her against a wall, twisting her wrists as she began, too late, to fight—a struggle to get to the door, get away, get to Henry.

This must be Habakkuk—why hadn't she noticed he had no limp . . . didn't talk like Nahum? Where was Nahum? Where were Margaret and Dulcey? Where was Henry?

The hard man was tying her hands, not with tape, but with a strip of cloth. He shoved her on the floor, tied her ankles too, and when she opened her mouth to cry out, shoved another strip of cloth in her mouth. She gagged, tried to swallow, fought to control the gagging, realizing that throwing up would be dangerous. She could choke on her own vomit.

Finally he was off her and stood, staring, cold, hard, cruel. Then he laughed.

All Carrie could think was: *Oh God, God.* No other prayer, no comforting words, came to calm the panic.

Eleanor had said, "You can pray fast and on your feet, Carrie McCrite." Oh, pray then, pray.

She couldn't make the thoughts come. She hoped . . . hoped that Eleanor . . . could. Was.

The man began to talk, more to himself than Carrie. "Don't think you're worth much, but this other one, now someone is gonna pay big money for Tracy Teal, famous recording star. They'll pay big money to redeem her." He laughed again. "I bet the music company'll pay a million at least for this one. I'll cut off her playin' fingers, one at a time, if they hesitate. With money like that, Zeph and me can go away, get outa this business. We're tired, and Micah's gettin' too old to be much help any more. Nahum, he's soft, stupid. My stupid twin left all his brains with me way back before we was born! As for our boys, well, they got other things to do, no interest in the family business, no matter how we taught them, raised them with money from the family business they claim to hate. Fancied-up sissies, all of 'em! But now here's big money all at once. No hard work, and we'll get away. Already got the place ready, outa here, far out." Again, he laughed. "Yes, we'll redeem this one for big money!"

Carrie's thoughts were churning. The man was cruel and dangerous, but that was a deep, real laugh. He was pleased, happy to have captives, or at least, happy to

240

have Tracy. Tracy was safe for now. But . . . ransom for Carrie McCrite? Who'd pay that? Rob, out of his university salary? If she could have, Carrie McCrite would have laughed too.

But she didn't, couldn't. Instead, prompted by what Habakkuk had said, verses from the Fifty-second chapter of Isaiah flowed into her thoughts. She was two people now. A terrified one, a strong one. Somehow, somehow, this must end up a blessing. Somehow God would reach her, blank out this terror—would keep them safe:

". . . o captive daughter of Zion . . . ye shall be
redeemed without money . . . therefore they shall
know in that day that I am he that doth speak:
behold it is I. How beautiful upon the mountains
are the feet of him that bringeth good tidings . . .
all the ends of the earth shall see the salvation of
our God."

Ye shall be redeemed, she thought, shall see the salvation of God.

Eventually Margaret or Henry would come. No, no, Henry would be with Margaret, with Dulcey. Now the two people inside her cried out, one for Henry to come, the other for him to stay away, stay safe and take Dulcey to safety.

Margaret would learn who Habakkuk's new captive was, then she'd at least come to help Tracy. But would she be in time?

241

Habakkuk was studying the two women in silence. He must be thinking what to do next. Carrie shut her eyes. Pray, pray.

She heard him leave the house, heard a motor starting, coming closer, softening to a low rumble in front of the porch. Could Henry hear the motor?

The man clumped back into the room and went through a door behind them, returning with a dish towel to tie around Carrie's head, blocking her eyes and knocking off her denim cap.

He left again, came back with something soft-sounding that he dropped on the floor. Then he was spreading it out. Fabric. Finally Carrie could hear him lift Tracy. There was a thump, scuffling, a grunt, a moan from Tracy, more fabric sounds.

After a silence, Carrie was picked up, laid back on the floor, shoved and rolled, over and over. Fabric came around her. It smelled clean, dried outdoors in the sun. Soft, lightly padded. A quilt. Nahum's quilt. She wondered if her lipstick had worn off. She didn't want to get lipstick on Nahum's quilt.

Tears squeezed out of her eyes, soaking into the dish towel. She was lifted, carried, dumped hard on the floor of a truck bed. The man's feet went up the porch steps, the screen slammed, and then, after a few moments, he returned. Tracy was put down, very gently, beside her. Yes, mustn't damage his valuable property.

A dusty tarp or canvas of some kind slid over them, and Carrie almost choked again. She heard heavy things—bricks, maybe—fall in place at the corners of the canvas.

The truck moved off. Now Henry could not find her. Each painful bounce of the truck was taking them farther away from Henry's help.

The bouncing, the thumping of cloth-wrapped skin and bone against metal, continued for a long time—forever. Carrie had no sense of direction or time or how long they'd been moving. Her mouth hurt, the towel was getting soggy, her saliva glands were working overtime. So thirsty . . . If her head would just stop bouncing. Maybe, if she passed out . . . she'd never fainted in her life, but now might be a good time to start.

Then the other person inside her shouted, *"No."*

"My God, I trust in thee . . . let not mine enemies triumph over me."*

At least she could be grateful for the thin padding of the quilt.

Almost immediately the bouncing stopped. All she heard, once more, was the rustle of branches and dry leaves in the wind; no traffic or people noises. They were still in the forest.

The truck shook as the man got out and slammed the door.

Carrie McCrite might not be on her feet, but she was sure praying fast, and, she hoped, Eleanor was too.

After a while Habakkuk came back, and she was lifted, carried up wooden steps, down what seemed

*Psalm 25:2

like a hall, put on the floor of a carpeted room, and left alone. In a few minutes the footsteps returned, and Tracy, too, went thump on the floor. The door shut, a lock turned, the footsteps faded. There were no voices.

When a time of silence had passed, Carrie began to twist and roll, back and forth. As she worked, she wondered how long it had been since Henry walked away into the woods.

Eventually, after bumping into what felt like bed legs and scooting away to roll again, she was free of the quilt. She turned on her back, and, sliding her head up and down against the carpet, pushed the towel that was covering her eyes over the top of her head. It yanked at her hair, and she was glad she couldn't see herself in a mirror. Then, digging in with her feet and using all the strength she could gather, she sat up.

In the moonlight she could tell that they were in a small room with two beds, a table, a chair. She eyed the room's one window. It wasn't barred.

She bumped on her bottom across the floor as quietly as she could and backed up to Tracy, pushing at her, making her rock from side to side. Finally Tracy understood, and she too began to roll, struggling to free herself from the quilt as Carrie had done. When Tracy finally shoved away from the binding fabric, Carrie backed against her and wiggled her fingers on Tracy's arm until, again, she understood, and moved around so Carrie's hands were against the tape binding her wrists.

With the tips of her fingers and nails, Carrie rubbed

against the end of the tape. Dig in and pull, dig in and pull. A piece came loose, and Carrie began unwinding the tape, helped by Tracy's wrist movements—now turning, then twisting—to release strip after strip of tape. At last, with a tug, a pull, and a slight murmur of pain, Tracy's hands were free.

She sat up, used her hands to pull the tape from her mouth and, with only one small whimper, from her eyes.

The two women stared at each other. Tracy's face looked splotchy, and, even in the dark, Carrie could see a sparkle of tears, whether from the pull of the tape, or emotion, or both, she didn't know. Then Tracy was moving again, bouncing closer, lifting her hands to pull the towel from Carrie's mouth.

As she bent to free her own ankles and Carrie's hands and feet, she asked, "Where's Dulcey? Is she safe?"

"Yes, safe," was all Carrie could manage to whisper. Surely, she thought, Henry must have managed to meet Margaret and get away with Dulcey. He'd know something was wrong the minute he returned to the place in the forest where she was supposed to be hiding, but surely his first priority would be to take Dulcey to . . . only to her father and grandmother now.

Carrie cleared her throat, swallowed, cleared her throat again. "How did you get here?" she whispered.

Tracy shut her eyes for a moment, then, instead of the tears and moaning that Carrie had expected, she said, in a whisper that was clear and unwavering, "I had to see about Dulcey. I wasn't asleep when Eleanor thought I was. Chase was sleeping soundly, though, and when I heard women's voices in Eleanor and Jason's room, I opened the first connecting door and put my ear against the second door. I could hear some of what you and Eleanor were saying. I heard about your plans for tonight, so I got back on the bed and pretended to be asleep until Chase left with the rest of you. Then I wrote a note for Eleanor—I didn't want her to worry about me, she's been so kind—left the room by the door on our side, and came here to get Dulcey.

"See, I just couldn't wait . . . so much had gone wrong, and it was my fault. I wanted to save her myself, to clean up the mess I'd made. I wanted my daughter to be safe . . . you can see why I couldn't wait, and the place was so easy to find after you mentioned the sewage plant. We used to play around there.

"That awful man caught me as I was trying to see in a window at the yellow house. I guess it wasn't dark enough yet."

Tracy paused, tilted her head sideways, looked into Carrie's eyes. "But, why was Margaret Culpeper willing to help us against her own sons? I can't figure that out. And how do you know Dulcey is safe?"

Yes, indeed, Carrie thought, why . . . and how? What should I tell her?

She swallowed again. "It's hard for me to talk, so I won't say much." She told an abridged version of the visit to Margaret's house, inventing a story about Margaret's compassion for a child without her mother, and

246

then went on with events up until the time Habakkuk had brought her into Nahum's living room.

"Enough," Carrie said. "I'm going to try and open that window before Habakkuk or someone else comes back. The window isn't barred, so if it'll open, we can get out and into the woods. I don't know where we are or where to run to, but just away from here sounds good enough right now.

"This could be Habakkuk's house, or maybe Micah's. Micah Culpeper has dogs. Habakkuk might too, but I haven't heard any barking. And, I don't hear anyone coming now, do you?"

Tracy shook her head, and Carrie got on her hands and knees, then stood up, wobbling on rubbery legs until her head cleared and she could walk to the window. She leaned on the wall for a moment, then reached for the catch. It turned easily. She tugged. The window didn't move. She tugged again. Nothing. She ran her hands down the sides of the frame. Maybe it was painted shut. Her fingers came to rough bumps. Screws! The window was screwed shut.

She stood, staring out the window into the moonlit forest, fighting panic. No! Think! She didn't have time to be afraid. Was there any way to break a window quietly? Impotently, she pushed against the glass. Think!

To keep her hands quiet she shoved them in her jacket pockets. Ouch! What . . . ? She lifted her right hand, looked at what it held. Then, after testing the object's strength by trying to bend it with her fingers, she felt for the slot in one of the screws. "Ever seen a guitar pick used as a screwdriver?" she asked Tracy as she worked.

"You can use them for that," Tracy said. "I have."

The guitar pick slid into the slot and Carrie twisted. If only it didn't break. She twisted harder. The screw began to turn. Steady, steady. It was going to work. It *was* working! In a moment she had the screw in her hands. Now the other one. Yes! It was coming out, just one more turn.

She froze as the second screw dropped free. Heavy footsteps were sounding along the bare wood floor of the hallway.

Hide the screws. They mustn't know. She threw the two screws behind a bed, shoved the guitar pick back in her pocket, and rushed to push Tracy over and roll her in her quilt. Then down on the floor. No—the quilt was dragging on the carpet! Roll, roll. Lock turning. Roll!

She stopped breathing. The door was open. A light went on. Three pounding steps, a pause; a yanking at the quilt, spilling her out on the floor. Habakkuk, his face wild with rage, jerked her to her feet. He held the forgotten blindfold in front of her face, then dropped it. She felt his whole body tense, draw up.

She was lifted off her feet, and like released high-tension springs, his arms shot out, flinging her into the wall.

*Broke the plaster board*, was the last thought she had before sinking into dead black nothing.

# Chapter XX

Her head hurt. Why? She never had headaches. Everything about her body felt funny . . . floating. Her hands, at the ends of arms stretched above her head, were tied to something cold and hard.

Somewhere, someone kept saying her name, over and over. The sound came from far away, so far away there would be no point in answering. Still it went on, pleading, "Carrie. Carrie." She wanted the voice to stop, but it didn't.

"Carrie. Carrie."

She opened her eyes. All . . . dark . . . black.

But now she recognized the feel and shape of the metal between her fingers. Metal spindles, like the spindles on the shiny brass bed she'd slept in as a teenager.

Strips of cloth bound her hands to the bedstead. Why was she tied to a bed?

Her feet were tied too, probably to the foot of the same bed and in a very unladylike posture. Her mother wouldn't have liked that. "Keep your legs together, Carrie," she'd have said. Well, Carrie couldn't, Carrie just couldn't. So there.

Someone was still calling her name, sounding closer now. She thought about answering. Maybe then, the person would shut up.

How could she keep her legs together when her feet were tied, wide apart, to the foot of a bed? She tried to laugh, but all that came out was, "Mmmp."

"Carrie! You've got to wake up."

She heard movement—the sound of metal bed-springs from her childhood—and turned her head, painfully, slowly. Black.

The voice sounded stronger. She knew that voice, it was . . . it was . . .

"Carrie, talk to me. Wake up. Please, Carrie, it's Tracy."

She concentrated. Tracy . . . ? She shut her eyes and wished her head would stop hurting. She needed to think.

Tracy's voice began again, but now it sounded like crying. "Carrie, you've got to wake up and talk to me. Please, are you all right? Please, please, say something. My hands are tied, and my nose is running and I can't blow it, so I mustn't cry anymore. Carrie? Carrie?" It was a wail now.

Carrie opened her eyes again, began to move her head sideways, turning in the direction of the voice. Oh, my. Moving her head that way was not the thing to do.

"Carrie, please, please."

Tracy? Oh! Dulcey, and the yellow house, and . . . Nahum-Habakkuk, and . . . Henry . . . gone . . .

"Mmmmp," she said again, louder this time.

"Carrie! Oh, thank goodness. Are you hurt? I heard the bang when he threw you at the wall."

And *that* Carrie did not want to remember, even though memories of a whole evening of peculiar hap-

250

penings, some of them very bad, now marched around and around in her head.

"Uh, yes, Tracy. I, um, o . . . kay. Maybe a cut . . . bled. Can't turn that way . . ."

"Oh, oh golly, I'm sorry, I'm so sorry," Tracy said.

Shapes began to form in the darkness. The moon must have set, but she couldn't turn her head far enough to see the window. And turning her head to see the window was certainly not the only thing she couldn't do.

Before long she was going to have to go the bathroom.

Don't think about that. Don't think about anything—where we are, or why we're here, or that, at any minute, Habakkuk might come. Talk! Talk to Tracy. Get her to talk. Don't think, talk . . . listen.

So Carrie asked, "What happened? How long we . . . here?"

"After that awful man threw you at the wall, he rolled me out of the quilt and tied me to this bed. Then he put you over there and tied you too. He's been gone a while. I don't know how long, maybe thirty minutes or more. Um, should I keep on talking? Does it help? Are you staying awake? Please stay awake."

"I'm awake. Talk."

"So, let's see, I came to the yellow house to find Dulcey, remember?"

"Umhmm."

"It's my fault. This mess is. Mostly. But if Chase

251

would just listen to someone besides himself. If he understood . . ."

"I . . . know." In fact, Carrie thought, I've really known for some time. "Chase wants career . . . being big music stars. You want family . . . home."

"Well, yes. How come you know that when Chase hasn't a clue? Oh, why won't he understand? Why? We have a family now, we have . . . ," her voice wavered, "Dulcey."

After a pause and a soggy snuffle, Tracy continued, "I don't know what to do, I just don't. Oh, I admit at first all the travel and late nights and push, push, push to be perfect was exciting. Like a picture magazine story come true. Things were good, we made big money, we were on a roll, there was all the applause, cheers, the interviews. Didn't have time to worry about other things, dumb little things like love. We sang about it, wasn't that enough? Did we ever have the real thing? I . . . I thought so. But it came to be that the only time we were a close, loving couple was on stage, play-acting at love." She laughed. "Wouldn't that make a good song, 'Play-acting at Love'? Well, gee, there I go . . ."

The voice in the dark stopped, and, in the silence, there was another snuffle. Carrie was thinking . . . yes, Tracy, you still love him. There is love, whether you know it or not.

"On stage. That, Carrie, is the only good thing about being on stage. I've begun to hate the performing, the practicing, even the applause. But, when we're on

252

stage, I can pretend Chase loves me, that we're a family."

"You said at first there was real love?"

This time Tracy's voice was pensive, quiet.

"Hmmm, maybe. I must have thought we were in love at the first. I wouldn't have married Chase if I didn't think so, would I? But I was only nineteen. He had big ideas, stardom for both of us. He offered to make me a star, and he did, he did that."

"Ever tell Chase how you feel?"

"He won't listen. He hears only himself. I even yelled it at him a couple of times when we were backstage. Thought that would get his attention. It didn't. He just acted like he hadn't heard me."

Carrie was feeling more alert every moment, alert enough to begin worrying about what might happen to them next. Henry and Dulcey should be safe by now, but she and Tracy weren't safe. They were in real danger, Carrie much more than Tracy, because by herself, Carrie McCrite was worth nothing in ransom. She had to pray . . . think what to do.

Tracy's voice was continuing in the background. It was as if her long-suppressed thoughts and words had been given permission to release and flow out. Now, here, in this anonymous darkness where they were bound together by shared peril, secrets could be spilled on the air freely, as if no one listened.

Well, they weren't going anywhere, and hadn't she promised herself earlier she'd find out what was wrong between Tracy and Chase? So, listening was a good thing to do. Yes, she thought, God, help me listen and know what to do.

". . . so Bobby Lee and Farel and me, we were friends, together all the time. Maybe we might have been just a little in love, all three of us. Of course it couldn't be real, since Farel and I were cousins, or at least we thought we were. But I did feel like they were, um, boyfriends, sometimes. Oh, it's so complicated. No matter about cousins, Bobby Lee and Farel were jealous of each other. So I couldn't be a real girlfriend to either of them without making the other one mad. I had to be so careful. It wore me out."

"Yes, I understand that," Carrie said.

"Then Chase Mason began performing in the Folk Center shows. He is gifted, he really is. People stopped breathing when he came on stage. They still do.

"One evening he and I were foolin' around back stage, singing together. All at once everything just clicked, and when he asked me to work with him, well, how could I not be flattered? It was like we *connected!* Everyone could hear it, especially Chase and me. It was magic. When we worked on stage together, we created a big, shining bubble filled with magic music." Tracy laughed, and repeated, "Magic music.

"So, we got married. Everyone expected it. We expected it. It was the next step, the right thing for our music."

"And 'Lying to Strangers'?"

"Oh, um . . . well, I had really learned the music and

different words from Farel and Bobby Lee, but I didn't think they'd care, so, one day I played it for Chase, and he all but jumped up and down. He assumed I wrote it, said I was his little genius song-writer. He grabbed hold of it, re-wrote the words. It was the first time I'd suggested music for us that he liked, and before I realized it, things had gone too far. The song was so big, and then I couldn't tell him, I just couldn't. Do you understand? I didn't think Farel'd mind, or even if he did mind, that he would ever have the nerve to say anything."

"I see. And . . . ?"

"Oh, well, Farel didn't say anything. Not until he came to Branson to see me a few months back, while Chase was gone to Nashville. Farel said then he'd found out from some of Uncle Ted's papers that we weren't really blood relations at all. He said I was adopted. We could have married.

"You can't imagine how that felt. Chase didn't really love me, and now Farel . . . But there was Dulcey. What was I gonna do?

"Imagine learning all of a sudden that you're adopted! One second I knew who I was, next I didn't. I didn't have anyone, not Chase, but not Farel either. It was like a platform under me collapsing. It wasn't that I hadn't felt like a real daughter to Mom and Dad. I had. They loved me, and I never, never guessed. I don't suppose they intended to tell me, and maybe I understand that . . . maybe I do.

"Now, though, I know I have true blood relations

somewhere, and I haven't been able to forget that. What if they're the kind of people Chase labels as trash, and he finds out about them? Goodness knows most Masons think Teals are bad enough, Chase won't let me forget that. But what if I turn out to be from a family Chase considers even worse than Teals, and he learns who they are?

"And, of course, Farel and I weren't related at all, but really, I knew it was way too late for anything with Farel—if it had ever been possible. Besides, Chase and I were at the top and had an image to uphold, didn't we?

"Funny thing, though. By myself I'm nothing anymore, not to anyone except Dulcey, Farel, and Bobby Lee. Chase? Dulcey and I mean most to him as performers. On stage, we're the perfect family, but . . ."

Tracy began to cry, hiccuped, said, "Oh, there, now I can't cry. Oh, ugh, ugh."

Carrie heard moist, rattling sounds and then another big snuffle. Poor Tracy.

"So Farel . . ." Carrie prompted.

"Farel has been having some bad times since Uncle Ted died. He always had dreams of something big happening, all at once, and he'd get lots of money. While Uncle Ted was here, Farel kept that dream pretty much under control. He did love his dad and knew he wouldn't put up with foolish schemes. Uncle Ted had worked hard and steady all his life. He believed in hard work, but that was part of the problem, because he never had much, and Farel saw that. He decided hard work just plain didn't get you anywhere.

"Now, you see, Farel never used drugs, or I didn't ever know him to, but, he admitted to me then, in Branson, that after Uncle Ted was gone, he got a job distributing drugs for some family around here that grows and manufactures. Not hard stuff—it's marijuana. Said he was supposed to get a big commission. But I guess he wasn't even very good at that.

"When he came to me in Branson, he wanted money for 'Lying to Strangers,' enough money to get away from the distribution job, away from Arkansas. He said the song should be doing that for him. It was his song. He deserved payment and royalties, and of course he was right. But I just couldn't let Chase know. Do you understand? I just couldn't. The song was the only thing he really admired me for."

A pause. "Carrie?" Tracy's voice quivered on the word.

"I'm listening."

"That song means more to Chase than Dulcey does. I gave him the song and I gave him Dulcey, and he thinks more of the *stupid song*."

"I don't believe that."

"It's true! So I couldn't tell him about it being Farel's song, not if I wanted to keep on performing with him, wanted to keep my job." She laughed, but there was no hint of pleasure there. "I hadn't thought of it that way before. I don't have a marriage or a family, Carrie. What I have is a job! And I brought

257

poor Dulcey into that. Gave her to a father who sees a performer, not a living, breathing, little girl . . ." Tracy's voice trailed off into silence.

"Hmmm, so the kidnapping idea was yours? A substitute way to get money, and Chase wouldn't have to find out about the song?"

"Yes. That's why it's all my fault."

"And, last night, in the dressmaker's shop?"

Tracy's stuffed-nose breathing sounds stopped, then she gasped air and began talking again. "Chase was more bothered by the kidnapping than I'd expected, and you know, I was glad he was. Maybe that meant he really did love Dulcey at least a little. So, I called Farel from an office in the administration building while you-all went ahead to the dining room. Told him he had to bring Dulcey back. I said I'd admit I stole the song from him, tell Chase everything. Chase would have to pay him royalty then. Farel said okay.

"We were to meet in the dressmaker's shop after the performance was over, after Chase and Momma Brigid went on to the auditorium. That's why I pretended to make a phone call. That way they'd go on ahead. Since Farel worked around the Folk Center and was part of the volunteer fire department, he had keys to all the buildings. He put the lights out of commission so we wouldn't be seen.

"But when we met, he admitted he'd stopped off in the parking lot to talk to a member of the family that he was selling drugs for. He left Dulcey in the car. Then he went to flip the breakers for the lights, but

258

when he got back to his car, Dulcey was gone, and he couldn't find her anywhere.

"I went wild. Flew at him, well, I just went wild. He tried to hold me off, got a little rough. Next thing I knew that man had rushed into the shop. He pulled Farel away from me, and . . . and . . . Farel fell on the floor. The man lit a cigarette lighter for a moment, I guess to look and see if Farel . . . if he . . . and Farel was there on the floor . . . with the knife . . ."

"Knife?"

"Farel brought it with him. A gift for me. I'd made the knife, back when the three of us, Bobby Lee and Farel and me, were so happy together." Tracy's voice broke. "It . . . it was a gift, a token, a reminder of happier times. Farel'd laid it there on the counter. Maybe the man thought Farel was going to stab me with it. Maybe it didn't look like what it really was, that I was attacking Farel. But, next I knew, Farel was dead, and the man had run off.

"It took a while for me to even move, or think what to do, but, of course I couldn't leave the knife. I, uh . . . pu-pulled it out and took the scissors, and, I, uh . . . I . . . oh, oh, dear God."

"Tracy, who was the man?"

"No, I won't answer that. He thought he was saving my life, Carrie. I can't ever say who he was. It was my fault he did what he did. If I hadn't . . . oh, if I hadn't . . . done any of this!

"So then, I wrapped the knife in some cloth scraps from the wastebasket there in the shop, put it in my pocket, and I buried it under a bush at Mama Brigid's when everyone thought I was in bed."

"You were never really in love with Farel." Carrie was making a statement, not asking a question.

Tracy was quiet for a long moment. "No . . . no," she said, her voice almost a whisper as her words followed her thoughts. "Oh, maybe a little, kid-dream stuff, when we were in high school, like I said, but really, I couldn't have been. I did think about it some more after Farel told me I was adopted, but then I realized if things had been good between Chase and me, I wouldn't care whether Farel was a cousin or not. When he came to see me in Branson, he talked about me leaving Chase and marrying him, but it was all talk. I really knew that, and I think he did too. We were good friends, very good friends, but marriage? No.

"So, see, Carrie, all of this is my fault. I'm a terrible mother, a terrible person."

"No, Tracy, you're not. You have made some bad choices, and things have gone horribly wrong, but you know inside yourself that you are not a bad person. You couldn't have foreseen any of this. And if you made the wrong choices, well, Farel sure did too, and so has Chase. But none of you intended evil. You just got caught in a terrible, terrible trap that all three of you helped make.

"And, Tracy, we are going to get out of this. We're going to survive and get out of this somehow, and then you are going to your husband, and you are going to tell him every single thing you've told me. The whole story, how you feel, everything. Do you understand?"

Tracy murmured, "Yes," and said no more.

Carrie wished she felt as confident as she was trying to sound. But no matter what, it was also time for her to tell the truth. Being tied to beds in the dark, it seemed, was making it very easy for her and Tracy to, at last, speak the truth.

"Now," Carrie said, "it's my turn to tell a story, and this is a true story too. It's about your mother, the mother who gave birth to you, and about her family. It's also the story of your song, 'Lying to Strangers.'

"The story begins with a woman named Margaret Culpeper . . ."

## Chapter XXI

Tracy was so still during the telling of the story that Carrie thought she must have fallen asleep. She didn't attempt to awaken her. The story could be re-told, and sleep would be good for Tracy. Carrie kept talking, holding her voice to a low, smooth flow—the same tone she'd used for reading bedtime stories to Rob.

But, finally, she ran out of words, let her voice lower and fade into silence. Then she lay there in the quiet, praying, telling God how grateful she was for life and for the fact her head had almost stopped hurting.

"Carrie?"

The small voice out of the darkness was as startling as a booming shout would have been.

261

"Yes, Tracy, I'm here." Again, she could have laughed. Tied as she was, where was Carrie McCrite going? Laughing, however, did not seem appropriate at the moment.

"That lady, Mad Margaret they call her, she's my granny?"

"Yes." Carrie held her breath.

"Ummm, well, I've never had a real granny before."

Quiet returned, and Carrie began breathing again.

"Ah . . ."

And, then, she slept. While she slept, she dreamed she heard Margaret's dulcimer, playing "Lying to Strangers" over and over and over.

Bang!

Door? But . . . she could still hear the music. Was she awake? She could hear the music that Margaret played . . .

Carrie opened her eyes just as an overhead light glared, and she shut them again. The music stopped.

She had to see. A moment passed. Silence. Finally, blinking painfully, she opened her eyes and squinted toward the door. Habbakuk stood there, and Margaret, like a black shadow, was just behind him.

Margaret's voice was low and commanding as she pushed past her son and came into the room. "Calm yerself, son, neither of 'em's any good dead, jes extra trouble, bring the law down upon us. Don't know how the chile got away, but niver ye mind, I'm glad she's gone, hit's God's honest truth! She were trouble, and she's too small to do or say anything sensible 'bout where she's bin, specially since she'll be wanderin' in th' woods fer a spell a'fore she comes out. She won't be eny worry.

"Takin' chillern means trouble, son, don't fergit that. Zeph shoulda thought more. Besides, ye got the big money right here, don't ye? That's what ye got!

"Now let me care fer yer guests. We gotta keep 'em healthy—fer now."

"Ma . . ." The big man's voice sounded fierce, but his mother interrupted him.

"Son, this 'un's hurt, her head's bleedin'. Go on now, bring me them clean strips o' wore-out sheet from the chest in the bathroom so's I can fix her up. Bring thet brown stoppered bottle too—the potion I made fer Tootie when he fell outa the tree—and them silver scissors. Then ye can be about yer bizness, 'n' leave me here t' tend these two fer ye."

Habakkuk went.

The bed creaked and tilted as Margaret sat next to Carrie. "Ah, thur, lady, kinda bad, ain't hit? Kin ye see right? Everthin' look straight?" She moved her finger back and forth in front of Carrie's face. "Look at my finger . . . foller it. Look here now. How's thet?"

Carrie considered, looked up at Margaret, and tried to nod, but decided saying, "Um hm," would be easier.

"Wahl, guess I shoulda put yer glasses on first. They's a little bent . . . um, mebbe I kin fix . . . ah, thur, straighter now. See me okay? Good. Now, kin ye turn

263

yer head t' this side? Here . . . I'll lift. Thet's hit. Hurt some?"

Margaret began to explore the side of Carrie's head with gentle fingers. "Cut ain't deep, just bled a lot. Got a bit of bump thur."

Carrie said, "Bathroom," and Margaret said, "Shhh."

Habakkuk was in the room again, but all he did was put a brown bottle, scissors, and a roll of sheeting on the table.

"Thankee, son. I'll fix this 'un up, then I reckon these ladies would like ter relieve thurselves. Kin ye untie 'em, one at a time then? I'll stay with 'em, prob'ly haf t' steady this one enyways. Thet okay? Or, would ye rather tend 'em in the bathroom yerself? Don't matter t' me none."

After saying this, Margaret—facing Carrie instead of her son—winked.

Hab, who had remained quiet during his mother's spout of conversation, shook his head and said, "It's okay, you take 'em. I'll stand watch outside the door while they . . . uh . . . I'll check on some other things now, be back in a bit."

After Habakkuk had disappeared and his footsteps were gone from the hall, Margaret turned back to Carrie. She splashed something from the brown bottle on a piece of sheet and began dabbing at Carrie's head.

"Thur now, thet's better, but think I'll snip just a bitty piece of hair off . . . right . . . . here. Ah, ye won't

264

miss thet if 'n ye comb this top hair over the spot. Now then . . ."

Margaret went back to the gentle dabs with her cloth.

The liquid from the brown bottle smelled spicy, but what spice? It was different from anything Carrie had encountered before. Cool and weedy too, maybe a bit like old wine. And now she noticed that her head's last little bit of hurt was gone.

After she'd finished swabbing, Margaret folded a fresh pad over the wet spot on Carrie's head and secured the dressing with a ribbon of sheeting, which she tied in a bow, hat fashion, on the opposite side.

Margaret leaned back, eyeing Carrie. "Thur, ye look right smart!" She smiled, obviously pleased with her work. "Don't think the wound's serious, cut's dryin'. Ye may feel tippy fer a spell." She leaned closer for a moment, whispering, "When Hab's back, act real tippy, hear me?"

Then, erect again, she said, "Ye jes rest easy whils't I see t' this other one." The bed springs under Carrie creaked, and, in a moment, a matching creak came from the bed across the room.

Carrie, with her head now turned to the side, could watch as Margaret sat, looking down at her grand-daughter. Tracy had been right. She did have a runny nose and looked a mess. One eye still had bits of tape stuck around it, and her other eye and mouth were out-lined in red streaks where the tape had been.

Margaret took some of the clean rag that Habakkuk

265

had brought and, as if she were helping a tiny child, held it against Tracy's nose while supporting her head. "Blow," she said.

Tracy blew, then immediately began crying again. "Oh, Granny." The words were jerky, but clearly identifiable.

Margaret raised her head and looked back across the room at Carrie, who pushed her own head up and down, nodding. The whispered words, "She knows," came out just fine.

Margaret reached down and put her arms around her granddaughter, who was sobbing in earnest now.

I think, Carrie mused, that we've got to get out of this soon so Tracy can stop crying.

Margaret was holding Tracy to her bosom, bending low over her, since Tracy was, after all, still tied to a bed. Carrie shut her eyes. Some kinds of love were almost too much to look at. Eyes still shut, she pictured Margaret and Nahum together and Henry's tender look as he watched them. Henry would have enjoyed seeing this sharing of love too.

She wished Henry *could* see it.

And then, Carrie McCrite fought back tears of her own.

A door slammed. After wiping Tracy's face once more, Margaret went to the hall and looked out.

In a moment, Habakkuk was beside her.

"I called the auditorium," he said. "Show was just out. Zeph'll not be long now."

Margaret nodded. "Thet's fine. Now, help me get this 'un up. Ye do the knots."

Carrie didn't have to pretend dizziness, but with Margaret's support she was finally seated properly in the bathroom. Margaret gave her a drink, then continued to run water, saying loudly, "I'll wipe yer face, Missus."

Instead, she leaned close to Carrie. "Now, kin ye manage to walk by yerself? Ye got t' git away. Dasn't risk what might happen when Zeph puts his head t'gether with Hab, 'n' Hab finds out the whole story of ye bein' at my house this day. Tracy's safe fer now, but I ain't so sure thet ye aire . . ."

Margaret shook her head, paused a moment, turned the faucet off, then back on again, and went on talking. "I see ye got the bedroom winder loose. I'll help ye both ter git out if 'n I kin send Hab off fer an errand."

Carrie whispered, "Where's Nahum? Is Dulcey safe? I told Tracy she was."

Margaret nodded. "I give her t' yer man on the path. They're away safe, 'n' we thought ye were safe, too, hidin' in the woods by the clearin'. When we found ye were gone, he were undone but had t' git away with Dulcey 'n' bring help. Then I found ye here. Hab sed he'd tricked ye into comin' into Nahum's house. He knows nothin' 'bout yer man bein' there, 'n' he thinks Dulcey got away by herself.

"I only learnt Hab 'n' Nahum traded places jes a'fore comin' t' meet ye. I saw t'was Nahum in the

267

truck, goin' t' Little Rock with Micah. Nahum wuz so proud to have new fam'ly . . . he musta said sumthin' 'bout hit ter Hab. Enyways, the boys insisted he 'n' Hab trade places ternight. Nahum were fussin' 'bout goin' away, but I guess he figured when his brothers learnt who Tracy really were, they'd be mighty pleased too. Nahum, he sees good in most ever'thin'. I allus hate ter spoil thet, 'n' I tol' him less 'n' I shoulda."

Carrie nodded.

"Now, we'll go back. Keep actin' tippy. When ye git ter thet bed, kinda fall in a faint. Thin mebbe Hab'll not tie ye back right away. I'll send him off ter write up a ransom fer Tracy, 'n' if he goes, I'll untie her too, so's she kin he'p ye walk. Ye two git out th' winder, head off from the back o'the house—thet-away." She pointed. "Hit's rough fer a bit, but keep in the same direction 'n' ye'll end up at th' Folk Center. Go as fast as ye kin, since Hab could git Micah's dogs. If 'n ye hear them dogs, walk in the creek if 'n ye kin git thur.

"Mebbe Hab'll stay away from the room 'til Zeph's come—give ye some time. Hit's chancy, but I don' know whut else t' do. If 'n they do come after ye—if 'n they git close—let Tracy distract 'em best she kin, 'n' ye get away. I kin pertect her fer now, but not ye."

That said, Margaret turned off the water, flushed the toilet, and, supporting Carrie, opened the bathroom door.

Carrie wobbled back into the bedroom and collapsed on the bed, moaning. She shut her eyes, jerked once, then stayed motionless and silent, hoping she hadn't overdone it.

Margaret was talking, "Son, how about ye go figure whut yer goin' t' say fer the ransom? Write it all out so ye'll remember. Yer good at makin' words like thet, so best ye do hit now, a'fore Zeph comes.

"Ye kin see this un's out o' things fer a while, 'n' that 'un's still tied. I'll holler if 'n I need ye. I want to watch this 'un enyways. She's purty bad, son. I hope she ain't gonna die on us. Go now, don't worry. I'll keep watch."

Habakkuk left, and the second he was out of the door, Margaret was cutting the cloth tying Tracy's hands and ankles, speaking softly to her, assuring her Dulcey was safe, explaining that now was the time to escape, to run to the Folk Center to be with her daughter.

Carrie got to her feet by herself, still woozy, but able to stand, and in a moment Tracy was standing too. Pushing Tracy in front of her, Margaret went to the window and shoved it up, then came back to help Carrie.

A truck's rumbling noise vibrated through the window, and Margaret paused, dismay clouding her face. "No, no, hit's Zeph's truck. He's early, what we gonter do?" She stood motionless by the window, fingers locked around Carrie's arm.

Then the thunder of a shotgun interrupted all thought. Tracy screamed, and Carrie stared toward the

269

door, feeling separated—as if she were part of the audience at a play.

In an instant, Habakkuk Culpeper was back in the room, shotgun raised, but he hadn't been shooting at them. His gun was pointing down the hall, and a sharp crack came from that direction. Simultaneously, Carrie heard a bullet hit the door frame next to Habakkuk. Finally she moved, dropping to the floor, pulling Margaret down beside her.

Habakkuk grabbed Tracy, who was still standing, and yanked her to him. He stood sideways in the door with Tracy as a shield and faced down the hall, shotgun pointed. Tracy looked frozen—unable, even, to scream.

Another shot came, this time from the black rectangle of the open window behind Habakkuk, and as he toppled to the floor, all Carrie could think was, no, no, it's not fair. Henry's come, and he had to shoot Margaret's son.

She raised to her knees and crawled toward Margaret, who had lifted Habakkuk's head into her lap and was pulling his bloody shirt away from the wound in his side. Margaret put her hand over the wound and leaned into Carrie, who touched her gently on the arm, feeling utterly miserable. She couldn't even manage to be frightened and simply could not look toward the window.

But Margaret looked. She gasped, and, at last, Carrie looked too. A man Carrie recognized—not Henry, praise God, not Henry—was climbing over the sill. He

270

went immediately to Tracy and pushed her behind him, ready to protect her from any coming danger. He, too, had a gun.

Margaret stared, her hand still against the wound in her son's side. "Benjamin? Benjamin Calhoun?" she said. "Is it ye? Aire ye come back?"

Then Carrie understood. It had not been Henry who fired at Habakkuk through the window. It was the man called Ben Yokum, and she knew who he must be. Tracy's father had, after all, come back to be closer to his daughter, and he'd been close enough to kill for her . . . twice.

Tracy was alert now, moving quickly around Ben, ignoring everyone but Habakkuk. She stamped her heel on Habakkuk's hand as it slid across the floor toward the gun.

Guess he's not very dead, after all, Carrie thought, because Habakkuk had definitely howled as Tracy's heel ground into his hand.

Tracy bent to pick up the gun and raised it to shooting position. "No, Uncle," she said. "No more." She stopped, then addressed her next remark to her grandmother. "Don't you worry, Granny, I'm not gonna shoot him . . . unless he moves."

Footsteps were thundering down the hall. This was too much. Carrie realized her wooziness had gone and just in time. Henry stood in the doorway, and a man in uniform was behind him, peering to see in the room. They both had guns, but now Tracy was the only one pointing a gun at anyone.

271

Henry's eyes swiveled around the room, stopping briefly on each person there. Carrie could almost see his mind working, taking it all in. Then he said, "It's all yours," to the man in uniform and came to wrap Carrie in his arms.

No matter how she felt about tears, hers began to soak the front of his jacket.

## Chapter XXII

Once more Margaret Culpeper was serving tea in her home, though, this time, it was three A.M. instead of three in the afternoon. Carrie doubted anyone there really wanted tea—what she wanted was her bed—but tea-making gave Margaret something to do. All of them, including the sheriff, seemed to understand that, so they were drinking tea.

During tea preparation the sheriff had been surveying each of them, sometimes thoughtfully, sometimes with *the look*. Carrie recognized *the look,* she remembered it from her childhood. Back then, the familiar glare had come from her father, and the misbehavior that caused it was less serious than failure to report a kidnapping or share information about drug dealing and murder.

Quiet ruled the room as the weary group sipped and the sheriff looked. All major activity was back at Habakkuk's house—though the homeowner was no longer there. After assuring Margaret that her son wasn't in mortal danger, medical technicians had

272

carted him off to the hospital under guard. The last Carrie heard from him as he disappeared inside the ambulance were loud complaints that Tracy Teal had broken every bone in his hand.

The EMTs had offered to take Carrie to the hospital along with Habakkuk, but there was no way she was going to leave this place. She proclaimed herself quite satisfied with Margaret's ministrations and stood her ground with Henry, Tracy, and Margaret. So, after quick phone calls to Brigid and Chase and the Stacks, the five of them had come to Margaret's home where they could talk without interruption.

Now the sheriff was just sitting there in Margaret's rocker, looking at them.

"Well," he said finally, "I need a good picture of what's happened here. From what King said when he called us, things got kinda deep, didn't they?" He smiled gently at Margaret, who had just returned the kettle to the grate and was sitting in her chair by the fire. "S'cuse me, Miz Culpeper, but how did you get hooked in with this crazy bunch of outsiders?"

He was probably just being kind, including her in his special circle, and Carrie decided she liked him for that, but Margaret took the man at his word. She began to tell her story, starting with when she first saw Carrie on the Folk Center path.

Carrie and Henry already knew most of what Margaret said, but Tracy's wide eyes were on her grandmother's face throughout. And Margaret didn't hold back. She didn't spare Micah, Habakkuk, and Zepha-

273

niah, or even her husband, as she told the involved tale of the family business and what she knew about the kidnapping of Dulcey and Tracy.

But she said nothing about Farel's murder, a daughter, or Tracy's relationship to her family.

"And thet's hit," Margaret finished. "I reckon ye'll be wantin' t' take me away too, but Nahum's innercent o' all this. Oh, he knowed about the fam'ly bizness, but, shuriff, how could one man like Nahum stop hit?"

"Or one woman?" the sheriff said. "Thank you, Miz Culpeper, we'll leave it at that. No need for you to be packin' your bag. But, after you've had some rest, you might pack clothing for your sons and get a lawyer for them. If you need help with that . . ."

"I'll help her," Tracy said, breaking her long silence. "I'll get a lawyer for my uncles."

The sheriff's jaw dropped. "S'cuse me, Miz Teal, but, uncles? How's that fit? Of course you don't need to say," he added quickly. It had been obvious all along that Sheriff Wylie—indeed almost everyone they'd seen this night—had been awed by Tracy's fame as a music star and very gentle and considerate of her well-being.

"Yes, my uncles," said Tracy, going to stand by Margaret's chair and putting her hand on her grandmother's shoulder. Her stance was theatrical, but Carrie doubted Tracy was acting or even conscious of how she looked, nor was Margaret as she raised her hand and put it over her granddaughter's.

Tracy looked straight at the sheriff and continued,

"My birth mother was this woman's youngest child, Elizabeth, who died just after I was born. I'm a Culpeper by birth."

*And proud of it,* Tracy's tone said plainly. Carrie wanted to leap to her feet and go hug her.

"Oh, well-uh, I'm sure Miz, uh, Culpeper . . . Margaret . . . will appreciate your help, Miz . . . Teal . . . ma'am. And, of course we know you and Mr. Mason had nothing to do with the drug business. I'm sorry to say, though, that Chief Bolen and I have suspected about those drugs for some time and were about ready to make a case. You see . . ." He hesitated, looked around, and stopped.

"We know Farel Teal was involved." That was Henry, helping out.

"Yes, sir, he was. He was easier to track than the others. In fact, we'd been thinkin' we might arrest Farel and get him to help us collect evidence on the Culpepers. I guess they must have found out about our plans and . . . and . . ."

"My sons don't hold with killin' fer sech a thing as that," Margaret said, fixing her black eyes on the sheriff's face.

"Um, yes, I'm sure, ma'am."

The sheriff turned toward Henry and Carrie. "Now, how about you two?" he said, obviously glad to change focus.

He nodded encouragingly at Carrie, and she began her story. She was sure Henry would be eager to hear what had happened to her after they separated. He leaned toward her as she talked and finally reached out for her hand as she told about being thrown into the wall by Habakkuk.

Carrie was just as eager to learn what Henry did after he walked away from her in the woods by Nahum's, and she was glad when her story was finished and he began to tell his.

"So, not long after I left Carrie, Margaret met me on the path. She had Dulcey with her and warned me that Habakkuk had changed places with Nahum. That's why she didn't dare meet us at the house. Then Margaret and I—with me carrying the child—made a large circle through the woods back to the place where I'd left Carrie. When she was gone . . . well, I didn't know what to do.

"After a bit, Margaret went up to the house to see who was there. It was empty, but she did find Carrie's denim hat on the floor." He tugged the hat out of his pocket and showed it to Carrie but, after looking at her bandaged head, stuffed it back in his pocket. "We didn't know that Tracy had been there too. Margaret didn't find out, as she said, until she went to Habakkuk's house. I only suspected it when I got back to the Folk Center Lodge with Dulcey and learned Tracy was gone and what she'd said in her note to Eleanor.

"That's when I called Sheriff Wylie. Sheriff, perhaps you can understand why we didn't involve you sooner? We had the safety of the child to consider. Everything else came after that. And, you must admit we had an inside advantage, with the family name, and as two older civilians . . . ."

The sheriff nodded and continued the story himself. "When King called, told us about the kidnapping, and asked us to stop Zephaniah, we were ready, you see. We got him in the parkin' lot with one lunch pail still full of merchandise. That made it easy to get close to this place since we had his truck and could hide deputies lyin' down in the back. First we parked on the road near here, listenin' and watchin', and when Ol' Mad Marg . . . ur, Miz Culpeper, began to play her music, King said he knew right where you all were. We should just follow the music."

He turned to Margaret. "You're pretty sharp, ma'am, pretty sharp! And accordin' to Ben Yokum, who had evidently caught on to the kidnapping some way, the music is what led him here too, lookin' fer the child. He says he just came because he thought there might be a reward. He didn't know Tracy was here either. None of us did know that for sure."

"What about Micah now?" Henry asked.

"They're watchin' the highways between here and Little Rock. I've warned the State Police to be gentle with Nahum Culpeper, and no violence if possible. Shucks, though, Micah and his wife must be near eighty. The others . . . not much younger, right?" He looked at Margaret. "They've got to be tired of all this, and I can't see they'll be a problem. Now, as to Habakkuk's wife, I'm not so sure. Accordin' to him she was out for the evening to a bridge game, but from all accounts, she's a wicked one.

"Thing is, the kidnapping would be enough without the drug charges. Kidnapping is serious stuff. It's obvious Habakkuk's wife was in on it, though Micah's wife's been away."

The sheriff turned toward Carrie. "Bobby Lee Logan knew about Farel's drug dealing, but he wouldn't talk to anyone about it until he found out we already knew. He told us last night he burned Farel's house to get rid of any evidence of Farel's dealings with the Culpepers. He wanted to protect his friend's reputation, and since he knew the murder had already been reported, he figured he didn't have time to search the whole house and clean out evidence Farel might have left. Of course that gets him an arson charge."

The sheriff paused, looking more closely at Carrie. "He heard you calling in that 911, Miz McCrite. That's how he found out about the murder.

"We know Bobby Lee didn't kill Farel. Never did suspect him. There are folks who saw him inside the auditorium all evening up until the time he left for Farel's. That was after he heard you call to report the murder, of course.

"Now, Miz Teal, do you have anything to add to clearing this up? The only thing we haven't solved yet is the murder of your cousin, Farel. Can you shed any light on that? Seems no one else here can." He gave them all *the look* again. "Unless a Culpeper . . ."

"No!" Tracy said, stopping him. Head bowed, she stood next to her grandmother and said no more.

What can she do now? Carrie was thinking. Implicate her birth father, or break Margaret's heart and imply that it was one of her uncles? Does she realize yet that Ben is her father? What can she do?

Heavy steps thunked on the wood porch, and a deputy beckoned to the sheriff from the doorway. After the two men had left the room, Carrie said, "Tracy, you know who killed Farel . . . you know it was not one of Margaret's sons."

Tracy raised her head to look at Carrie, then walked around to kneel in front of her grandmother, putting her hands in Margaret's lap and looking up into her face like a small child in prayer. "It was Ben, Granny. It was Ben, but he thought he was protecting me . . . same as he did with Habakkuk."

Margaret had just placed a hand on each side of Tracy's head, cradling her face, when the sheriff came back into the room. He noticed Margaret and Tracy and looked at them thoughtfully for a moment before he said, "Well, now, that's interesting. Ben Yokum has confessed to the murder of Farel Teal. He says they had an argument. Says Farel was threatening him, so he took the knife from Farel and just stabbed out. Didn't mean to kill him."

Margaret stood, pulling Tracy up with her. Together they turned to face the sheriff, meeting his gaze for a long moment of silence.

Then Tracy said, "I was the one fighting with Farel, not Ben. It was there in the dressmaker's shop, after I learned Dulcey was gone. See, Farel had her before

279

the Culpepers did, and he left her alone in the car, so anyone could have taken her. He and I were fighting about that when Ben saw us. He went after Farel only to protect me. He thought Farel would hurt me, maybe use the knife that was there. I can tell you all about it. Ben was just protecting me."

Carrie sure hoped Margaret Culpeper felt proud of the strong woman she had for a granddaughter, and she hoped too that Tracy told her story quickly. It would be daylight soon. If Tracy talked very long, Carrie was going to fall asleep . . . and then she'd fall off her chair.

When they were finally ready to leave, Margaret walked out on the porch with Carrie, leaving Tracy, Henry, and the sheriff in a last-minute conversation.

"I'll stay by my boys," Margaret said as they stood together in the light that filtered through the cabin's window. "I hope Tracy 'n' you understand thet. They've done wrong, but thur still my own, no matter how much they seek punishin'. I'll stay by my boys 'n' not turn away from them like Robert E. did from Elizabeth when she were in trouble."

She took hold of Carrie's arm and looked into her face. "Ye'll watch over Tracy fer me now?"

"I'm sure you can do that yourself," Carrie said. "We'll come back to visit and make plans tomorrow, er, no, this afternoon, if it's all right, and if you don't need to be with your boys."

Margaret smiled, but her eyes were sad. "Oh, I

reckon all three of 'em'll be in good enough hands, 'n' I don't think Hab's hurt serious. The three'll be whur they need t' be fer a spell, and Nahum'll be here with me."

Carrie wondered just how long the "spell" in prison might be for men who were already senior citizens, but she didn't mention that to Margaret. Instead, she decided now was the right time to speak up about Nahum, because that was news full of hope—something Margaret could look forward to.

"Margaret, have you ever heard of dyslexia?"

"Dys . . ." She shook her head. "Niver. What's hit?"

"Well, it's what may be keeping Nahum from learning to read. It's not a disease but the name we call it when people are born with brains that aren't organized quite like yours and mine. Dyslexics see and learn things in a different way than you and I do. Doesn't mean they're dumb, not at all, but sometimes people with dyslexia find it very hard to read. They mix up letters. The problems it causes can vary. I suspect Nahum is dyslexic and that he can be helped. He can learn to read."

Margaret was watching her face, looking at her as if the intent gaze would help her understand what Carrie was saying. "How do ye know 'bout this . . . dyslessics? Whut makes ye think Nahum . . . ?"

"I helped teach dyslexic students back in Tulsa when I worked at the library. We had a special program for them. Watching Nahum, well, I think he shows many of the symptoms. And dyslexia is sup-

281

posedly passed down in families. Since his father couldn't read either . . .

"Margaret, what I'd like to do is have Nahum tested, and then we'll know what help to get for him. Some of the tests, like one called the Irlen Syndrome Test, can be expensive, but I think Tracy will be glad to help pay for all this. She'll be proud to be able to help you and Nahum. And, I just wanted you to know, Nahum isn't dumb. I'm sure he's very smart."

Margaret lifted her chin. "Knowed thet," she said, " 'n' we got money. Don't need Tracy's help. She's got Dulcey ter tek care of. So, how'd we go about gittin' this thing done?"

Carrie decided Margaret had no concept yet of just how wealthy her granddaughter probably was, so she let that pass and left Margaret with her pride.

"We'll get together and talk about it more this afternoon, after Nahum's home."

Margaret nodded, accepting that, then changed the subject. "I reckon ye figured who Benjamin is?"

Carrie nodded.

"Wahl, fer now, I don't see no reason t' tell Tracy 'bout thet, they's bin so much . . ."

"Umm, yes, but she may have figured it out already, Margaret. If she hasn't, she will soon. She's smart too, you know. I think Ben saw Farel turn off the breakers for the craft shops and followed him, simply because he was acting suspiciously. Ben didn't like Farel anyway, and when he got to the dressmaker's shop, I'm sure it did look to him like Farel was hurting

282

Tracy. There was the knife there, and Ben may have thought Farel was planning to use it on Tracy. I think it happened just like Tracy says. I don't believe he planned to kill him at all."

"Why wur they fightin'? I didn't quite see thet."

"Farel had taken Dulcey to begin with. It was a scheme to get money from Tracy and Chase. Tracy can tell you all about it later—I'm so tired I don't think I can manage to get it straight right now. But when Tracy learned Farel went off and left Dulcey alone in his unlocked car and someone had taken her, she was frightened, of course, and she was furious. It's no wonder she flew at Farel.

"Margaret, are Zephaniah and Ben friends? Zephaniah asked Ben to put his kidnapping note in the bird house."

"Don't know, but Zeph has a way of gittin' others to do fer him. He were spoiled, bein' the youngest 'til Elizabeth come along." She paused, then went on, "Mebbe Benjamin read Zeph's note 'n' thet's why he come here—t' save the chile."

"There's something else, Margaret. I think Tracy really needs you and Nahum as family right now. She's not very happy with her career or her marriage . . . wants to spend more time at home with Dulcey. She doesn't want the two of them to be performing all the time, and she says her husband doesn't understand that. So maybe you can help her there."

Again, Margaret lifted her chin. "Wahl, thet's a new kind of trouble ter fix, ain't hit! But, I'm here. I'm

283

allus here, and now ain't no man gonna hurt Tracy nur Dulcey. Sure, they kin come ter me. I imagine Lee Ellen'll go away to her 'n' Micah's kids now, iff 'n she don't end up in jail, too. Enyways, she won't stay in thet house alone. Tracy kin have Micah's house, if 'n she wants hit."

"Good. That will give her some freedom, though—who knows—maybe she and Chase will work things out. Anyway, now she's got options and can spend time close to you and Nahum. Thank you, Margaret, thank you for everything."

"She's my granddaughter," Margaret reminded her. Then she smiled so deeply that her eyes vanished in wrinkles. "'N' don't ye fergit, Carrie, yer a Culpeper, too. Fam'lies gotter stay together."

The two women were silent for a moment before Carrie took out a tissue, blew her nose, and began, "Margaret . . . ," but could say no more.

"I'm all right," said the older woman, understanding.

There was a pause before she said, "Ye say ye've got chillern?"

"One son."

"We kin pertect 'em from lots o' things when they's small," Margaret said, "but when they's growed, we sure cain't pertect 'em from theyselves, now kin we!"

Her head dropped, and she seemed to be looking at her feet. "Wahl, I got Nahum, and, mebbe, I got Tracy."

"You do have Tracy," Carrie said, "and you always will."

# Chapter XXIII

At least it was still dark. Maybe she'd actually see her bed before daylight.

On the ride back to the lodge, Carrie decided she was in no mood to do anything but go to bed. Mason-Teal-Culpeper problems that needed any more sorting out could just wait about eight hours, or they could do it on their own.

During the drive Henry and Tracy were as quiet as Carrie, either lost in thought, or simply numb. On the other hand, the young sheriff's deputy driving the car was decidedly chirpy, chattering about his own fiddle playing and occasional appearances on the Folk Center stage. He actually had the nerve to ask Tracy for her autograph as he let them out in the parking lot, and that made Carrie even grumpier. It was true. Famous people had no privacy.

Tracy accepted the paper graciously, scrawled her name, and said a quiet, "Thank you," as she handed it back. Stardom, it seemed, was a never-over job.

Silence returned as the three of them walked toward Eleanor and Jason's lighted motel room. When they stopped at the door, Carrie saw Tracy's face in the glow from the porch lamp.

Margaret's special salve had cleaned the lovely skin, and the red marks were almost gone. Tracy's face was beautiful and should be. Dulcey was safe, she had gained a whole new family, and now she had a way to escape constant performing, which is exactly what she'd said she wanted. But there was no joy in the face Carrie saw in the porch light.

Yes, no matter what she said or how he'd treated her, Tracy Teal was still in love with her husband. If Carrie was any judge of humans, Tracy was having a difficult time deciding what to do about that now that she had options.

Part of Carrie wanted to tell Tracy to dump Chase. The man simply wasn't worth fretting over. But then she would be denying that change and reformation were always possible, as well as overlooking the importance of working to make a marriage succeed. Carrie puffed her cheeks and blew out air. It seemed there was still something to settle here.

Jason opened the door to Henry's light knock and had to turn aside quickly as Tracy rushed past him into the room. She fell on her knees by the rocking chair where Brigid Mason sat, the sleeping Dulcey sprawled across most of her lap. A worn rag doll with a smile made lopsided by missing embroidery threads filled the rest of Brigid's lap space. Tracy knelt, still as a statue, staring at her daughter.

"She's fine," Brigid whispered. "She wanted to stay awake 'til you got here, but jest couldn't make it."

Chase was in the room, but Tracy ignored him. He had been lying, fully clothed, on one of the beds. Now he sat up, slid to the edge of the bed, and spoke Tracy's name. She seemed not to hear him, and he didn't stand.

"Tracy?" he said again.

She looked at him.

"Tracy . . ."

She said nothing.

His voice went on, low, faltering. "I guess . . . guess I've made a botch-up of things. Don't know exactly what to tell you . . . what to say. I'm still sortin' out what I think, and maybe it's too late to say anything. If I could think what to do . . . If I . . ."

She interrupted him. "Chase, stop. There are things you need to know before you try and talk to me. See, I got all this started, and it sure caused a mess I didn't expect, but it also opened doors I didn't know about. You need to listen and hear me out before you say anything."

She took a deep breath and looked around the room. After another swish of air—in, out—she began. "One thing is, I wasn't born a Teal, so your jokes about a feud won't work anymore."

There was a pause. In the silence, Chase got to his feet and held his hands up and out at each side, palms toward Tracy. A theatrical gesture of helplessness, Carrie thought. Theatrics seemed to be built into this family.

"You've called my Teal relatives scummy. Well, tonight I found out who I really am by birth—a Culpeper. Yes, that's right, part of the infamous Culpeper family of Mountain View. My birth mother was Margaret Culpeper's daughter, Elizabeth, and that's another thing. Elizabeth Culpeper never married. I was born to a single mother." Tracy paused, looked down at her folded hands. "She died a week after I was born, and I was adopted by my Teal parents.

"So now I have a whole second family here, and some of them are in jail. They've done bad things—drugs, kidnapping. I'm sure you'd call them scummy. I can't really defend every Culpeper from that label, though it's not true of my Granny Margaret or my Uncle Nahum. Neither was it true of the Teals who raised me and loved me. The Culpepers, though, they're probably not people you'd ever want to associate with.

"I found out who my biological father is, too. You know him as Ben Yokum. He's going to be charged with Farel's murder.

"So, you'd better stop right now, Chase Mason. These people are my family, and the tabloids are going to love it. I'm sure you're already picturing the headlines. You'd better get Dulcey and me out of your life while you can."

She bowed her head again, and her defiant tone softened. "So, how did I get this started? Well, see, *I* arranged for Farel to take Dulcey. It was to keep him from blackmailing us and so you wouldn't find out I didn't write the music for 'Lying to Strangers.'

"No, Chase, don't you talk. You listen to me.

"I lied to you about writing that song. I got it from Farel, and all along I thought Farel wrote it for me, back when we were kids. I heard it first from him.

Bobby Lee knew that, of course. When Farel needed to get away from here and make a fresh start, he decided to blackmail you and me . . . claim the royalty we owed him for his song. If we didn't do what he asked, he said he'd tell the world I didn't write it. I thought I couldn't let you know about the song not being mine, so I convinced Farel to let me fake the kidnapping and get money for him that way.

"But, you know what's funny, Chase? Farel didn't write the song either. My mother, Elizabeth Culpeper, was the one who really wrote what we've called our song. Farel must have heard Granny Margaret playing my mother's song out in the woods and picked it up. Granny told me she often does that—sits in the woods playing music."

Chase wasn't moving at all. He might have been carved from a block of wood. He'd stopped opening and closing his mouth, trying to talk, and was now just staring at his wife.

"So there you are," she said. "And I'm ready to get out of your life, bring Dulcey here to Mountain View, let her keep regular hours, play like a regular kid, go to a real school at proper times. I'm ready to be her mother. I don't want strangers to raise her while I only get to spend little bits of time with her.

"I've got money of my own. You did that for us, saw to it I had my share of our take. And I reckon I can get a job in one of the music shows here. Granny Margaret can baby-sit, and maybe Mama Brigid will help out too. I want her to stay a big part of Dulcey's life.

289

And . . . you'll always be her daddy."

At this, Tracy's voice broke, and everyone stayed statuestill, ignoring Brigid's murmured, "Whoo-eee."

Tracy swallowed, lifted her chin higher. "I know who I am. I know who I want to be. I know that doesn't fit in your scheme of things, so Dulcey and I will relieve you of the bother of worrying about it. You're on your own."

During this speech, Chase had dropped to the bed again, and Carrie wasn't surprised he looked frozen. Talk about a double whammy!

Well, hadn't she told Tracy just a couple of hours ago, there in the bedroom at Habakkuk's house, that it was time to tell Chase everything? And now Tracy had gotten just about everything out at once. Maybe that was best. Maybe that had more chance of getting around Chase Mason's enormous self-centered ego.

No one in the room seemed to be breathing. Finally, Chase spoke, his words rolling out quietly, slowly, without inflection. "Mama said this would come. She said things had gone too good for my own good. Those were her very words. She said that to me last summer."

He was still looking at Tracy, but his real seeing was far away, in some secret world.

"You know I was a music star from the time I was in my teens. Praise, applause, money, all of it. Mama said to me it was time I grew to be a man, a family man, a real man. Time I recognized a strength beyond my own, time I knew Him who gave me my talent.

She said all that. But just last summer—those few months ago—I couldn't see it with her. How could things get better? I was a *star*. That was good, wasn't it? Nothing could be better, right?"

Again there was that theatrical gesture, hands out, palms up, but now, tears were streaming down Chase's face.

Glory be, thought Carrie.

He looked at his mother. "Well, maybe things couldn't get better, Mama, but they sure could get worse . . . they could get a whole lot worse."

He turned back to his wife, his voice faltering now. "I just didn't need anyone and even told myself I didn't need you, because I thought it wouldn't be long and I wouldn't have you anyway. See, Trace, I've known you were adopted since our last visit here. Bobby Lee was very pleased to be able to tell me all about it after that fund-raiser we did. At first I didn't believe him, because I'd-a thought you'd have told me. But, see, I also knew Farel had come to you in Branson when I was gone. A couple of guys in the band saw him. I was sure the man they described was Farel. So, when Bobby Lee said all that, and I thought about it, I saw that you . . . you and Farel . . . well, you were so quiet about it, why else wouldn't you have told me unless you were in love with Farel Teal and planned to go with him? I figured the kidnapping was somehow part of that, to get more money for you and Farel and . . . Dulcey. That's what I figured, and it was hard to pretend I didn't know . . ."

Now Chase looked at his feet. "Though I thought I'd already lost you, and it was tearin' me up, still I told myself I could deal with it. But then Farel was killed, and, God forgive me, I was almost glad. I thought you'd stay with me then, because of Dulcey, you know, even if you didn't love me. I could handle that, couldn't I? But the one thing I couldn't handle was that you . . . that . . . you and Dulcey might be . . . dead, which is what came on me this night."

Now Chase's whole body was shaking with sobs. He covered his face with his hands and said, "Oh, God, Tracy, it doesn't matter, Culpeper or Teal, I . . . I . . . love you, I love our daughter. Oh, dear God, what am I gonna do?"

This time Carrie knew Chase was not swearing. This time he was really speaking to God. Tracy must have realized it too, because she went to him and she was holding out a piece of Margaret's clean white rag.

Tracy touched her husband's face. "Blow," she said. After a polite pause, Brigid cleared her throat and said, in a matter-of-fact tone, "How about pickin' up yer daughter, Chase Mason, 'n' takin' her to the car? It's sure past ever'one's bedtime. It's time we let these poor folks alone and went home."

## Chapter XXIV

Saying goodbye took a while, and Carrie didn't even mind. She was beyond tired anyway, and there was so much to think about.

It helped to see that Brigid was full of hope. She'd said so the last thing before she shut the door of the van. "Future's full of hope, Carrie, hit shore is."

When the four friends were back in the room, Jason leaned against the door he had just closed and said, "Still can't believe it. It's just like a TV story—not real. But I sure hope the Branson vacation Chase offered is real enough."

Carrie, who'd plopped in a rocker still warm from Brigid's recent presence, said, "Oh, yes, it's real. And now I imagine you two want to hear the whole story . . ."

"Plenty of time for that," Eleanor said. "We've put together quite a bit of it already, and we'll get your part later, after we've all had some sleep."

She turned to Henry. "And you can have your room back. I got fresh sheets and towels from the house-keeper. It won't take a minute . . ."

Henry looked thoughtful. "My things are already unpacked in Carrie's room, and you know she got that bump on her head. Never can tell about head bumps. I don't think she should be alone."

Carrie, who had forgotten all about the bump—though she realized now that Margaret's bandage was still wrapped around her head—nodded in agreement.

Carrie watched two adults and one child skip through a field of wildflowers. Ox-eye daisies. Oh! She knew the people. The Masons. Chase, Tracy, and their little girl, Dulcey . . . skipping in daisies.

293

A slight rustle. Paper sound.

Consciousness grabbed her, the meadow faded.

Another paper rustle. Carrie wanted to open her eyes and see what it was, but there was a bright light, too hot against her eyelids. Instead of looking, she stretched her body, sliding arms and legs against smooth sheets.

A rocker creaked, ever so slightly, and after a space of silence, there was another paper rustle.

Umpf. She pushed pillows against the headboard, scooted back to lean against them, and popped her eyes open into the sunlight coming through the window.

Oh, my! There appeared to be an enormous cherub in a white robe sitting in the rocking chair at the foot of the bed. The cherub looked up and said, "Good morning."

For goodness sake. Henry slept in a night shirt! She'd never seen one of those on a real person.

And she remembered why she hadn't seen Henry in his big cherub shirt. She'd fallen asleep while he was still in the shower. That would be earlier this morning.

She looked back at Henry. He had her Bible open on his lap. Well, now. There was certainly a lot she didn't know about this man . . .

"Good morning." Had she said it out loud?

His face was hidden in the glare of the sun, but she thought he smiled.

"You were sleeping soundly. I guess you feel okay?"

"Yes. Yes, I do."

"I've been sitting here thinking about how much we have to be grateful for," he said.

"You're right." She looked down and arranged the ruffles on the sleeves of her nightgown. There were so many things she wanted to ask, and she might as well do it now.

"Um . . . Henry, I'm wondering, will the sheriff do anything to Margaret or Nahum? I guess they really did break the law. At the least they knew about the family business . . . and Nahum helped with growing that stuff."

"I think Sheriff Wylie's got what he wants. He closed down the business. It sounded like he has no plans to charge either of them. Besides, kidnapping is a more serious crime, and he knows Margaret and Nahum had nothing to do with that. Margaret did her best to get all of you away to safety."

"What about the three boys?" She giggled as she realized what she'd said, and Henry smiled too.

"Their age may be a factor, but they'll pay for what they've done. Exactly to what degree is up to the law."

"Benjamin Calhoun?"

"I don't believe he's really a violent man, do you? He acted violently, but I'm sure it was for what he saw as justifiable reasons. I think the testimony Tracy has offered will make a difference there, though he may still serve time. Tracy may not avoid having a father in prison—whatever the tabloids want to make of it. I've thought about that since last night. Seems to me her reaction to what the tabloids say is going to be more important than any black headline words by themselves."

"You've been thinking a lot, haven't you! Did you get any sleep?"

"Oh, yes. Enough. I'm used to long nights on duty, remember? And your questions are things anyone in law enforcement thinks about, or should."

After a moment of silence, she asked, "Would you go back to police work now if you could?"

He smiled again. "Would you want me to?"

"No. But that's selfish."

"I wouldn't go back. That part of my story is over."

There was another space of silence before Henry continued. "Now is the beginning of other things, though."

She played with the ruffle on her gown, wondering exactly what he meant. Finally she said, "Henry, you had to shoot at Habakkuk, didn't you? There in the hall? The shot barely missed. If he hadn't backed into the room . . ."

"He had you captive, Carrie, you and Tracy. I wasn't shooting to kill, and it was for a reason I understood completely and had already justified. As it turned out, I wasn't the one who stopped him anyway."

"But the shotgun . . . Habakkuk shot at you."

"Yes."

"He might have hit you."

"Carrie, look at me."

"I am."

296

"He didn't hit anyone. Not me, not anyone else. He just messed up his house a bit. The end of the story matters, Carrie. It matters a lot. Neither of us has any reason to feel guilty or frightened. Sometimes we might. But not this time."

His voice changed, became softer, and she had to listen carefully to hear his next words.

"When I learned you were in danger . . . that was very hard for me. Oh, not that it wouldn't have been hard for any law officer who's trained to help people in danger . . ."

"But, I understa . . ."

"Shhh, now let me finish. I've been in similar situations many times before, of course, where the lives and safety of innocent people were involved, but this was much more than that. *You* were in danger. I cared about that, rather like, it seems, Chase found out he cared about his wife and child. What was different for me this time, Carrie, was that it was you."

He paused, looked at her, dropped his eyes to the book in his lap, then looked up again.

"Do you understand?"

She sat in silence, thinking he would surely be able to see the wiggle of her nightgown as her heart bumped vigorously in her chest. Questions rattled through her thoughts with the drumbeats of her heart: What's coming next? Does this mean Henry and I are in love? Do I know what that kind of love is like? Have I ever really known?

Amos and she had enjoyed a good, companionable

297

marriage, but . . . but now . . . And she just couldn't say, "Henry King, act your age." She didn't even know what *that* meant.

She thought back to last November when, not long after they met, Henry had kissed her. Amos hadn't kissed her more than a brief brush on the cheek for many years before he died, but even when they were first married and he kissed her, it hadn't been like that, not ever.

But when Henry kissed her, held her, and the warmth of their coming together was so overwhelming, well, it had turned quite a few of her ideas topsy-turvy. She'd never imagined that a kiss could mean that much, do that much, for Carrie Culpeper McCrite.

Love? Henry was such fun, they talked together like old friends, they understood lots of things without even saying them. Yes, they had become very close friends, but now . . . ?

She was still picking at the ruffle on the sleeve of her nightgown. The fabric was doubled there. It wasn't doubled anywhere else on the gown. Though there was a high neck and long sleeves, she knew quite well the light-weight cotton didn't conceal . . . everything.

She looked up at Henry, who was watching her with that funny, quirky little smile dimpling at the corners of his mouth. The sun was overhead now, and its glare was off the windows. She could see Henry's face quite clearly. Yes, he was smiling, but he also looked . . .

scared . . . was that it? And hesitant. She'd never seen him look that way before.

"We've talked a lot about enjoying our single independence," she said.

"Thursdays?"

*"What?"*

"We can be independent on Thursdays. That is . . . if . . . I mean I have no right . . . to . . ." He finished weakly, "I have no right to say what you want to do about Thursdays."

"Oh, my goodness, Henry," she said in the most matter-of-fact tone she could manage, "I will very definitely love you on Thursdays, too."

She kicked off the rest of the covers and stood. "I'm going to take a shower," she said, "and we need to think about breakfast or whatever meal comes at this time of day. I'm hungry."

As she passed the rocker, Henry reached out and touched her arm. He pointed. "I found your box of food. You have apples, bananas, breakfast bars. Why don't we eat a picnic breakfast here? We can have a late lunch with Jason and Eleanor before we pick up Tracy and Dulcey—and Chase, too, I'd bet—and go to Margaret's house. But for now, let's don't even think about that. Let's just be us."

She turned to face him. "Henry?"

"Yes, Little One."

"I'm glad you're here."

"Me too," he said.

He stood up. Night shirts were really rather cute.

Then she couldn't see the night shirt because her face was mashed against it, and Henry's arms were around her.

After a while she pulled away and turned toward the bathroom. "I'll be ready in ten minutes," she said, "and it's your turn to fix breakfast."

# Recipes

## Apple Chunky

12 cups cooked apples (Approx. one dozen large cooking apples, peeled and sliced, or one #10 can.)

2 cups apple cider

2 cups sugar (To taste, and depending on whether fresh or canned apples are used. Canned apples take less sugar.)

1 tsp. ground cinnamon

¼ tsp. ground cloves

¼ tsp. Allspice

Cook apples slowly in cider until soft (or drain canned apples and cook in cider until flavors blend). Mash cooked apples with a potato masher until chunky. Add sugar and spices, cook on low heat, stirring to keep from sticking, until the mixture has thickened and is the proper consistency to spread on biscuits.

Will keep in the refrigerator several weeks. To can, put hot mixture in hot, sterilized jars, put lids on, process in boiling water bath ten minutes. Can also be frozen.

Recipe makes about four quarts.

# Peach Chunky

12 cups cooked peaches (Approx. a dozen and a half medium, fully ripe peaches, or one #10 can.)

Scant 2 cups sugar (To taste, and depending on whether fresh or canned peaches are used. Canned peaches take less sugar.)

½ tsp. ground cinnamon

¼ tsp. ground cloves

¼ tsp. nutmeg

¼ tsp. ground ginger

Wash, scald, and peel fresh peaches. Cook slowly until soft in enough water to prevent sticking. (Or cook canned peaches until soft in enough water/juice to prevent sticking.) Mash cooked peaches with potato masher until chunky. Add sugar and spices. Cook until thick, stirring to prevent sticking.

Process or store as for Apple Chunky.

**Center Point Publishing**
600 Brooks Road ● PO Box 1
Thorndike ME 04986-0001 USA

(207) 568-3717

US & Canada:
1 800 929-9108